Conan, the hairs of his neck prickling with a barbarian's horror of supernatural menaces, recognized the newcomers as the dreaded *brylukas* of Zaporoskan legend—creatures neither man nor beast nor demon, but a little of all three. Their near-human intelligence served their bestial lust for human blood, while their supernatural powers enabled them to survive even though entombed for centuries. Creatures of darkness, they had been held at bay by the light of the flame. When this was put out they emerged, as ferocious as ever and even more avid for blood.

Those that struck the floor near Conan rushed upon him, claws outstretched. With an inarticulate roar he whirled, making wide sweeps with his great sword to keep them from him. Still they clustered, twittering . . .

Chronological order of the CONAN series:

CONAN
CONAN OF CIMMERIA
CONAN THE FREEBOOTER
CONAN THE WANDERER
CONAN THE ADVENTURER
CONAN THE BUCCANEER
CONAN THE WARRIOR
CONAN THE USURPER
CONAN THE CONQUEROR
CONAN THE AVENGER
CONAN OF AQUILONIA
CONAN OF THE ISLES

Illustrated CONAN novels:

CONAN AND THE SORCERER
THE TREASURE OF TRANICOS
CONAN THE MERCENARY

CONAN
THE FREEBOOTER

Robert E. Howard and L. Sprague de Camp

SF
ace books
A Division of Charter Communications Inc.
A GROSSET & DUNLAP COMPANY
51 Madison Avenue
New York, New York 10010

CONAN THE FREEBOOTER

Hawks over Shem was rewritten by L. Sprague de Camp from an original story by Robert E. Howard called *Hawks over Egypt*, laid in 11th-century Egypt. *Hawks over Shem* was first published in *Fantastic Universe Science Fiction* for October, 1955; copyright © 1955 by King-Size Publications, Inc. It was reprinted in *Tales of Conan*, N.Y.: Gnome Press, Inc., 1955.

Black Colossus was first published in *Weird Tales* for June, 1933; copyright 1933 by Popular Fiction Publishing Co. It was reprinted in *Conan the Barbarian*, N.Y.: Gnome Press, Inc., 1954.

Shadows in the Moonlight was first published in *Weird Tales* for April, 1934; copyright 1934 by Popular Fiction Publishing Co. It was reprinted in *Conan the Barbarian* and in *Swords and Sorcery*, ed. by L. Sprague de Camp, N.Y.: Pyramid Publications, Inc., 1963.

The Road of the Eagles was rewritten by L. Sprague de Camp from an original story by Robert E. Howard of the same title, but laid in the 16th century Turkish Empire. It was published in *Fantastic Universe Science Fiction* for December, 1955, under the title *Conan, Man of Destiny;* copyright © 1955 by King-Size Publications, Inc. It was reprinted under its present title in *Tales of Conan*.

A Witch Shall Be Born was first published in *Weird Tales* for December, 1934; copyright 1934 by Popular Fiction Publishing Co. It was reprinted in *Avon Fantasy Reader No. 10, 1949*, and in *Conan the Barbarian*.

The biographical paragraphs between the stories are based upon *A Probable Outline of Conan's Career*, by P. Schuyler Miller and Dr. John D. Clark, published in *The Hyborian Age* (1938), and on the expanded version of this essay, *An Informal Biography of Conan the Cimmerian*, by P. Schuyler Miller, John D. Clark, and L. Sprague de Camp, published in *Amra*, Vol. 2, No. 4, copyright © 1959 by G. H. Scithers; used by permission of G. H. Scithers.

An ACE Book

4 6 8 0 9 7 5 3
Manufactured in the United States of America

Contents

INTRODUCTION, by L. Sprague de Camp 8
HAWKS OVER SHEM, by Robert E. Howard
& L. Sprague de Camp 15
BLACK COLOSSUS, by Robert E. Howard 54
SHADOWS IN THE MOONLIGHT,
by Robert E. Howard 99
THE ROAD OF THE EAGLES,
by Robert E. Howard &
L. Sprague de Camp 133
A WITCH SHALL BE BORN,
by Robert E. Howard 172

Pages 6 and 7: A map of the world of Conan in the Hyborian Age, based upon notes and sketches by Robert E. Howard and upon previous maps by P. Schuyler Miller, John D. Clark, David Kyle, and L. Sprague de Camp, with a map of Europe and adjacent regions superimposed for reference.

VANAHEIM
ASGARD
CIMMERIA
PICTISH WILDERNESS
WESTERN OCEAN
BORDER KIN
MARCHES
GUNDERLAND
Galparan
NEMEDIA
TAURAN
Tanasul
BOSSONIAN
Black River
AQUILONIA
Belverus
Shirki R.
Num
Thunder River
Khorotas R.
Tarantia
Shamar
OPHIR
POITAIN
Tybor R.
Kordava
Alimane R.
Khorshemish
ZINGARA
ARGOS
Barachan Isles
Messantia
SHEM
Isle of the Black Ones
Asgalun
River
Khemi
Luxur
Sukhmet
KUSH
DARF
Xuthal
Xuchotl
Zarkheba R.

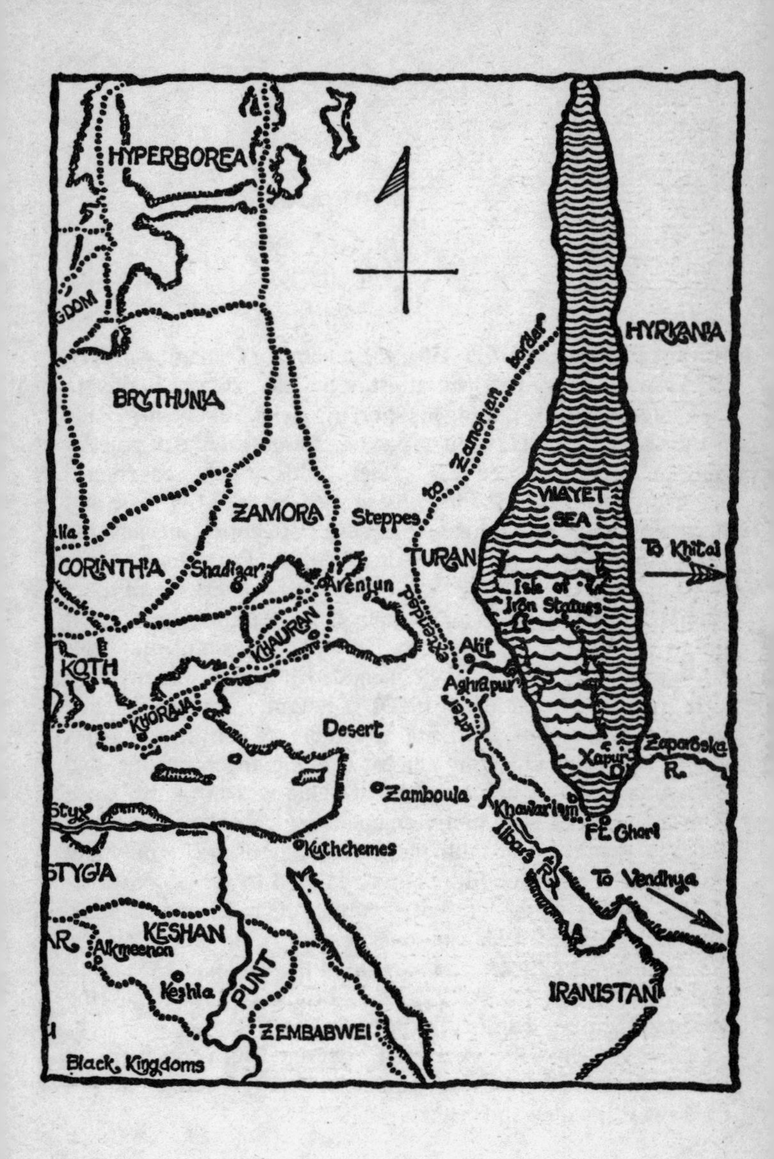
HYPERBOREA
BRYTHUNIA
ZAMORA
Steppes
to Zamorian border
TURAN
HYRKANIA
VILAYET SEA
To Khitai
CORINTHIA
Shadizar
Arenjun
Isle of Iron Statues
KHAURAN
Later extended
Akif
Aghrapur
KOTH
KHORAJA
Desert
Xapur
Zaporoska R.
Zamboula
Khawarizm
Ft. Ghori
Styx
Kuthchemes
Ilbars R.
To Vendhya
STYGIA
KESHAN
Alkmeenon
Keshia
PUNT
IRANISTAN
ZEMBABWEI
Black Kingdoms

Introduction

ROBERT E. HOWARD (1906–36), the creator of Conan, was born in Peaster, Texas, and spent most of his life in Cross Plains. in the center of Texas. During his short life (which ended in suicide at the age of thirty) Howard turned out a large volume of popular fiction: sport, detective, western, historical, adventure, science-fiction, weird, and ghost stories, besides his verse and his many fantasies. Of his several series of heroic fantasies, the most popular have been the Conan stories. Eighteen of these were published in Howard's lifetime; eight others, from mere fragments and outlines to complete manuscripts, have been found among his papers since 1950. The incomplete stories have been completed by my colleague Lin Carter and myself.

In addition, in the early 1950s, I rewrote four unpublished Howard manuscripts of oriental adventure, to convert them into Conan stories by changing names, deleting anachronisms, and introducing a supernatural element. This was not hard, since Howard's heroes were pretty much all cut from the same cloth, and the resulting posthumous collaborations are still about three-quarters or four-fifths Howard. Two of these converted stories appear in the present volume: "Hawks over Shem" (originally called "Hawks over Egypt"), a story laid in eleventh-century Egypt, in the reign of the mad Caliph Hakîm; and "The Road of the Eagles," originally placed in the sixteenth-century Turkish Empire.

Moreover, my colleagues Lin Carter and Björn Nyberg and I have collaborated on several Conan pastiches, based upon hints in Howard's notes and letters.

The Conan stories are laid in Howard's fictional Hyborian Age, about twelve thousand years ago between the sinking of Atlantis and the beginnings of recorded history. Conan, a gigantic barbarian adventurer from the backward northern land of Cimmeria, arrived as a youth in the kingdom of Zamora (see the map) and for several years made a precarious living there and in neighboring lands as a thief. Then he served as a mercenary soldier, first in the oriental realm of Turan and then in the Hyborian kingdoms.

Forced to flee from Argos, Conan became a pirate along the coasts of Kush, in partnership with a Shemitish she-pirate, Bêlit, with a crew of black corsairs. After Bêlit's death and some hairsbreadth adventures among the black tribes, he returned to the trade of mercenary in Shem. Here the present volume begins.

Nearly twenty years ago, my old friend John D. Clark, a chemist and a Conan buff long before I was, edited the then-known Conan stories for the volumes published by Gnome Press. He wrote an eloquent introduction to the first volume of this series to be issued, *Conan the Conqueror*. This essay gives a free-swinging impression of Howard's fiction in general and the Conan stories in particular. Dr. Clark has allowed me to quote it here:

> It was almost seventeen years ago when I collided with the Hyborian Age. It was a notable collision, occurring when I was caught by the somewhat juicy cover on the September 1933 *Weird Tales*, read "The Slithering Shadow," and met Conan for the first time. It was an introduction that stuck, and from then on I followed the adventures of that slightly unconventional character with more than casual interest. A little later (1935 or so) Schuyler Miller and I decided to make a try at plotting out Conan's world. It turned out to be ridiculously easy. The countries flopped out on the paper, squirmed about a bit, and clicked together into an indubitable and obviously authentic map. We wrote to Howard then and found that his own map was practically identical with ours; his biography of Conan was also identical in all important respects with the one Miller and I had concocted from the internal evidence in the stories. As I remember, the most important point of disagreement was a two years' difference in Conan's age at one point in the stories.

We knew then that we had a story-teller on our hands who knew his business. And when we read the manuscript of "The Hyborian Age," some time before it was first published, we were sure of it.

Anyhow, in the next few years I managed to pick up the rest of Howard's fantasies, including King Kull and all the rest. It was obvious, of course, that although some of them had apparently been written before that gorgeous concept filtered into his mind, they might be fitted into the pattern with a little stretching. . . .

Among the Conan stories are fragments of the biography of that remarkable character, as deduced by Miller and myself, accounting for most of Conan's travels and adventures that are not recounted in the tales themselves. They do *not*, however, explain how he managed to get rid of the woman of which he was usually possessed by the end of a story in time for him to acquire another in the next. I might, by the way, recommend that question as a subject for literary research to some budding Ph.D. in English. The results of the inquiry might be at least as useful as a publication purporting finally to decide whether Francis Bacon or the Earl of Oxford really wrote the works of the alleged W. Shakespeare. . . .

I do not intend to write about Robert E. Howard himself. I never knew him personally and those who did can do a better job than I. I knew him only as the writer of some incredibly good fantasy. The parts of a writer that don't die with his body are his stories—and Howard's yarns are not going to die among those who frankly and whole-heartedly like adventure on the grand scale. You are probably one of those readers or you wouldn't have bought this book in the first place.

Howard was a first-rate teller of tales, with a remarkable technical command of his tools and with a complete lack of inhibitions. With a fine and free hand he took what he liked from the more spectacular aspects of all ages and climes: proper names of every conceivable linguistic derivation, weapons from everywhere and everywhen under the sun, customs and classes from the whole ancient and medieval world, and fitted the whole together into a coherent and self-consistent cosmos without a visible joint. Then he added a king-sized portion of the supernatural to add zest to the whole, and the result was a purple and golden and crimson universe where anything can happen—except the tedious.

His heroes are never profound—but they are never dull. Kull, Solomon Kane, Bran Mak Morn, Conan himself, walk and talk and are alive and of one piece. They may not be exactly the types of persons whom we would invite to a polite party, but they're not exactly the sort of persons whom we would forget if they came anyway. Conan, the hero of all Howard's heroes, is the armored swashbuckler, indestructible and irresistible, that we've all wanted to be at one time or another; the women, in appearance, manner, and costume (or lack of it) are the inmates of the sort of harem that harems ought to be but aren't (and isn't it a shame, and wouldn't it be nice, if they were commoner?); the villains are villainous as only perfect villains can be; the sorcerers are sorcerers in spades; and the apparitions they conjure up, or who appear under their own power, are (thank God!) out of this world.

And above all Howard was a story-teller. The story came first, last, and in between. Something is always happening, and the flow of action never hesitates from beginning to end, as one incident flows smoothly and inevitably into the next with never a pause for the reader to take breath. Don't look for hidden philosophical meanings or intellectual puzzles in the yarns—they aren't there. *Howard was a story-teller.* The tales are the sword-and-cloaker carried to the ultimate limit and a little beyond, with enough extra sex to keep the results off the more tedious library shelves.

So here is the book. If you have read of Conan before, you know what to expect. If you haven't, and are addicted to fantastic adventure, you can repair the omission and sit down now and read of the gods and demons and of the warriors and their women and of their adventures in a world that never was but should have been. If the history propounded doesn't agree with what you know of history—if the ethnology is remarkable and the geology more so—don't let it worry you. Howard was writing of another Earth than this one—one painted in brighter colors and on a grander scale.

If, on the other hand, you insist on realism in your reading—if you must have novels about introverts suffering in a brutal world—if your meat is something "close to the soil" or concerned with psychopathology or the state of the world, then, my friend, this book is not for you. You'd better find yourself a hole and read *Crime and Punishment*. But I won't be there with you—I have an engagement in the Hyborian Age, and will be busy all evening.

John D. Clark, Ph.D.

New York City
April 5, 1950.

For further information on and opinions about Howard, the Conan stories, and heroic fantasy in general, see the other volumes of this series.

L. Sprague de Camp

Hawks over Shem

Following the events of the story The Snout in the Dark, *Conan, dissatisfied with his accomplishments in the black countries, wanders northward across the deserts of Stygia to the meadowlands of Shem. During this trek, his reputation stands him in good stead. He presently finds himself in the army of King Sumu-abi of Akkharia, one of the southerly Shemitish city-states. Through the treachery of one Othbaal, cousin of the mad King Akhîrom of Pelishtia, the Akkharian forces are ambushed and wiped out—all but Conan, who survives to track the renegade to Asgalun, the Pelishti capital.*

The tall figure in the white cloak wheeled, cursing softly, hand at scimitar hilt. Not lightly did men walk the nighted streets of Asgalun, capital of Shemitish Pelishtia. In this dark, winding alley of the unsavory river quarter, anything might happen.

"Why do you follow me, dog?" The voice was harsh, slurring the Shemitic gutturals with the accents of Hyrkania.

Another tall figure emerged from the shadows, clad, like the first, in a cloak of white silk but lacking the other's spired helmet.

"Did you say, 'dog'?" The accent differed from the Hyrkanian's.

"Aye, dog. I have been followed—"

Before the Hyrkanian could get further, the other rushed with the sudden blinding speed of a pouncing tiger. The Hyrkanian snatched at his sword. Before the blade cleared the scabbard, a huge fist smote the side of his head. But for the Hyrkanian's powerful build and the protection of the camail of ring mail that hung down from his helmet, his neck might have been broken. As it was, he was hurled sprawling to the pavement, his sword clattering out of his grasp.

As the Hyrkanian shook his head and groped back to consciousness, he saw the other standing over him with drawn saber. The stranger rumbled: "I follow nobody, and I let nobody call me dog! Do you understand that, dog?"

The Hyrkanian glanced about for his sword and saw that the other had already kicked it out of reach. Thinking to gain time until he could spring for his weapon, he said: "Your pardon if I wronged you, but I have been followed since nightfall. I heard stealthy footsteps along the dark alleys. Then you came unexpectedly into view, in a place most suited for murder."

"Ishtar confound you! Why should I follow you? I have lost my way. I've never seen you before, and I hope never to—"

A stealthy pad of feet brought the stranger round, springing back and wheeling to keep both the Hyrkanian and the newcomers before him.

Four huge figures loomed menacingly in the shadows, the dim starlight glinting on curved blades. There was also a glimmer of white teeth and eyeballs against dark skins.

For an instant there was tense stillness. Then one muttered in the liquid accents of the black kingdoms: "Which is our dog? Here be two clad alike, and the darkness makes them twins."

"Cut down both," replied another, who towered half a head above his tall companions. "We shall then make no mistake and leave no witness."

So saying, the four Negroes came on in deadly silence.

The stranger took two long strides to where the Hyrkanian's sword lay. With a growl of "Here! he kicked the weapon at the Hyrkanian, who snatched it up; then rushed upon the advancing blacks with a snarling oath.

The giant Kushite and one other closed with the stranger while the other two ran at the Hyrkanian. The stranger, with that same feline speed he had shown earlier, leaped in without awaiting attack. A quick feint, a clang of steel, and a lightning slash sheared the head of the smaller black from his shoulders. As the stranger struck, so did the giant, with a long forehand sweep that should have cut the stranger in two at the waist.

But, despite his size, the stranger moved even faster than the blade as it hissed through the night air. He dropped to the ground in a crouch so that the scimitar passed over him. As he squatted in front of his antagonist, he struck at the black's legs. The blade bit into muscle and bone. As the black reeled on his wounded leg and swung his sword up for another slash, the stranger sprang up and in, under the lifted arm, and drove his blade to the hilt in the Negro's chest. Blood spurted along the stranger's wrist. The scimitar fell waveringly, to cut through the silken kaffia and glance from the steel cap beneath. The giant sank down dying.

The stranger tore out his blade and whirled. The Hyrkanian had met the attack of his two Negroes coolly, retreating slowly to keep them in front of him. He suddenly slashed one across the chest and shoulder so that he dropped his sword and fell to his knees with a moan. As he fell he gripped his foe's knees and hung on like a leech. The Hyrkanian kicked and struggled in vain. Those black arms, bulging with iron muscles, held him fast, while the remaining Negro redoubled the fury of his strokes.

Even as the Kushite swordsman drew breath for a stroke that the hampered Hyrkanian could not have parried, he heard the rush of feet behind him. Before he could turn, the stranger's saber drove through him with such fury that the blade sprang half its length out of his chest, while the hilt smote him fiercely between the shoulders. Life went out of him with a cry.

The Hyrkanian caved in the skull of his other antagonist with his hilt and shook himself free of the corpse. He turned to the stranger, who was pulling his saber out of the body it transfixed.

"Why did you come to my aid after nearly knocking my head off?" he asked.

The other shrugged. "We were two men beset by rogues. Fate made us allies. Now, if you like, we'll take up our quarrel again. You said I spied upon you."

"I see my mistake and crave your pardon," answered the Hyrkanian promptly. "I know now who has been skulking after me."

He wiped and sheathed his scimitar and bent over each corpse in turn. When he came to the body of the giant, he paused and murmured:

"Soho! Keluka the Sworder! Of high rank the archer whose shaft is paneled with pearls!" He wrenched from the limp black finger a heavy, ornate ring, slipped the ring into his sash, and laid hold of the garments of the dead man. "Help me to dispose of this carrion, brother, so that no questions shall be asked."

The stranger grasped a bloodstained jacket in each hand and dragged the bodies after the Hyrkanian down a reeking black alley, in which rose the broken curb of a ruined and forgotten well. The corpses plunged into the abyss and struck far below with sullen splashes. With a light laugh the Hyrkanian turned.

"The gods have made us allies," he said. "I owe you a debt."

"You owe me naught," answered the other in a surly tone.

"Words cannot level a mountain. I am Farouz, an archer of Mazdak's Hyrkanian horse. Come with me to a more seemly spot, where we can converse in comfort. I hold no grudge for the buffet you dealt me, though, by Tarim! my head still rings from it."

The stranger grudgingly sheathed his saber and followed the Hyrkanian. Their way led through the gloom of reeking alleys and along narrow, winding streets. Asgalun was a contrast of splendor and decay, where opulent palaces rose among the smoke-stained ruins of buildings of forgotten ages. A swarm of suburbs clustered about the walls of the forbidden inner city where dwelt King Akhîrom and his nobles.

The two men came to a newer and more respectable quarter, where the latticed windows of overhanging balconies almost touched one another across the street.

"All the shops are dark," grunted the stranger. "A few days ago the city was lighted like day, from dusk to sunrise."

"One of Akhîrom's whims. Now he has another, that no lights shall burn in Asgalun. What his mood will be tomorrow, Pteor only knows."

They halted before an iron-bound door in a heavy stone arch, and the Hyrkanian rapped cautiously. A voice challenged from within and was answered by a password. The door opened, and the Hyrkanian pushed into thick darkness, drawing his companion with him. The door closed behind them. A heavy leather curtain was pulled back, revealing a lamplit corridor and a scarred old Shemite.

"An old soldier turned to wine-selling," said the Hyrkanian. "Lead us to a chamber where we can be alone, Khannon."

"Most of the chambers are empty," grumbled Khannon, limping before them. "I'm a ruined man. Men fear to touch the cup, since the king banned wine. Pteor smite him with gout!"

The stranger glanced curiously into the larger chambers that they passed, where men sat at food and drink. Most of Khannon's customers were typical Pelishtim: stocky, swarthy men with hooked noses and curly blue-black beards. Occasionally one saw men of the more slender type that roamed the deserts of eastern Shem, or Hyrkanians or black Kushites from the mercenary army of Pelishtia.

Khannon bowed the two men into a small room, where he spread mats for them. He set before them a great dish of fruits and nuts, poured wine from a bulging skin, and limped away muttering.

"Pelishtia has come upon evil days, brother," drawled the Hyrkanian, quaffing the wine of Kyros. He was a tall man, leanly but strong built. Keen black eyes, slightly aslant, danced restlessly in a face with a yellowish tinge. His hawk nose overhung a thin, black, drooping mustache. His plain cloak was of costly fabric, his spired helmet was chased with silver, and jewels glittered in the hilt of his scimitar.

He looked at a man as tall as himself, but who contrasted with him in many ways. The other had thicker limbs and greater depth of chest: the build of a mountaineer. Under his white kaffia his broad brown face, youthful but already seamed with the scars of brawls and battles, showed smooth-shaven. His natural complexion was lighter than that of the Hyrkanian, the darkness of his features being more of the sun than of nature. A hint of stormy fires smoldered in his cold blue eyes. He gulped his wine and smacked his lips.

Farouz grinned and refilled his goblet. "You fight well, brother. If Mazdak's Hyrkanians were not so infernally jealous of outsiders, you'd make a good trooper."

The other merely grunted.

"Who are you, anyway?" persisted Farouz. "I've told you who I am."

"I am Ishbak, a Zuagir from the eastern deserts."

The Hyrkanian threw back his head and laughed loudly,

bringing a scowl to the face of the other, who said: "What's so funny?"

"Do you expect me to believe that?"

"Do you say I lie?" snarled the stranger.

Farouz grinned. "No Zuagir ever spoke Pelishtic with an accent like yours, for the Zuagir tongue is but a dialect of Shemitish. Moreover, during our fight with the Kushites, you called upon strange gods—Crom and Manannan—whose names I have heard before from barbarians of the far North. Fear not; I am in your debt and can keep a secret."

The stranger half started up, grasping his hilt. Farouz merely took a sip of wine. After an instant of tension the stranger sank back. With an air of discomfiture he said:

"Very well. I am Conan, a Cimmerian, late of the army of King Sumuabi of Akkharia."

The Hyrkanian grinned and stuffed grapes into his mouth. Between chews he said: "You could never be a spy, friend Conan. You are too quick and open in your anger. What brings you to Asgalun?"

"A little matter of revenge."

"Who is your enemy?"

"An Anaki named Othbaal, may the dogs gnaw his bones!"

Farouz whistled. "By Pteor, you aim at a lofty target! Know you that this man is the general of all King Akhîrom's Anakian troops?"

"Crom! It matters as little to me as if he were a collector of offal."

"What has Othbaal done to you?"

Conan said: "The people of Anakia revolted against their king, who's an even bigger fool than Akhîrom. They asked help of Akkharia. Sumuabi hoped they would succeed and choose a friendlier king than the one in power, so he called for volunteers. Five hundred of us marched to help the Anakim. But this damned Othbaal had been playing both sides. He led the revolt to encourage the king's enemies to come out into the open, and then betrayed the rebels into the arms of this king, who butchered the lot.

"Othbaal also knew we were coming, so he set a trap for us. Not knowing what had happened, we fell into it. Only I escaped with my life, and that by shamming death. The rest of us either fell on the field or were put to death with the fanciest tortures the king's Sabatean torturer could devise." The moody blue eyes narrowed. "I've fought men before this and thought no more of them afterwards, but in this case I swore I'd pay back Othbaal for some of my dead friends. When I got back to Akkharia I learned that Othbaal had fled from Anakia for fear of the people and had come here. How has he risen so high so fast?"

"He's a cousin of King Akhîrom," said Farouz. "Akhîrom, though a Pelishti, is also a cousin of the king of Anakia and was reared at that court. The kings of these little Shemitish city-states are all more or less related, which makes their wars all quarrels within the family and all the bitterer in consequence. How long have you been in Asgalun?"

"Only a few days. Long enough to learn that the king is mad. No wine indeed!" Conan spat.

"There is more to learn. Akhîrom is indeed mad, and the people murmur under his heel. He holds his power by means of three bodies of mercenary troops, with whose aid he overthrew and slew his brother, the previous king. First, the Anakim, whom he recruited while an exile at the court of Anakia. Secondly, the black Kushites, who under their general, Imbalayo, yearly gain more power. And thirdly, the Hyrkanian horse, like myself. Their general is Mazdak, and among him and Imbalayo and Othbaal there is enough hatred and jealousy to have started a dozen wars. You saw some of it in this evening's encounter.

"Othbaal came here last year as a penniless adventurer. He has risen partly by his relationship to Akhîrom, and partly by the intrigues of an Ophirean slave-woman named Rufia, whom he won at gaming from Mazdak and then refused to return when the Hyrkanian had sobered up. That's another reason for there being little love between them. There is a woman behind Akhîrom, too: Zeriti the Stygian, a witch. Men say she has driven him mad by the potions she has fed him to keep him under her government. If that's true, then she defeated her own ends, for now nobody can control him."

Conan set down his goblet and looked straight at Farouz. "Well, what now? Will you betray me, or did you speak truth when you said you would not?"

Turning in his fingers the ring he had taken from Keluka, Farouz mused. "Your secret is safe with me. For one reason, I too owe Othbaal a heavy debt. If you succeed in your quest ere I find means to discharge it, I shall bear the loss with serenity."

Conan started forward, his iron fingers gripping the Hyrkanian's shoulder. "Do you speak truth?"

"May these potbellied Shemitish gods smite me with boils if I lie!"

"Then let me aid you in your vengeance!"

"You? An outsider, who knows nought of the secret ways of Asgalun?"

"Of course! So much the better; having no local ties, I can be trusted. Come on; let's make a plan. Where is the swine and how do we get to him?"

Farouz, though no weakling, recoiled a little before the primitive elemental force that blazed in the eyes and showed in the manner of the other. "Let me think," he said. "There is a way, if one is swift and daring . . ."

Later, two hooded figures halted in a group of palms among the ruins of nighted Asgalun. Before them lay the waters of a canal, and beyond it, rising from its bank, the great bastioned wall of sun-dried brick which encircled the inner city. The inner city was really a gigantic fortress, sheltering the king and his trusted nobles and mercenary troops, forbidden to common men without a pass.

"We could climb the wall," muttered Conan.

"And find ourselves no nearer our foe," answered Farouz, groping in the shadows. "Here!"

Conan saw the Hyrkanian fumble at a shapeless heap of marble. "An ancient ruined shrine," grumbled Farouz. "But—ah!"

He lifted a broad slab, revealing steps leading down into darkness. Conan frowned suspiciously.

Farouz explained: "This tunnel leads under the wall and up into the house of Othbaal, which stands just beyond."

"Under the canal?"

"Aye. Once Othbaal's house was the pleasure-house of King Uriaz, who slept on a down-cushion floating on a pool of quicksilver, guarded by tame lions—yet fell before the avenger's dagger in spite of all. He prepared secret exits from all parts of his houses. Before Othbaal took the house, it belonged to his rival Mazdak. The Anaki knows nothing of this secret, so come!"

Swords drawn, they groped down a flight of stone steps and advanced along a level tunnel in blackness. Conan's groping fingers told him that the walls, floor, and ceiling were composed of huge blocks of stone. As they advanced, the stones became slippery and the air grew dank. Drops of water fell on Conan's neck, making him shiver and swear. They were passing under the canal. Later, this dampness abated. Farouz hissed a warning, and they mounted another flight of stairs.

At the top, the Hyrkanian fumbled with a catch. A panel slid aside, and a soft light streamed in. Farouz slipped through the opening and, after Conan had followed, closed it behind them. It became one of the inlaid panels of the wall, not differing to the sight from the other panels. They stood in a vaulted corridor, while Farouz pulled his kaffia around to hide his face and motioned Conan to do likewise. Farouz then led the way down the corridor without hesitation. The Cimmerian followed, sword in hand, glancing to right and left.

They passed through a curtain of dark velvet and came upon an arched doorway of gold-inlaid ebony. A brawny black, naked but for a silken loincloth, started up from his doze, sprang to his feet, and swung a great scimitar. But he did not cry out; his open mouth revealed the cavernous emptiness of the mouth of a mute.

"Quietly!" snapped Farouz, avoiding the sweep of the mute's sword. As the Negro stumbled from his wasted effort, Conan tripped him. He fell sprawling, and Farouz passed his sword through the dark body.

"That was quick and silent enough!" breathed Farouz with a grin. "Now for the real prey!"

Cautiously he tried the door, while the giant Cimmerian crouched at his shoulder, eyes burning like those of a hunting tiger. The door gave inward, and they sprang into the chamber. Farouz closed the door behind them and set his back to it, laughing at the man who leaped up from his divan with a startled oath. Beside him, a woman half-rose from the cushions and screamed. Farouz said: "We've run the buck to cover, brother!"

For a fraction of a second, Conan took in the spectacle. Othbaal was a tall, lusty man, his thick black hair gathered in a knot at his nape and his black beard oiled, curled, and precisely trimmed. Late as the hour was, he was fully clad in silken kilt and velvet vest, under which gleamed the links of a mail shirt. He dove for a scabbarded sword that lay on the floor beside the couch.

As for the woman, she was not conventionally pretty but still good to look at: red-haired, with a broad, slightly freckled face, and brown eyes sparkling with intelligence.

She was rather broadly built, with shoulders wider than the average, a big bust, and full hips. She gave the impression of great physical vigor.

"Help!" shouted Othbaal, rising to meet the Cimmerian's rush. "I am beset!"

Farouz started across the wide floor not more than a step behind Conan, but then leaped back to the door through which they had come. With half an ear, Conan was aware of a commotion in the corridor and heard the thump of some heavy object rammed against the door. Then his blade crossed that of the Anaki. The swords clanged in mid-air, showering sparks, flashing and flickering in the lamplight.

Both men attacked, smiting furiously, each too intent on the life of the other to give much thought to showy swordplay. Each stroke had full weight and murderous will behind it. They fought in silence. As they circled, Conan saw, over Othbaal's shoulder, that Farouz had braced his shoulder against the door. From the other side came increasingly heavy blows, which had already torn loose the bolt. The woman had vanished.

"Can you deal with him?" said Farouz. "If I let this door go, his slaves will pour in."

"All right so far," grunted Conan, parrying a ferocious slash.

"Hasten, then, for I cannot hold them much longer."

Conan plunged in with fresh ferocity. Now it was the Anaki whose attention was devoted to parrying the Cimmerian's sword, which beat on his blade like a hammer on an anvil. The sheer strength and fury of the barbarian began to tell. Othbaal paled under his swarthy skin. His breath came in gasps as he gave ground. Blood streamed from gashes on arms, thigh, and neck. Conan bled, too, but there was no slackening in the headlong fury of his attack.

Othbaal was close to the tapestried wall when suddenly he sprang aside as Conan lunged. Carried off-balance by his wasted thrust, the Cimmerian plunged forward and his sword point clashed against the stone beneath the tapestries. At the same instant, Othbaal slashed at his foe's head with all his waning power.

But Conan's sword of Stygian steel, instead of snapping like a lesser blade, bent and sprang straight again. The falling scimitar bit through Conan's helmet into the scalp beneath. Before Othbaal could recover his balance, Conan's heavy blade sheared upward through steel links and hip bone to grate into the spinal column.

The Anaki reeled and fell with a choking cry, his entrails spilling out on the floor. His fingers clawed briefly at the nap of the heavy carpet, then went limp.

Conan, blind with blood and sweat, was driving his sword in silent frenzy again and again into the form at his feet, too drunken with fury to realize that his antagonist was dead, until Farouz called:

"Cease, Conan! They've stopped their attack to bring up a heavier ram, and we can run for it."

"How?" said Conan, dazedly raking the blood from his eyes, for he was still dizzy from the stroke that had cloven his helmet. He tore off the riven, blood-filled headpiece and threw it aside, exposing his square-cut black mane. A crimson torrent descended into his face, blinding him anew. He stooped and tore a strip from Othbaal's kilt to bind up his head.

"That door!" said Farouz, pointing. "Rufia fled that way, the slut! If you're ready, we'll run."

Conan saw an inconspicuous little door to one side of the couch. It had been concealed by draperies, but Rufia in her flight had disarranged these and left the door open behind her.

The Hyrkanian took from his girdle the ring that he had pulled from the finger of the black slayer, Keluka. He ran across the floor, dropped the ring near Othbaal's body, and continued on toward the small door. Conan followed him, though he had to crouch and almost turn sideways to get through the door.

They emerged into another corridor. Farouz led Conan by a roundabout route, turning and twisting through a maze of passages, until Conan was hopelessly lost. By this means they avoided the main body of household retainers, gathered in the corridor outside the principal entrance to the room where they had slain Othbaal. Once they aroused feminine screams from a room they passed, but Farouz kept on. Presently they reached the secret panel, entered it, and groped in darkness until they emerged once more into the silent grove.

Conan stopped to get his breath and re-tie his bandage. Farouz said: "How is your wound, brother?"

"A scratch only. Why did you drop that ring?"

"To blind the avengers of blood. Tarim! All that trouble, and the strumpet got away."

Conan grinned wryly in the darkness. Rufia evidently did not regard Farouz as a rescuer. The brief picture that Conan had obtained, in the second before he closed with Othbaal, stuck in his mind. Such a woman, he thought, would suit him very well.

Within the massive wall of the inner city, a stupendous event was coming to pass. Under the shadows of the balconies stole a veiled and hooded figure. For the first time in three years, a woman was walking the streets of Asgalun.

Knowing her peril, she trembled with fear not wholly inspired by the lurking shadows. The stones hurt her feet in her tattered velvet slippers; for three years the cobblers of Asgalun had been forbidden to make street shoes for women. King Akhîrom had decreed that the women of Pelishtia should be shut up like reptiles in cages.

Rufia, the red-haired Ophirean, favorite of Othbaal,

had wielded more power than any woman in Pelishtia save Zeriti, the king's witch-mistress. And now, as she stole through the night, an outcast, the thought that burned her like a white-hot brand was the realization that the fruits of all her scheming had been spilt in a second by the sword of one of Othbaal's enemies.

Rufia came of a race of women accustomed to swaying thrones with their beauty and wit. She scarcely remembered her native Ophir from which she had been stolen by Kothian slavers. The Argossean magnate who had bought her and raised her for his household had fallen in battle with the Shemites, and as a supple girl of fourteen Rufia had passed into the hands of a prince of Stygia, a languorous, effeminate youth whom she came to twist around her pink fingers. Then, after some years, had come the raid of a band of wandering freebooters from the half-mythical lands beyond the Sea of Vilayet, upon the prince's pleasure island on the upper Styx, with slaughter, fire, and plunder, crashing walls and shrieks of death, and a red-haired girl screaming in the arms of a tall Hyrkanian chieftain.

Because she came of a race whose women were rulers of men, Rufia neither perished nor became a whimpering toy. When Mazdak enlisted his band under Akhîrom in Anakia, as part of Akhîrom's plan to seize Pelishtia from his hated brother, Rufia had gone along.

She had not liked Mazdak. The sardonic adventurer was coldly masterful in his relations with women, keeping a large harem and letting none command or persuade him in the slightest. Because Rufia could endure no rival, she had not been displeased when Mazdak had gambled her away to his rival Othbaal.

The Anaki was more to her taste. Despite a streak of cruelty and treachery, the man was strong, vital, and intelligent. Best of all, he could be managed. He only needed a spur to his ambition, and Rufia supplied that. She had started him up the shining rungs of the ladder—and now he had been slain by a pair of masked murderers who had sprung from nowhere.

Engrossed in her bitter thoughts, she looked up with a start as a tall, hooded figure stepped from the shadows of an overhanging balcony and confronted her. Only his eyes burned at her, almost luminous in the starlight. She cowered back with a low cry.

"A woman on the streets of Asgalun!" The voice was hollow and ghostly. "Is this not against the king's commands?"

"I walk not the streets by choice, lord," she answered. "My master has been slain, and I fled from his murderers."

The stranger bent his hooded head and stood statue-like. Rufia watched him nervously. There was something gloomy and portentous about him. He seemed less like a man pondering the tale of a chance-met slave-girl than a somber prophet weighing the doom of a sinful people. At last he lifted his head.

"Come," said he. "I will find a place for you."

Without pausing to see if she obeyed, he stalked away up the street. Rufia hurried after him. She could not walk the streets all night, for any officer of the king would strike off her head for violating the edict of King Akhîrom. This stranger might be leading her into worse slavery, but she had no choice.

Several times she tried to speak, but his grim silence struck her silent in turn. His unnatural aloofness frightened her. Once she was startled to see furtive forms stealing after them.

"Men follow us!" she exclaimed.

"Heed them not," answered the man in his weird voice.

Nothing was said until they reached a small arched gate in a lofty wall. The stranger halted and called out. He was answered from within. The gate opened, revealing a black mute holding a torch. In its light, the height of the robed stranger was inhumanly exaggerated.

"But this—this is a gate of the Great Palace!" stammered Rufia.

For answer, the man threw back his hood, revealing a long pale oval of a face, in which burned those strange, luminous eyes.

Rufia screamed and fell to her knees. "King Akhîrom!"

"Aye, King Akhîrom, O faithless and sinful one!" The hollow voice rolled out like a bell. "Vain and foolish woman, who ignores the command of the Great King, the King of Kings, the King of the World, which is the word of the gods! Who treads the street in sin, and sets aside the mandates of the Good King! Seize her!"

The following shadows closed in, becoming a squad of Negro mutes. As their fingers seized her flesh, Rufia fainted.

The Ophirean regained consciousness in a windowless chamber whose arched doors were bolted with bars of gold. She stared wildly about for her captor and shrank down to see him standing above her, stroking his pointed, graying beard while his terrible eyes burned into her soul.

"O Lion of Shem!" she gasped, struggling to her knees. "Mercy!"

As she spoke, she knew the futility of the plea. She was crouching before the man whose name was a curse in the mouths of the Pelishtim; who, claiming divine guidance, had ordered all dogs killed, all vines cut down, all grapes and honey dumped into the river; who had banned all wine, beer, and games of chance; who believed that to disobey his most trivial command was the blackest sin conceivable. He roamed the streets at night in disguise to see that his orders were obeyed. Rufia's flesh crawled as he stared at her with unblinking eyes.

"Blasphemer!" he whispered. "Daughter of evil! O Pteor!" he cried, flinging up his arms. "What punishment shall be devised for this demon? What agony terrible enough, what degradation vile enough to render justice? The gods grant me wisdom!"

Rufia rose to her knees and pointed at Akhîrom's face. "Why call on the gods?" she shrieked. "Call on Akhîrom! You are a god!"

He stopped, reeled, and cried out incoherently. Then he straightened and looked down at her. Her face was white, her eyes staring. To her natural acting ability was added the terror of her position.

"What do you see, woman?" he asked.

"A god has revealed himself to me! In your face, shining like the sun! I burn, I die in the blaze of thy glory!"

She sank her face in her hands and crouched trembling. Akhîrom passed a shaking hand over his brow and bald pate.

"Aye," he whispered. "I am a god! I have guessed it; I have dreamed it. I alone possess the wisdom of the infinite. Now a mortal has seen it also. I see the truth at last—no mere mouthpiece and servant of the gods, but the God of gods himself! Akhîrom is the god of Pelishtia; of the earth. The false demon Pteor shall be cast down from his place and his statues melted up . . ."

Bending his gaze downward, he ordered: "Rise, woman, and look upon thy god!"

She did so, shrinking before his awful gaze. A change clouded Akhîrom's eyes as he seemed to see her clearly for the first time.

"Your sin is pardoned," he intoned. "Because you were the first to hail your god, you shall henceforth serve me in honor and splendor."

She prostrated herself, kissing the carpet before his feet. He clapped his hands. A eunuch entered and bowed.

"Go quickly to the house of Abdashtarth, the high priest of Pteor," he said, looking over the servant's head. "Say to him: 'This is the word of Akhîrom, who is the one true god of the Pelishtim, and shall soon be the god of all the peoples of the earth: that on the morrow shall be the beginning of beginnings. The idols of the false Pteor shall be destroyed, and statues of the true god shall be erected in their stead. The true religion shall be proclaimed, and a sacrifice of one hundred of the noblest children of the Pelishtim shall celebrate it . . .' "

Before the temple of Pteor stood Mattenbaal, the first assistant to Abdashtarth. The venerable Abdashtarth, his hands tied, stood quietly in the grip of a pair of brawny Anaki soldiers. His long white beard moved as he prayed. Behind him, other soldiers stoked the fire in the base of the huge, bull-headed idol of Pteor, with his obscenely exaggerated male characteristics. In the background towered the great seven-storied zikkurat of Asgalun, from which the priests read the will of the gods in the stars.

When the brazen sides of the idol glowed with the heat within, Mattenbaal stepped forward, raised a piece of papyrus, and read:

"For that your divine king, Akhîrom, is of the seed of Yakin-Ya, who was descended from the gods when they walked the earth, so is a god this day among ye! And now I command ye, all loyal Pelishtim, to recognize and bow down to and worship the greatest of all gods, the God of gods, the Creator of the Universe, the Incarnation of Divine Wisdom, the king of gods, who is Akhîrom the son of Azumelek, king of Pelishtia! And inasmuch as the wicked and perverse Abdashtarth, in the hardness of his heart, has rejected this revelation and has refused to bow down before his true god, let him be cast into the fire of the idol of the false Pteor!"

A soldier tugged open the brazen door in the belly of the statue. Abdashtarth cried:

"He lies! This king is no god, but a mortal madman! Slay the blasphemers against the true god of the Pelishtim, the mighty Pteor, lest the all-wise one turn his back upon his people—"

At this point, four Anakim picked up Abdashtarth as if he had been a log of wood and hurled him feet-first through the opening. His shriek was cut off by the clang of the closing door, through which these same soldiers had, in times past, tossed hundreds of the children of the Pelishtim in times of crisis under the direction of this same Abdashtarth. Smoke poured from the vents in the statue's ears, while a look of smug satisfaction spread over the face of Mattenbaal.

A great shudder rippled across the throng. Then a frenzied yell broke the stillness. A wild-haired figure ran forward, a half-naked shepherd. With a shriek of "Blasphemer!" he hurled a stone. The missile struck the new high priest in the mouth, breaking his teeth. Mattenbaal staggered, blood streaming down his beard. With a roar, the mob surged forward. High taxes, starvation, tyranny, rapine, and massacre—all these the Pelishtim had endured from their mad king, but this tampering with their religion was the last straw. Staid merchants became madmen; cringing beggars turned into hot-eyed fiends.

Stones flew like hail, and louder rose the roar of the mob. Hands were clutching at the garments of the dazed Mattenbaal when the armored Anakim closed in around him, beat the mob back with bowstaves and spear shafts, and hustled the priest away.

With a clanking of weapons and a jingling of bridle chains, a troop of Kushite horse, resplendent in headdresses of ostrich feathers and lions' manes and corselets of silvered scales, galloped out of one of the streets leading into the great Square of Pteor. Their white teeth shone in their dark faces. The stones of the mob bounced off their bucklers of rhinoceros hide. They urged their horses into the press, slashing with curved blades and thrusting long lances through the bodies of the Asgalunim. Men rolled howling under the stamping hooves. The rioters gave way, fleeing wildly into shops and alleys, leaving the square littered with writhing bodies.

The black riders leaped from their saddles and began crashing in the doors of shops and dwellings and heaping their arms with plunder. Screams of women sounded from within the houses. A crash of latticework, and a white-clad body struck the street with bone-crushing impact. Another horseman, laughing, passed his lance through the body as it lay.

The giant Imbalayo, in flaming silk and polished steel, rode roaring among his men, beating them into order with a heavy leaded ship. They mounted and swung into line behind him. In a canter they swept off down the street, gory human heads bobbing on their lances as an object lesson to the maddened Asgalunim who crouched in their coverts, panting with hate.

The breathless eunuch who brought news of the uprising to King Akhîrom was swiftly followed by another, who prostrated himself and cried: "O divine king, the general Othbaal is dead! His servants found him murdered in his palace, and beside him the ring of Keluka the Sworder. Wherefore the Anakim cry out that he was murdered by the order of the general Imbalayo. They search for Keluka in the Kushites' quarter and fight with the Kushites!"

Rufia, listening behind a curtain, stifled a cry. Akhîrom's faraway gaze did not alter. Wrapped in aloofness he replied:

"Let the Hyrkanians separate them. Shall private quarrels interfere with the destiny of a god? Othbaal is dead, but Akhîrom lives forever. Another man shall lead my Anakim. Let the Kushites handle the mob until they realize the sin of their atheism. My destiny is to reveal myself to the world in blood and fire, until all the tribes of the earth know me and bow down before me! You may go."

Night was falling on a tense city as Conan, his head wound now healed, strode through the streets adjoining the quarter of the Kushites. In that section, occupied mostly by soldiers, lights shone and stalls were open by tacit agreement. All day, revolt had rumbled in the quarters. The mob was like a thousand-headed serpent; stamp it out here and it broke out there. The hooves of the Kushites had clattered from one end of the city to the other, spattering blood.

Only armed men now traversed the streets. The great iron-bound wooden gates of the quarters were locked as in times of civil war. Through the lowering arch of the great gate of Simura cantered troops of black horsemen, the torchlight crimsoning their naked scimitars. Their silken cloaks flowed in the wind, and their black arms gleamed like polished ebony.

Conan entered a cookshop where girdled warriors gorged and secretly guzzled forbidden wine. Instead of taking the first place open he stood, head up, his smoldering eyes roaming the place. His gaze came to rest on a far corner where a plainly-dressed man with a kaffia pulled well down over his face sat cross-legged on the floor in a dim alcove. A low table of food stood on the floor in front of the man.

Conan strode across, swerving around the other tables. He kicked a cushion into the alcove opposite the seated man and dropped down upon it.

"Greetings, Farouz!" he rumbled. "Or should I say General Mazdak?"

The Hyrkanian started. "What's that?"

Conan grinned wolfishly. "I knew you when we entered the house of Othbaal. No one but the master of the house could know its secrets so well, and that house had once belonged to Mazdak the Hyrkanian."

"Not so loud, friend! How did you pick me out when my own men don't know me in this Zuagir's headcloth?"

"I used my eyes. Well, now that our first venture has paid us so well, what shall we do next?"

"I know not. I should be able to do something with one

of your brawn and force. But you know how it is with the dog-brothers."

"Aye," snarled Conan. "I tried to get mercenary service, but your three rival armies hate each other so and strive so fiercely for the rule of the state that none will have me. Each thinks I'm a spy for one of the other two." He paused to order a joint of beef.

"What a restless dog you are!" said Mazdak. "Will you then go back to Akkharia?"

Conan spat. "Nay. It's small, even for one of these little Shemitish fly-specks of a state, and has no great wealth. And the people are as crazily touchy about their racial and national pride as you all are here, so I couldn't hope to rise very high. Perhaps I'd do better under one of the Hyborian rulers to the north, if I could find one who'd pick men for fighting ability only. But look you, Mazdak, why don't you seize the rule of this nation for yourself? Now that Othbaal's gone, you have only to find an excuse for putting a blade into Imbalayo's guts, and . . ."

"*Tarim!* I'm as ambitious as the next man, but not so headlong as that! Know that Imbalayo, having gotten the confidence of our mad monarch, dwells in the Great Palace, surrounded by his black swordsmen. Not that one could not kill him by a sudden stab during some public function—if one did not mind being cut to bits instantly afterward. And then where's ambition?"

"We should be able to think up something," said Conan, eyes narrowed.

"We, eh? I suppose you'd expect a reward for your part?"

"Of course. What sort of fool do you think me?"

"No more foolish than the next. I see no immediate prospect of such an enterprise, but I'll bear your words in mind. And fear not but that you'd be well repaid. Now fare you well, for I must go back into the toils of politics."

Conan's joint arrived as Mazdak left. Conan dug his

teeth into the meat with even more than his usual gusto, for the success of his vengeance had made his spirits soar. While devouring a mass that would have satisfied a lion, he listened to the talk around him.

"Where are the Anakim?" demanded a mustached Hyrkanian, cramming his jaws with almond cakes.

"They sulk in their quarter," answered another. "They swear the Kushites slew Othbaal and show Keluka's ring to prove it. Keluka has disappeared, and Imbalayo swears he knows naught of it. But there's the ring, and a dozen had been slain in brawls when the king ordered us to beat them apart. By Asura, this has been a day of days!"

"Akhîrom's madness brought it on," declared another in a lowered voice. "How soon before this lunatic dooms us all by some crazy antic?"

"Careful," cautioned his mate. "Our swords are his as long as Mazdak orders. But if revolt breaks out again, the Anakim are more likely to fight against the Kushites than with them. Men say Akhîrom has taken Othbaal's concubine Rufia into his harem. That angers the Anakim the more, for they suspect that Othbaal was slain by the king's orders, or at least with his consent. But their anger is naught beside that of Zeriti, whom the king has put aside. The rage of the witch, they say, makes the sandstorm of the desert seem like a spring breeze."

Conan's moody blue eyes blazed as he digested this news. The memory of the red-haired wench had stuck in his mind during the last few days. The thought of stealing her out from under the nose of the mad king, and keeping her out of sight of her former owner Mazdak, gave spice to life. And, if he had to leave Asgalun, she would make a pleasant companion on the long road to Koth. In Asgalun there was one person who could best help him in this enterprise: Zeriti the Stygian, and if he could guess human motives she would be glad to do so.

He left the shop and headed towards the wall of the inner city. Zeriti's house, he knew, was in this part of

Asgalun. To get to it he would have to pass the great wall, and the only way he knew of doing this without discovery was through the tunnel that Mazdak had shown him.

Accordingly, he approached the canal and made his way to the grove of palms near the shore. Groping in the darkness among the marble ruins, he found and lifted the slab. Again he advanced through blackness and dripping water, stumbled on the other stair, and mounted it. He found the catch and emerged into the corridor, now dark. The house was silent, but the reflection of lights elsewhere showed that it was still occupied, doubtless by the slain general's servants and women.

Uncertain as to which way led to the outer stair, he set off at random, passed through a curtained archway—and confronted six black slaves who sprang up glaring. Before he could retreat, he heard a shout and a rush of feet behind him. Cursing his luck, he ran straight at the blacks. A whirl of steel and he was through, leaving a writhing form on the floor behind him, and dashed through a doorway on the other side of the room. Curved blades sought his back as he slammed the door behind him. Steel rang on the wood and glittering points showed through the panels. He shot the bolt and whirled, glaring about for an exit. His gaze found a gold-barred window.

With a headlong rush, he launched himself full at the window. The soft bars tore out with a crash, taking half the casement with them, before the impact of his hurtling body. He shot through space as the door crashed inward and howling figures flooded into the room.

In the Great East Palace, where slave-girls and eunuchs glided on bare feet, no echo reverberated of the hell that seethed outside the walls. In a chamber whose dome was of gold-filagreed ivory, King Akhîrom, clad in a white silken robe that made him look even more ghostly, sat cross-legged on a couch of gemmed ivory and stared at Rufia kneeling before him.

Rufia wore a robe of crimson silk and a girdle of satin sewn with pearls. But amidst all this splendor, the Ophirean's eyes were shadowed. She had inspired Akhîrom's latest madness, but she had not mastered him. Now he seemed withdrawn, with an expression in his cold eyes that made her shudder. Abruptly he spoke:

"It is not meet for a god to mate with mortals."

Rufia started, opened her mouth; then feared to speak.

"Love is a human weakness," he continued. "I will cast it from me. Gods are beyond love. Weakness assails me when I lie in your arms."

"What do you mean, my lord?" she ventured.

"Even the gods must sacrifice, and therefore I give you up, lest my divinity weaken." He clapped his hands, and a eunuch entered on all fours. "Send in the general Imbalayo," ordered Akhîrom, and the eunuch banged his head against the floor and crawled out backwards. These were the most recently instituted customs of the court.

"No!" Rufia sprang up. "You cannot give me to that beast—" She fell to her knees, catching at his robe, which he drew back from her.

"Woman!" he thundered. "Are you mad? Would you assail a god?"

Imbalayo entered uncertainly. A warrior of barbaric Darfar, he had risen to his present high estate by wild fighting and crafty intrigue. But shrewd, brawny, and fearless though the Negro was, he could not be sure of the mad Akhîrom's intentions from moment to moment.

The king pointed to the woman cowering at his feet. "Take her!"

Imbalayo grinned and caught up Rufia, who writhed and screamed in his grasp. She stretched her arms towards Akhîrom as Imbalayo bore her from the chamber. But Akhîrom answered not, sitting with hands folded and gaze detached.

Another heard. Crouching in an alcove, a slim brown-skinned girl watched the grinning Kushite carry his captive up the hall. Scarcely had he vanished when she fled in another direction.

Imbalayo, the favored of the king, alone of the generals dwelt in the Great Palace. This was really an aggregation of buildings united into one great structure and housing the three thousand servants of Akhîrom. Following winding corridors, crossing an occasional court paved with mosaics, he came to his own dwelling in the southern wing. But even as he came in sight of the door of teak, banded with arabesques of copper, a supple form barred his way.

"Zeriti!" Imbalayo recoiled in awe. The hands of the handsome, brown-skinned woman clenched and unclenched in controlled passion.

"A servant brought me word that Akhîrom has discarded the red-haired slut," said the Stygian. "Sell her to me! I owe her a debt that I would pay."

"Why should I?" said the Kushite, fidgeting impatiently. "The king has given her to me. Stand aside, lest I hurt you."

"Have you heard what the Anakim shout in the streets?"

"What is that to me?"

"They howl for the head of Imbalayo, because of the murder of Othbaal. What if I told them their suspicions were true?"

"I had naught to do with it!" he shouted.

"I can produce men to swear they saw you help Keluka cut him down."

"I'll kill you, witch!"

She laughed. "You dare not! Now will you sell me the red-haired jade, or will you fight the Anakim?"

Imbalayo let Rufia slip to the floor. "Take her and begone!" he snarled.

"Take your pay!" she retorted and hurled a handful of coins into his face. Imbalayo's eyes burned red and his hands opened and closed with suppressed blood-lust.

Ignoring him, Zeriti bent over Rufia, who crouched, dazed with the hopeless realization that against this new possessor the wiles she played against men were useless. Zeriti gathered the Ophirean's red locks in her fingers and forced her head back, to stare fiercely into her eyes. Then she clapped her hands. Four eunuchs entered.

"Take her to my house," Zeriti ordered, and they bore the shrinking Rufia away. Zeriti followed, breathing softly between her teeth.

When Conan plunged through the window, he had no idea of what lay in the darkness ahead of him. Shrubs broke his crashing fall. Springing up, he saw his pursuers crowding through the window he had just shattered. He was in a garden, a great shadowy place of trees and ghostly blossoms. His hunters blundered among the trees while he reached the wall unopposed. He sprang high, caught the coping with one hand, and heaved himself up and over.

He halted to locate himself. Though he had never been in the inner city, he had heard it described often enough so that he carried a mental map of it. He was in the Quarter of the Officials. Ahead of him, over the flat roofs, loomed a structure that must be the Lesser West Palace, a great pleasure house giving into the famous Garden of Abibaal. Sure of his ground, he hurried along the street into which he had dropped and soon emerged on the broad thoroughfare that traversed the inner city from north to south.

Late as it was, there was much stirring abroad. Armed Hyrkanians strode past. In the great square between the two palaces, Conan heard the jingle of reins on restive horses and saw a squadron of Kushite troopers sitting their steeds under the torchlight. There was reason for their alertness. Far away he heard tom-toms drumming sullenly among the quarters. The wind brought snatches of wild song and distant yells.

With his soldierly swagger, Conan passed unnoticed among the mailed figures. When he plucked the sleeve of a Hyrkanian to ask the way to Zeriti's house, the man readily gave him the information. Conan, like everyone else in Asgalun, knew that however much the Stygian regarded Akhîrom as her personal property, she by no means considered herself his exclusive possession in return. There were mercenary captains as familiar with her chambers as was the king of Pelishtia.

Zeriti's house adjoined a court of the East Palace, to whose gardens it was connected so that Zeriti, in the days of her favor, could pass from her house to the palace without violating the king's order for the seclusion of women. Zeriti, the daughter of a free chieftain, had been Akhîrom's mistress but not his slave.

Conan did not expect difficulty in gaining entrance to her house. She pulled hidden strings of intrigue and politics, and men of all races and conditions were admitted to her audience chamber, where dancing girls and the fumes of the black lotus offered entertainment. That night there were no dancing girls or guests, but a villainous-looking Zuagir opened the arched door under a burning cresset and admitted Conan without question. He showed Conan across a small court, up an outer stair, down a corridor, and into a broad chamber bordered by fretted arches hung with curtains of crimson velvet.

The softly lit room was empty, but somewhere sounded the scream of a woman in pain. Then came a peal of musical laughter, also feminine, indescribably vindictive and malicious.

Conan jerked his head to catch the direction of the sounds. Then he began examining the drapes behind the arches to see which of them concealed doors.

Zeriti straightened up from her task and dropped the heavy whip. The naked figure bound to the divan was crossed by red weals from neck to ankles. This, however, was but a prelude to a more ghastly fate.

The witch took from a cabinet a piece of charcoal, with which she drew a complex figure on the floor, adding words in the mysterious glyphs of the serpent-folk who ruled Stygia before the Cataclysm. She set a small golden lamp at each of the five corners of the figure and tossed into the flame of each a pinch of the pollen of the purple lotus, which grows in the swamps of southern Stygia. A strange smell, sickeningly sweet, pervaded the chamber. Then she began to incant in a language that was old before purple-towered Python rose in the lost empire of Acheron, over three thousand years before.

Slowly a dark something took form. To Rufia, half dead with pain and fright, it seemed like a pillar of cloud. High up in the amorphous mass appeared a pair of glowing points that might have been eyes. Rufia felt an all-pervading cold, as if the thing were drawing all the heat out of her body by its mere presence. The cloud gave the impression of being black without much density. Rufia could see the wall behind it through the shapeless mass, which slowly thickened.

Zeriti bent and snuffed out the lamps—one, two, three, four. The room, lit by the remaining lamp, was now dim. The pillar of smoke was hardly discernible except for the glowing eyes.

A sound made Zeriti turn: a distant, muffled roar, faint and far-off but of vast volume. It was the bestial howling of many men.

Zeriti resumed her incantation, but there came another interruption: angry words and the voice of the Zuagir, a cry, the crunch of a savage blow, and the thud of a body. Imbalayo burst in, a wild-looking figure with his eyeballs and teeth gleaming in the light of the single lamp and blood dripping from his scimitar.

"Dog!" exclaimed the Stygian, drawing herself up like a serpent from its coil. "What do you here?"

"The woman you took from me!" roared Imbalayo. "The city has risen and all Hell is loose! Give me the woman before I kill you!"

Zeriti glanced at her rival and drew a jeweled dagger, crying: "Hotep! Khafra! Help me!"

With a roar, the black general lunged. The Stygian's supple quickness was futile; the broad blade plunged through her body, standing out a foot between her shoulders. With a choking cry she stumbled, and the Kushite wrenched his scimitar free as she fell. At that instant Conan appeared at the door, sword in hand.

Evidently taking the Cimmerian for one of the witch's servants, the Kushite bounded across the floor, his saber whistling in a fearful slash. Conan leaped back; the sword missed his throat by a finger's breadth and nicked the doorframe. As he leaped, Conan struck backhanded in return. It was incredible that the black giant should recover from his missed cut in time to parry, but Imbalayo somehow twisted his body, arm, and blade all at once to catch a blow that would have felled a lesser man by sheer impact.

Back and forth they surged, swords clanging. Then recognition dawned in Imbalayo's features. He fell back with a cry of "Amra!"

Now Conan knew that he must kill this man. Though he did not remember ever seeing him before, the Kushite had recognized him as the leader of a crew of black corsairs who, under the name of Amra, the Lion, had plundered the coasts of Kush and Stygia and Shem. If Imbalayo revealed Conan's identity to the Pelishtim, the vengeful Shemites would tear Conan apart with their bare hands if need be. Bitterly though the Shemites fought among themselves, they would unite to destroy the red-handed barbarian who had raided their coast.

Conan lunged and drove Imbalayo back a step, feinted, and struck at the Kushite's head. The force of the blow beat down Imbalayo's scimitar and came down stunningly on the bronze helmet—and Conan's sword, weakened by deep notches in the blade, broke off short.

For the space of two heartbeats, the two barbarian-warriors confronted each other. Imbalayo's bloodshot eyes sought a vulnerable spot on Conan's form; his muscles tensed for a final, fatal spring and slash.

Conan hurled his hilt at Imbalayo's head. As the Kushite ducked the missile, Conan whirled his cloak around his left forearm and snatched out his poniard with his right hand. He had no illusions about his chances with Imbalayo in this Zingaran-style fighting. The Kushite, now stalking forward on the balls of his feet like a cat, was no slow-moving mountain of muscle like Keluka, but a superbly-thewed fighting machine almost as lightning-fast as Conan himself. The scimitar whipped up . . .

And a shapeless mass of cloudy something, hitherto unnoticed in the gloom, swept forward and fastened itself on Imbalayo's back. Imbalayo screamed like a man being roasted alive. He kicked and squirmed and tried to reach back with his sword. But the luminous eyes glowed over his shoulder and the smoky substance lapped around him, drawing him slowly backwards.

Conan reeled back from the sight, his barbarian's fears of the supernatural rising like a choking lump in his throat.

Imbalayo's shrieks ceased. The black body slid to the ground with a soft, squashy sound. The cloudy thing was gone.

Conan advanced cautiously. Imbalayo's body had a curiously pallid, collapsed appearance, as if the demon had extracted all the bones and blood, leaving only a man-shaped bag of skin with a few organs inside it. The Cimmerian shuddered.

A sob from the divan called his attention to Rufia. With two strides he reached her and cut her bonds. She sat up, weeping silently, when a voice shouted:

"Imbalayo! In the name of all the fiends, where are you? It's time to mount and ride! I saw you run in here!"

A mailed and helmeted figure dashed into the chamber. Mazdak recoiled at the sight of the bodies and cried: "Oh, you cursed savage, why must you slay Imbalayo at this time? The city has risen. The Anakim are fighting the Kushites, who had their hands full already. I ride with my men to aid the Kushites. As for you—I still owe you my life, but there's a limit to all things! Get out of this city and never let me see you again!"

Conan grinned. "It wasn't I who killed him, but one of Zeriti's demons after he slew the witch. Look at his body if you don't believe me." As Mazdak bent to see, Conan added: "And have you no greeting for your old friend Rufia?"

Rufia had been cowering behind Conan. Mazdak plucked at his mustache. "Good. I'll take her back to my house; we have—"

The distant roaring of the mob became louder.

"No," said Mazdak distractedly. "I must go to put down the sedition. But how can I leave her to wander the streets naked?"

Conan said: "Why not throw in your lot with the Anakim, who will be as glad to get rid of this mad king as are the Asgalunim? With Imbalayo and Othbaal dead, you're the only general alive in Asgalun. Become leader of the revolt, put down the crazy Akhîrom, and set some feeble cousin or nephew in his place. Then you'll be the real ruler of Pelishtia!"

Mazdak, listening like a man in a dream, gave a sudden shout of laughter. "Done!" he cried. "To horse! Take Rufia to my house, then join the Hyrkanians in battle. Tomorrow I shall rule Pelishtia, and you may ask of me what you will. Farewell for now!"

Off went the Hyrkanian with a swirl of his cloak. Conan turned to Rufia. "Get some clothes, wench."

"Who are you? I heard Imbalayo call you Amra . . ."

"Don't say that name in Shem! I am Conan, a Cimmerian."

"Conan? I heard you spoken of when I was intimate with the king. Do not take me to Mazdak's house!"

"Why not? He'll be the real ruler of Pelishtia."

"I know that cold snake too well. Take me with you instead! Let's loot this house and flee the city .With all this uproar, nobody will stop us."

Conan grinned. "You tempt me, Rufia, but it's worth too much to me right now to keep on Mazdak's good side. Besides, I told him I would deliver you, and I like to keep my word. Now get into a garment or I'll drag you as you are."

"Well," said Rufia in a temporizing tone, but then stopped.

A gurgling sound came from the sprawled body of Zeriti. As Conan watched with his hair standing up in horror, the witch slowly rose to a sitting position, despite a wound that any fighter would have said would be instantly fatal. She struggled to her feet and stood, swaying, regarding Conan and Rufia. A little blood ran down from the wounds in her back and chest. When she spoke, it was in a voice choked with blood.

"It takes—more than—a sword-thrust—to kill—a daughter of Set." She reeled towards the door. In the doorway she turned back to gasp: "The Asgalunim—will be interested to know—that Amra and his woman—are in their city."

Conan stood irresolutely, knowing that for his own safety he ought to rush upon the witch and hew her in pieces, but restrained by his rude barbarian's chivalry from attacking a woman.

"Why bother us?" he burst out. "You can have your mad king back!"

Zeriti shook her head. "I know—what Mazdak plans.

And ere I quit this body—for good—I will have—my revenge—on this drab."

"Then—" growled Conan, snatching up Imbalayo's scimitar and starting towards the witch. But Zeriti made a gesture and spoke a word. A line of flame appeared across the floor between Conan and the doorway, extending from wall to wall. Conan recoiled, throwing up a hand to shade his face from the fierce heat. Then Zeriti was gone.

"After her!" cried Rufia. "The fire is but one of her illusions."

"But if she can't be killed—"

"Nevertheless, heads do not tell secrets when sundered from their bodies."

Grimly, Conan rushed for the exit, leaping across the line of flame. There was an instant of heat, and then the flames vanished as he passed through them.

"Wait here!" he barked at Rufia, and ran after Zeriti.

But when he reached the street, there was no witch to be seen. He ran to the nearest alley and looked up it, then to the alley in the opposite direction. Still there was no sign of her.

In seconds he was back in Zeriti's house. "You were right the first time," he grunted at Rufia. "Let's grab what we can and go."

In the great Square of Adonis, the tossing torches blazed on a swirl of straining figures, screaming horses, and lashing blades. Men fought hand-to-hand: Kushites and Shemites, gasping, cursing, and dying. Like madmen the Asgalunim grappled the black warriors, dragging them from their saddles, slashing the girths of the frenzied horses. Rusty pikes clanged against lances. Fire burst out here and there, mounting into the skies until the shepherds on the Libnun Hills gaped in wonder. From the suburbs poured a torrent of figures converging on the great square. Hundreds of still shapes, in mail or striped robes, lay under the trampling hooves, and over them the living screamed and hacked.

The square lay in the Kushite quarter, into which the Anakim had come ravening while the bulk of the Negroes had been fighting the mob elsewhere. Now withdrawn in haste to their own quarter, the ebony swordsmen were overwhelming the Anakian infantry by sheer numbers, while the mob threatened to engulf both bodies. Under their captain, Bombaata, the Kushites retained a semblance of order that gave them an advantage over the unorganized Anakim and the leaderless mob. Their squadrons clattered back and forth across the square, charging to keep a space clear in the midst of he swarming thousands, so that they could use their horses to advantage.

Meanwhile the maddened Asgalunim were smashing and plundering the houses of the blacks, dragging forth howling women. The blaze of burning buildings made the square swim in an ocean of fire, while the shrieks of their women and children as they were torn to pieces by the Shemites made the Negroes fight with even more than their usual ferocity.

Somewhere arose the whir of Hyrkanian kettledrums above the throb of many hooves.

"The Hyrkanians at last!" panted Bombaata. "They've loitered long enough. And where in Derketa's name is Imbalayo?"

Into the square raced a frantic horse, foam flying from its bit rings. The rider, reeling in the saddle, screamed: "Bombaata! Bombaata!" as he clung to the mane with bloody hands.

"Here, fool!" roared the Kushite, catching the other's bridle.

"Imbalayo is dead!" shrieked the man above the roar of the flames and the rising thunder of the kettledrums.

"The Hyrkanians have turned against us! They have slain our brothers in the palaces! Here they come!"

With a deafening thunder of hooves and drums, the squadrons of mailed lancers burst upon the square, riding down friend and foe. Bombaata saw the lean, exultant face of Mazdak beneath the blazing arc of his scimitar, and then a sword fell and the Kushite with it.

On the rocky spurs of Libnun the herdsmen watched and shivered, and the clangor of swords was heard miles up the river, where pallid nobles trembled in their gardens. Hemmed in by mailed Hyrkanians, furious Anakim, and shrieking Asgalunim, the Kushites died fighting to a man.

It was the mob that first turned its attention to Akhîrom. They rushed through the unguarded gates into the inner city, and through the great bronze doors of the East Palace. Ragged hordes streamed yelling down the corridors through the Golden Gates into the great Golden Hall, tearing aside the curtain of cloth-of-gold to reveal an empty throne. Silken tapestries were ripped from the walls by grimed and bloody fingers. Sardonyx tables were overthrown with a clatter of golden vessels. Eunuchs in crimson robes fled squeaking, and slave-girls shrieked in the hands of ravishers.

In the Great Emerald Hall, King Akhîrom stood like a statue on a fur-strewn dais, his white hands twitching. At the entrance to the hall clustered a handful of his faithful servants, beating back the mob with swords. A band of Anakim plowed through the throng and burst the barrier of black slaves. As the wedge of swarthy Shemitish soldiers clattered forward, Akhîrom seemed to come to himself. He dashed to an exit in the rear. Anakim and Pelishtim, mingling as they ran, chased the fleeing king. After them came a band of Hyrkanians with the blood-splashed Mazdak at their head.

Akhîrom ran down a corridor, then turned aside to dash

up a winding stair. The stair curled up and up until it came out on the roof of the palace. But it did not stop there; it continued on up into the slender spire that rose from the roof, from which Akhîrom's father, King Azumelek, had observed the stars.

Up went Akhîrom, and after him came the pursuers, until the stair became so narrow that only one man could negotiate it, and the pursuit slowed for lack of breath.

King Akhirom came out on the small circular platform at the top of the tower, surrounded by a low wall. He slammed down the stone trapdoor and bolted it. Then he leaned over the wall. Men swarmed on the roof, and below them others gazed up from the main courtyard.

"Sinful mortals!" screeched Akhîrom. "You do not believe I am a god! I will show you! I am not bound to the surface of the earth as worms like you are, but can soar through the heavens like a bird! You shall see, and then you will bow down and worship me as you ought! Here I go!"

Akhîrom climbed to the top of the wall, balanced an instant, and dove off, spreading his arms like wings. His body described a long, steep parabola downward, missing the edge of the roof and plunging on down, the wind whistling in his garments, until he struck the stones of the courtyard below with the sound of a melon hit by a sledgehammer.

Not even the extermination of the Kushites and the death of Akhîrom brought peace to troubled Asgalun. Other mobs roamed the city, incited by a mysterious rumor that Amra, the pirate chief of the black corsairs, was there, and that the Ophirean woman Rufia was with him. The rumors grew and changed with each retelling until men said that Amra had sent Rufia to Asgalun as a spy for the pirates, and that a pirate navy was waiting off the coast for word from Amra to march overland against the city. But, though they combed the whole town over, no sign did the searchers find of Amra and his doxy.

North from Asgalun, through the meadowlands of western Shem, ran the long road to Koth. Along this road, as the sun rose, Conan and Rufia rode at a canter. Conan bestrode his own horse; the Ophirean woman, a riderless horse which Conan had caught on the streets of Asgalun that night. She wore clothes from the chests of Zeriti—tight for her full figure, but adequate.

Rufia said: "If you had stayed in Asgalun, Conan, you could have risen high under Mazdak."

"And who begged me not to turn her back to him?"

"I know. He was a cold, unfeeling master. But . . ."

"Besides, I rather liked the fellow. If I had stayed there, sooner or later one of us would have had to kill the other over you." The Cimmerian chuckled and slapped the bag of loot from Zeriti's house, so that the coins and ornaments jingled. "I shall do as well in the North. Come on there, beat some speed out of that nag!"

"But I'm still sore where she beat me—"

"If you don't hurry, I'll see that you get even sorer. Do you want Mazdak's Hyrkanians to catch us before we've even had breakfast?"

Black Colossus

Rufia's interest seems to have lasted no longer than the loot that Conan brought from Asgalun, or he may have traded her for a better horse before taking service under Amalric of Nemedia, mercenary general of Queen-Regent Yasmela of the little border kingdom of Khoraja. Here he soon works his way up to the rank of captain. Yasmela's brother, the king of Khoraja, is a prisoner in Ophir, and her borders are assailed by nomadic forces gathered by a mysterious veiled sorcerer, Natohk.

"The Night of Power, when Fate stalked through the corridors of the world like a colossus just risen from an age-old throne of granite—"

—*E. Hoffmann Price,* The Girl from Samarcand

1

Only the age-old silence brooded over the mysterious ruins of Kuthchemes, but Fear was there; Fear quivered in the mind of Shevatas, the thief, driving his breath quick and sharp against his clenched teeth.

He stood, the one atom of life admidst the colossal monuments of desolation and decay. Not even a vulture hung like a black dot in the vast blue vault of the sky that the sun glazed with its heat. On every hand rose the grim relics of another, forgotten age: huge broken pillars, thrusting up their jagged pinnacles into the sky; long, wavering lines of crumbling walls; fallen cyclopean blocks of stone; shattered images, whose horrific features the corroding winds and dust storms had half erased. From horizon to horizon no sign of life: only the sheer breathtaking sweep of the naked desert, bisected by the wandering line of a long-dry river course; in the midst of that vastness the glimmering fangs of the ruins, the columns standing up like broken masts of sunken ships—all dominated by the towering ivory dome before which Shevatas stood trembling.

The base of this dome was a gigantic pedestal of marble, rising from what had once been a terraced eminence on the banks of the ancient river. Broad steps led up to a great bronze door in the dome, which rested on its base like the half of some titanic egg. The dome itself was of pure ivory, which shone as if unknown hands kept it polished. Likewise shone the spired gold cap of the pinnacle, and the inscription which sprawled about the curve of the dome in golden hieroglyphics yards long. No man on earth could read those characters, but Shevatas shuddered at the dim conjectures they raised. For he came of a very old race, whose myths ran back to shapes undreamed of by contemporary tribes.

Shevatas was wiry and lithe, as became a master thief of Zamora. His small, round head was shaven, his only garment a loincloth of scarlet silk. Like all his race, he was very dark, his narrow vulture-like face set off by his keen black eyes. His long, slender, and tapering fingers were quick and nervous as the wings of a moth. From a gold-scaled girdle hung a short, narrow, jewel-hilted sword in a sheath of ornamented leather. Shevatas handled the weapon with apparently exaggerated care. He even seemed to flinch away from the contact of the sheath with his naked thigh. Nor was his care without reason.

This was Shevatas, a thief among thieves, whose name was spoken with awe in the dives of the Maul and the dim shadowy recesses beneath the temples of Bel, and who lived in songs and myths for a thousand years. Yet fear ate at the heart of Shevatas as he stood before the ivory dome of Kuthchemes. Any fool could see there was something unnatural about the structure; the winds and suns of three thousand years had lashed it, yet its gold and ivory rose bright and glistening as the day it was reared by nameless hands on the bank of the nameless river.

This unnaturalness was in keeping with the general aura of these devil-haunted ruins. This desert was the mysterious expanse lying southeast of the lands of Shem. A few days' ride on camel back to the southwest, as Shevatas knew, would bring the traveler within sight of the great river Styx at the point where it turned at right angles with its former course and flowed westward to empty at last into the distant sea. At the point of its bend began the land of Stygia, the dark-bosomed mistress of the South, whose domains, watered by the great river, rose sheer out of the surrounding desert.

Eastward, Shevatas knew, the desert shaded into steppes stretching to the Hyrkanian kingdom of Turan, rising in barbaric splendor on the shores of the great inland sea. A week's ride northward, the desert ran into a tangle of barren hills, beyond which lay the fertile uplands of Koth, the southernmost realm of the Hyborian races. Westward the desert merged into the meadowlands of Shem, which stretched away to the ocean.

All this Shevatas knew without being particularly conscious of the knowledge, as a man knows the streets of his town. He was a far traveler and had looted the treasures of many kingdoms. But now he hesitated and shuddered before the highest adventure and the mightiest treasure of all.

In that ivory dome lay the bones of Thugra Khotan, the dark sorcerer who had reigned in Kuthchemes three thousand years ago, when the kingdoms of Stygia and Acheron stretched far northward of the great river, over the meadows of Shem, and into the uplands. Then the great drift of the Hyborians swept southward from the cradleland of their race near the northern pole. It was a titanic drift, extending over centuries and ages. But in the reign of Thugra Khotan, the last magician of Kuthchemes, gray-eyed, tawny-haired barbarians in wolfskins and scale mail had ridden from the North into the rich uplands to carve out the kingdom of Koth with their iron swords. They had stormed over Kuthchemes like a tidal wave, washing the marble towers in blood, and the kingdom of Acheron had gone down in fire and ruin.

But while they were shattering the streets of this city and cutting down his archers like ripe corn, Thugra Khotan had swallowed a strange terrible poison, and his masked priests had locked him into the tomb he himself had prepared. His devotees died about that tomb in a crimson holocaust, but the barbarians could not burst the door, nor ever mar the structure by maul or fire. So they rode away, leaving the great city in ruins, and in his ivory-domed sepulcher great Thugra Khotan slept unmolested, while the lizards of desolation gnawed at the crumbling pillars, and the very river that watered his land in old times sank into the sands and ran dry.

Many a thief sought to gain the treasure which fables said lay heaped about the moldering bones inside the dome. And many a thief died at the door of the tomb, and many another was harried by monstrous dreams to die at last with the froth of madness on his lips.

So Shevatas shuddered as he faced the tomb, nor was his shudder altogether occasioned by the legend of the serpent said to guard the sorcerer's bones. Over all myths of Thugra Khotan hung horror and death like a pall. From where the thief stood he could see the ruins of the great hall wherein chained captives had knelt by the hundreds during festivals to have their heads hacked off by the priest-king in honor of Set, the Serpent god of Stygia. Somewhere near by had been the pit, dark and awful, wherein screaming victims were fed to a nameless amorphic monstrosity, which came up out of a deeper, more hellish cavern. Legend made Thugra Khotan more than human; his worship yet lingered in a mongrel degraded cult, whose votaries stamped his likeness on coins to pay the way of their dead over the great river of darkness of which the Styx was but the material shadow. Shevatas had seen this likeness, on coins stolen from under the tongues of the dead, and its image was etched indelibly in his brain.

But he put aside his fears and mounted to the bronze door, whose smooth surface offered no bolt or catch. Not for naught had he gained access into darksome cults, had harkened to the grisly whispers of the votaries of Skelos under midnight trees, and read the forbidden iron-bound books of Vathelos the Blind.

Kneeling before the portal, he searched the sill with nimble fingers; their sensitive tips found projections too small for the eye to detect or for less-skilled fingers to discover. These he pressed carefully and according to a peculiar system, muttering a long-forgotten incantation as he did so. As he pressed the last projection, he sprang up with frantic haste and struck the exact center of the door a quick sharp blow with his open hand.

There was no rasp of spring or hinge, but the door retreated inward, and the breath hissed explosively from Shevatas' clenched teeth. A short, narrow corridor was disclosed. Down this the door had slid and was now in place at the other end. The floor, ceiling, and sides of the tunnel-like aperture were of ivory, and now from an opening on one side came a silent writhing horror that reared up and glared on the intruder with awful luminous eyes: a serpent twenty feet long, with shimmering, iridescent scales.

The thief did not waste time in conjecturing what night-black pits lying below the dome had given sustenance to the monster. Gingerly he drew the sword, and from it dripped a greenish liquid exactly like that which slavered from the scimitar-fangs of the reptile. The blade was steeped in the poison of the snake's own kind, and the obtaining of that venom from the fiend-haunted swamps of Zingara would have made a saga in itself.

Shevatas advanced warily on the balls of his feet, knees bent slightly, ready to spring either way like a flash of light. And he needed all his coordinate speed when the snake arched its neck and struck, shooting out its full length like a stroke of lightning. For all his quickness of nerve and eye, Shevatas had died then but for chance. His well-laid plans of leaping aside and striking down on the outstretched neck were put at naught by the blinding speed of the reptile's attack. The thief had but time to extend the sword in front of him, involuntarily closing his eyes and crying out. Then the sword was wrenched from his hand and the corridor was filled with a horrible thrashing and lashing.

Opening his eyes, amazed to find himself still alive, Shevatas saw the monster heaving and twisting its slimy form in fantastic contortions, the sword transfixing its giant jaws. Sheer chance had hurled it full against the point he had held out blindly. A few moments later the serpent sank into shining, scarcely quivering coils, as the poison on the blade struck home.

Gingerly stepping over it, the thief thrust against the door, which this time slid aside, revealing the interior of the dome. Shevatas cried out; instead of utter darkness he had come into a crimson light that throbbed and pulsed almost beyond the endurance of mortal eyes. It came from a gigantic red jewel high up in the vaulted arch of the dome. Shevatas gaped, inured though he was to the sight of riches. The treasure was there, heaped in staggering profusion—piles of diamonds, sapphires, rubies, turquoises, opals, emeralds; zikkurats of jade, jet, and lapis lazuli; pyramids of gold wedges; teocallis of silver ingots; jewel-hilted swords in cloth-of-gold sheaths; golden helmets with colored horsehair crests, or black and scarlet plumes; silver-scaled corselets; gem-crusted harness worn by warrior-kings three thousand years in their tombs; goblets carven of single jewels; skulls plated with gold, with moonstones for eyes; necklaces of human teeth set with jewels. The ivory floor was covered inches deep with gold dust that sparkled and shimmered under the crimson glow with a million scintillant lights. The thief stood in a wonderland of magic and splendor, treading stars under his sandaled feet.

But his eyes were focused on the dais of crystal which rose in the midst of the shimmering array, directly under the red jewel, and on which should be lying the moldering bones, turning to dust with the crawling of the centuries. And as Shevatas looked, the blood drained from his dark features; his marrow turned to ice, and the skin of his back crawled and wrinkled with horror, while his lips worked soundlessly. But suddenly he found his voice in one awful scream that rang hideously under the arching dome. Then again the silence of the ages lay among the ruins of mysterious Kuthchemes.

2

Rumors drifted up through the meadowlands, into the cities of the Hyborians. The word ran along the caravans, the long camel trains plodding through the sands, herded by lean, hawk-eyed men in white kaftans. It was passed on by the hook-nosed herdsmen of the grasslands, from the dwellers in tents to the dwellers in the squat stone cities, where kings with curled blue-black beards worshipped round-bellied gods with curious rites. The word passed up through the fringe of hills, where gaunt tribesmen took toll of the caravans. The rumors came into the fertile uplands, where stately cities rose above blue lakes and rivers: the rumors marched along the broad white roads thronged with ox-wains, with lowing herds, with rich merchants, knights in steel, archers, and priests.

They were rumors from the desert that lies east of

Stygia, far south of the Kothian hills. A new prophet had risen among the nomads. Men spoke of tribal war, of a gathering of vultures in the southeast, and a terrible leader who led his swiftly increasing hordes to victory. The Stygians, ever a menace to the northern nations, were apparently not connected with this movement; for they were massing armies on their eastern borders and their priests were making magic to fight that of the desert sorcerer, whom men called Natohk, the Veiled One; for his features were always masked.

But the tide swept northwestward, and the blue-bearded kings died before the altars of their potbellied gods, and their squat-walled cities were drenched in blood. Men said that the uplands of the Hyborians were the goal of Natohk and his chanting votaries.

Raids from the desert were not uncommon, but this latest movement seemed to promise more than a raid. Rumor said Natohk had welded thirty nomadic tribes and fifteen cities into his following, and that a rebellious Stygian prince had joined him. This latter lent the affair an aspect of real war.

Characteristically, most of the Hyborian nations were prone to ignore the growing menace. But in Khoraja, carved out of Shemite lands by the swords of Kothic adventurers, heed was given. Lying southeast of Koth, it would bear the brunt of the invasion. And its young king was captive to the treacherous king of Ophir, who hesitated between restoring him for a huge ransom, or handing him over to his enemy, the penurious king of Koth, who offered no gold, but an advantageous treaty. Meanwhile, the rule of the struggling kingdom was in the white hands of young princess Yasmela, the king's sister.

Minstrels sang her beauty throughout the western world, and the pride of a kingly dynasty was hers. But on that night her pride was dropped from her like a cloak. In her chamber whose ceiling was a lapis lazuli dome, whose marble floor was littered with rare furs, and whose walls were lavish with golden frieze work, ten girls, daughters of nobles, their slender limbs weighted with gem-crusted armlets and anklets, slumbered on velvet couches about the royal bed with its golden dais and silken canopy. But princess Yasmela lolled not on that silken bed. She lay naked on her supple belly upon the bare marble like the most abased suppliant, her dark hair streaming over her white shoulders, her slender fingers intertwined. She lay and writhed in pure horror that froze the blood in her lithe limbs and dilated her beautiful eyes, that pricked the roots of her dark hair and made goose-flesh rise along her supple spine.

Above her, in the darkest corner of the marble chamber, lurked a vast, shapeless shadow. It was no living thing of form or flesh and blood. It was a clot of darkness, a blur in the sight, a monstrous night-born incubus that might have been deemed a figment of a sleep-drugged brain but for the points of blazing yellow fire that glimmered like two eyes from the blackness.

Moreover, a voice issued from it—a low, subtle, inhuman sibilance that was more like the soft, abominable hissing of a serpent than anything else, and that apparently could not emanate from anything with human lips. Its sound as well as its import filled Yasmela with a shuddering horror so intolerable that she writhed and twisted her slender body as if beneath a lash, as though to rid her mind of its insinuating vileness by physical contortion.

"You are marked for mine, princess," came the gloating whisper. "Before I wakened from the long sleep I had marked you and yearned for you, but I was held fast by the ancient spell by which I escaped mine enemies. I am the soul of Natohk, the Veiled One! Look well upon me, princess! Soon you shall behold me in my bodily guise and shall love me!"

The ghostly hissing dwindled off in lustful titterings, and Yasmela moaned and beat the marble tiles with her small fists in her ecstasy of terror.

"I sleep in the palace chamber of Akbitana," the sibilances continued. "There my body lies in its frame of bones and flesh. Yet it is but an empty shell from which the spirit has flown for a brief space. Could you gaze from that palace casement, you would realize the futility of resistance. The desert is a rose garden beneath the moon, where blossom the fires of a hundred thousand warriors. As an avalanche sweeps onward, gathering bulk and momentum, I will sweep into the lands of mine ancient enemies. Their kings shall furnish me skulls for goblets, their women and children shall be slaves of my slaves' slaves. I have grown strong in the long years of dreaming. . . .

"But thou shalt be my queen, O princess! I will teach thee the ancient forgotten ways of pleasure. We——" Before the stream of cosmic obscenity which poured from the shadowy colossus, Yasmela cringed and writhed as if from a whip that flayed her dainty bare flesh.

"Remember!" whispered the horror. "The days will not be many before I come to claim mine own!"

Yasmela, pressing her face against the tiles and stopping her pink ears with her dainty fingers, yet seemed to hear a strange sweeping noise, like the beat of batwings. Then, looking fearfully up, she saw only the moon that shone through the window with a beam that rested like a silver sword across the spot where the phantom had lurked. Trembling in every limb, she rose and staggered to a satin couch, where she threw herself down, weeping hysterically. The girls slept on; but one, who roused, yawned, stretched her slender figure, and blinked about. Instantly she was on her knees beside the couch, her arms about Yasmela's supple waist.

"Was it—was it——?" her dark eyes were wide with fright. Yasmela caught her in a convulsive grasp.

"Oh, Vateesa, *It* came again! I saw It—heard It speak! It spoke Its name—Natohk! It is Natohk! It is not a nightmare—it towered over me while the girls slept like drugged ones. What—oh, *what* shall I do?"

Vateesa twisted a golden bracelet about her rounded arm, in meditation.

"O Princess," she said, "it is evident that no mortal power can deal with It, and the charm is useless that the priests of Ishtar gave you. Therefore seek you the forgotten oracle of Mitra."

In spite of her recent fright, Yasmela shuddered. The gods of yesterday become the devils of tomorrow. The Kothians had long since abandoned the worship of Mitra, forgetting the attributes of the universal Hyborian god. Yasmela had a vague idea that, being very ancient, it followed that the deity was very terrible. Ishtar was much to be feared, and all the gods of Koth. Kothian culture and religion had suffered from a subtle admixture of Shemite and Stygian strains. The simple ways of the Hyborians had become modified to a large extent by the sensual, luxurious, yet despotic habits of the East.

"Will Mitra aid me?" Yasmela caught Vateesa's wrist in her eagerness. "We have worshipped Ishtar so long——"

"To be sure he will!" Vateesa was the daughter of an Ophirean priest who had brought his customs with him when he fled from political enemies to Khoraja. "Seek the shrine! I will go with you."

"I will!" Yasmela rose, but objected when Vateesa prepared to dress her. "It is not fitting that I come before the shrine clad in silk. I will go naked, on my knees, as befits a suppliant, lest Mitra deem I lack humility."

"Nonsense!" Vateesa had scant respect for the ways of what she deemed a false cult. "Mitra would have folks stand upright before him—not crawling on their bellies like worms, or spilling blood of animals all over his altars."

Thus objurgated, Yasmela allowed the girl to garb her in the light, sleeveless silk shirt, over which was slipped a silken tunic, bound at the waist by a wide velvet girdle.

Satin slippers were put upon her slender feet, and a few deft touches of Vateesa's pink fingers arranged her dark, wavy tresses. Then the princess followed the girl, who drew aside a heavy, gilt-worked tapestry and threw the golden bolt of the door it concealed. This let into a narrow winding corridor, and down this the two girls went swiftly, through another door and into a broad hallway. Here stood a guardsman in crested gilt helmet, silvered cuirass, and gold-chased greaves, with a long-shafted battle-ax in his hands.

A motion from Yasmela checked his exclamation, and saluting, he took his stand again beside the doorway, motionless as a brazen image. The girls traversed the hallway, which seemed immense and eery in the light of the cressets along the lofty walls and went down a stairway where Yasmela shivered at the blots of shadows which hung in the angles of the walls. Three levels down, they halted at last in a narrow corridor whose arched ceiling was crusted with jewels, whose floor was set with blocks of crystal, and whose walls were decorated with golden frieze work. Down this shining way they stole, holding hands, to a wide portal of gilt.

Vateesa thrust open the door, revealing a shrine long forgotten except by a faithful few, and royal visitors to Khoraja's court, mainly for whose benefit the fane was maintained. Yasmela had never entered it before, though she was born in the palace. Plain and unadorned in comparison to the lavish display of Ishtar's shrines, there was about it a simplicity of dignity and beauty characteristic of the Mitran religion.

The ceiling was lofty, but it was not domed and was of plain white marble, as were the walls and floor, the former with a narrow gold frieze running about them. Behind an altar of clear green jade, unstained with sacrifice, stood the pedestal whereon sat the material manifestation of the deity. Yasmela looked in awe at the sweep of the magnificent shoulders, the clear-cut features—the wide straight eyes, the patriarchal beard, the thick curls of the hair, confined by a simple band about the temples. This, though she did not know it, was art in its highest form—the free, uncramped artistic expression of a highly aesthetic race, unhampered by conventional symbolism.

She fell on her knees and thence prostrate, regardless of Vateesa's admonition, and Vateesa, to be on the safe side, followed her example; for after all, she was only a girl, and it was very awesome in Mitra's shrine. But even so she could not refrain from whispering in Yasmela's ear.

"This is but the emblem of the god. None pretends to know what Mitra looks like. This but represents him in idealized human form, as near perfection as the human mind can conceive. He does not inhabit this cold stone, as your priests tell you Ishtar does. He is everywhere—above us, and about us, and he dreams betimes in the high places among the stars. But here his being focuses. Therefore call upon him."

"What shall I say?" whispered Yasmela in stammering terror.

"Before you can speak, Mitra knows the contents of your mind——" began Vateesa. Then both girls started violently as a voice began in the air above them. The deep, calm, bell-like tones emanated no more from the image than from anywhere else in the chamber. Again Yasmela trembled before a bodiless voice speaking to her, but this time it was not from horror or repulsion.

"Speak not, my daughter, for I know your need," came the intonations like deep musical waves beating rhythmically along a golden beach. "In one manner may you save your kingdom and, saving it, save all the world from the fangs of the serpent which has crawled up out of the darkness of the ages. Go forth upon the streets alone, and place your kingdom in the hands of the first man you meet there."

The unechoing tones ceased, and the girls stared at

each other. Then, rising, they stole forth, nor did they speak until they stood once more in Yasmela's chamber. The princess stared out of the gold-barred windows. The moon had set. It was long past midnight. Sounds of revelry had died away in the gardens and on the roofs of the city. Khoraja slumbered beneath the stars, which seemed to be reflected in the cressets that twinkled among the gardens and along the streets and on the flat roofs of houses where folk slept.

"What will you do?" whispered Vateesa, all a-tremble.

"Give me my cloak," answered Yasmela, setting her teeth.

"But alone, in the streets, at this hour!" expostulated Vateesa.

"Mitra has spoken," replied the princess. "It might have been the voice of the god, or a trick of a priest. No matter. I will go!"

Wrapping a voluminous silken cloak about her lithe figure and donning a velvet cap from which depended a filmy veil, she passed hurriedly through the corridors and approached a bronze door, where a dozen spearmen gaped at her as she passed through. This was in a wing of the palace which let directly onto the street; on all other sides it was surrounded by broad gardens, bordered by a high wall. She emerged into the street, lighted by cressets placed at regular intervals.

She hesitated; then, before her resolution could falter, she closed the door behind her. A slight shudder shook her as she glanced up and down the street, which lay silent and bare. This daughter of aristocrats had never before ventured, unattended, outside her ancestral palace. Then, steeling herself, she went swiftly up the street. Her satin-slippered feet fell lightly on the pave, but their soft sound brought her heart into her throat. She imagined their fall echoing thunderously through the cavernous city, rousing ragged, rat-eyed figures in hidden lairs among the sewers. Every shadow seemed to hide a lurking assassin, every blank doorway to mask the slinking hounds of darkness.

Then she started violently. Ahead of her a figure appeared on the eery street. She drew quickly into a clump of shadows, which now seemed like a haven of refuge, her pulse pounding. The approaching figure went not furtively, like a thief, or timidly, like a fearful traveler. He strode down the nighted street as one who has no need or desire to walk softly. An unconscious swagger was in his stride, and his footfalls resounded on the pave. As he passed near a cresset she saw him plainly—a tall man, in the chain-mail hauberk of a mercenary. She braced herself, then darted from the shadow, holding her cloak close about her.

"Sa-ha!" His sword flashed half out of his sheath. It halted when he saw it was only a woman that stood before him, but his quick glance went over her head, seeking the shadows for possible confederates.

He stood facing her, his hand on the long hilt that jutted forward from beneath the scarlet cloak which flowed carelessly from his mailed shoulders. The torchlight glinted dully on the polished blue steel of his greaves and basinet. A more baleful fire glittered bluely in his eyes. At first glance she saw he was no Kothian; when he spoke she knew he was no Hyborian. He was clad like a captain of the mercenaries, and in that desperate command there were men of many lands, barbarians as well as civilized foreigners. There was a wolfishness about this warrior that marked the barbarian. The eyes of no civilized man, however wild or criminal, ever blazed with such a fire. Wine scented his breath, but he neither staggered nor stammered.

"Have they shut you into the street?" he asked in barbarous Kothic, reaching for her. His fingers closed lightly about her rouned wrist, but she felt that he could splinter its bones without effort. "I've but come from the last wineshop open—Ishtar's curse on these white-livered reformers who close the grog-houses! 'Let men sleep rather than guzzle,' they say—aye, so they can work and fight better for their masters! Soft-gutted eunuchs, I call them. When I served with the mercenaries of Corinthia, we swilled and wenched all night and fought all day—aye, blood ran down the channels of our swords. But what of you, my girl? Take off that cursed mask——"

She avoided his clutch with a lithe twist of her body, trying not to appear to repulse him. She realized her danger, alone with a drunken barbarian. If she revealed her identity, he might laugh at her, or take himself off. She was not sure he would not cut her throat. Barbaric men did strange inexplicable things. She fought a rising fear.

"Not here," she laughed. "Come with me——"

"Where?" His wild blood was up, but he was wary as a wolf. "Are you taking me to some den of robbers?"

"No, no, I swear it!" She was hard put to avoid the hand which was again fumbling at her veil.

"Devil bite you, hussy!" he growled disgustedly. "You're as bad as a Hyrkanian woman, with your damnable veil. Here—let me look at your figure, anyway!"

Before she could prevent it, he wrenched the cloak from her, and she heard his breath hiss between his teeth. He stood holding the cloak, eyeing her as if the sight of her rich garments had somewhat sobered him. She saw suspicion flicker sullenly in his eyes.

"Who the devil are you?" he muttered. "You're no street waif—unless your leman robbed the king's seraglio for your clothes."

"Never mind." She dared to lay her white hand on his massive ironclad arm. "Come with me off the street."

He hesitated, then shrugged his mighty shoulders. She saw that he half believed her to be some noble lady, who, weary of polite lovers, was taking this means of amusing herself. He allowed her to don the cloak again, and followed her. From the corner of her eye she watched him as they went down the street together. His mail could not conceal his hard lines of tigerish strength. Everything about him was tigerish, elemental, untamed. He was alien as the jungle to her in his difference from the debonair courtiers to whom she was accustomed. She feared him, told herself she loathed his raw brute strength and unashamed barbarism, yet something breathless and perilous inside her leaned toward him; the hidden primitive chord that lurks in every woman's soul was sounded and responded. She had felt his hardened hand on her arm, and something deep in her tingled to the memory of that contact. Many men had knelt before Yasmela. Here was one she felt had never knelt before any one. Her sensations were those of one leading an unchained tiger; she was frightened, and fascinated by her fright.

She halted at the palace door and thrust lightly against it. Furtively watching her companion, she saw no suspicion in his eyes.

"Palace, eh?" he rumbled. "So you're a maid-in-waiting?"

She found herself wondering, with a strange jealousy, if any of her maids had ever led this war eagle into her palace. The guards made no sign as she led him between them, but he eyed them as a fierce dog might eye a strange pack. She led him through a curtained doorway into an inner chamber, where he stood, naively scanning the tapestries, until he saw a crystal jar of wine on an ebony table. This he took up with a gratified sigh, tilting it toward his lips. Vateesa ran from an inner room, crying breathlessly, "Oh, my princess——"

"*Princess!*"

The wine jar crashed to the floor. With a motion too quick for sight to follow, the mercenary snatched off Yasmela's veil, glaring. He recoiled with a curse, his sword leaping into his hand with a broad shimmer of blue steel. His eyes blazed like a trapped tiger's. The air was supercharged with tension that was like the pause before the bursting of a storm. Vateesa sank to the floor, speechless with terror, but Yasmela faced the infuriated barbarian without flinching. She realized her very life hung in the balance: maddened with suspicion and unreasoning panic, he was ready to deal death at the slightest provocation. But she experienced a certain breathless exhilaration in the crisis.

"Do not be afraid," she said. "I am Yasmela, but there is no reason to fear me."

"Why did you lead me here?" he snarled, his blazing eyes darting all about the chamber. "What manner of trap is this?"

"There is no trickery," she answered. "I brought you here because you can aid me. I called on the gods—on Mitra—and he bade me go into the streets and ask aid of the first man I met."

This was something he could understand. The barbarians had their oracles. He lowered his sword, though he did not sheathe it.

"Well, if you're Yasmela, you need aid," he grunted. "Your kingdom's in a devil of a mess. But how can I aid you? If you want a throat cut, of course——"

"Sit down," she requested. "Vateesa, bring him wine."

He complied, taking care, she noticed, to sit with his back against a solid wall, where he could watch the whole chamber. He laid his naked sword across his mail-sheathed knees. She glanced at it in fascination. Its dull blue glimmer seemed to reflect tales of bloodshed and rapine; she doubted her ability to lift it, yet she knew that the mercenary could wield it with one hand as lightly as she could wield a riding whip. She noted the breadth and power of his hands; they were not the stubby undeveloped paws of a troglodyte. With a guilty start she found herself imagining those strong fingers locked in her dark hair.

He seemed reassured when she deposited herself on a divan opposite him. He lifted off his basinet and laid it on the table, and drew back his coif, letting the mail folds fall upon his massive shoulders. She saw more fully now his unlikeness to the Hyborian races. In his dark, scarred face there was a suggestion of moodiness; and without being marked by depravity, or definitely evil, there was more than a suggestion of the sinister about his features, set off by his smoldering blue eyes. A low, broad forehead was topped by a square-cut, tousled mane as black as a raven's wing.

"Who are you?" she asked abruptly.

"Conan, a captain of the mercenary spearmen," he answered, emptying the wine cup at a gulp and holding it out for more. "I was born in Cimmeria."

The name meant little to her. She only knew vaguely that it was a wild, grim hill country, which lay far to the North, beyond the last outposts of the Hyborian nations, and was peopled by a fierce, moody race. She had never before seen one of them.

Resting her chin on her hands, she gazed at him with the deep, dark eyes that had enslaved many a heart.

"Conan of Cimmeria," she said, "you said I needed aid. Why?"

"Well," he answered, "any man can see that. Here is the king your brother in an Ophirean prison; here is Koth plotting to enslave you; here is this sorcerer screaming hell-fire and destruction down in Shem—and what's worse, here are your soldiers deserting every day."

She did not at once reply; it was a new experience for a man to speak so forthrightly to her, his words not couched in courtier phrases.

"Why are my soldiers deserting, Conan?" she asked.

"Some are being hired away by Koth," he replied, pulling at the wine jar with relish. "Many think Khoraja is doomed as an independent state. Many are frightened by tales of this dog Natohk."

"Will the mercenaries stand?" she asked anxiously.

"As long as you pay us well," he answered frankly.

"Your politics are nothing to us. You can trust Amalric, our general, but the rest of us are only common men who love loot. If you pay the ransom Ophir asks, men say you'll be unable to pay us. In that case we might go over to the king of Koth, though that cursed miser is no friend of mine. Or we might loot this city. In a civil war the plunder is always plentiful."

"Why would you not go over to Natohk?" she inquired.

"What could he pay us?" he snorted. "With fat-bellied brass idols he looted from the Shemite cities? As long as you're fighting Natohk, you may trust us."

"Would your comrades follow you?" she asked abruptly.

"What do you mean?"

"I mean," she answered deliberately, "that I am going to make you commander of the armies of Khoraja!"

He stopped short, the goblet at his lips, which curved in a broad grin. His eyes blazed with a new light.

"Commander? Crom! But what will your perfumed nobles say?"

"They will obey me!" She clapped her hands to summon a slave, who entered, bowing deeply. "Have Count Thespides come to me at once, and the chancellor Taurus, lord Amalric, and the Agha Shupras.

"I place my trust in Mitra," she said bending her gaze on Conan, who was now devouring the food placed before him by the trembling Vateesa. "You have seen much war?"

"I was born in the midst of a battle," he answered, tearing a chunk of meat from a huge joint with his strong teeth. "The first sound my ears heard was the clang of swords and the yells of the slaying. I have fought in blood feuds, tribal wars, and imperial campaigns."

"But can you lead men and arrange battle lines?"

"Well, I can try," he returned imperturbably. "It's no more than swordplay on a larger scale. You draw his guard, then—stab, slash! And either his head is off, or yours."

The slave entered again, announcing the arrival of the men sent for, and Yasmela went into the outer chamber, drawing the velvet curtains behind her. The nobles bent the knee, in evident surprise at her summons at such an hour.

"I have summoned you to tell you of my decision," said Yasmela. "The kingdom is in peril——"

"Right enough, my princess." It was Count Thespides who spoke—a tall man, whose black locks were curled and scented. With one white hand he smoothed his pointed mustache, and with the other he held a velvet chaperon with a scarlet feather fastened by a golden clasp. His pointed shoes were satin, his cote-hardie of gold-broidered velvet. His manner was slightly affected, but the thews under his silks were steely. "It were well to offer Ophir more gold for your royal brother's release."

"I strongly disagree," broke in Taurus the chancellor, an elderly man in an ermine-fringed robe, whose features were lined with the cares of his long service. "We have already offered what will beggar the kingdom to pay. To offer more would further excite Ophir's cupidity. My princess, I say as I have said before: Ophir will not move until we have met this invading horde. If we lose, he will give King Khossus to Koth; if we win, he will doubtless restore his majesty to us on payment of the ransom."

"And in the meantime," broke in Amalric, "The soldiers desert daily, and the mercenaries are restless to know why we dally." He was a Nemedian, a large man with a lion-like yellow mane. "We must move swiftly, if at all——"

"Tomorrow we march southward," she answered. "And there is the man who shall lead you!"

Jerking aside the velvet curtains, she dramatically indicated the Cimmerian. It was perhaps not an entirely happy moment for the disclosure. Conan was sprawled in his chair, his feet propped on the ebony table, busily engaged in gnawing a beef bone which he gripped firmly in both hands. He glanced casually at the astounded nobles, grinned faintly at Amalric, and went on munching with undisguised relish.

"Mitra protect us!" exploded Amalric. "That's Conan the northron, the most turbulent of all my rogues! I'd have hanged him long ago, were he not the best swordsman that ever donned hauberk——"

"Your highness is pleased to jest!" cried Thespides, his aristocratic features darkening. "This man is a savage—a fellow of no culture or breeding! It is an insult to ask gentlemen to serve under him! I——

"Count Thespides," said Yasmela, "you have my glove under your baldric. Please give it to me, and then go."

"Go?" he cried, starting. "Go where?"

"To Koth or to Hades!" she answered. "If you will not serve me as I wish, you shall not serve me at all."

"You wrong me, princess," he answered, bowing low, deeply hurt. "I would not forsake you. For your sake I will even put my sword at the disposal of this savage."

"And you, my lord Amalric?"

Amalric swore beneath his breath, then grinned. A true soldier of fortune, no shift of fortune, however outrageous, surprised him much.

"I'll serve under him. A short life and a merry one, say I—and with Conan the Throat-slitter in command, life is likely to be both merry and short. Mitra! If the dog ever commanded more than a company of cutthroats before, I'll eat him, harness and all!"

"And you, my Agha?" She turned to Shupras.

He shrugged his shoulders resignedly. He was typical of the race evolved along Koth's southern borders—tall and gaunt, with features leaner and more hawklike than his purer-blooded desert kin.

"Ishtar gives, princess." The fatalism of his ancestors spoke for him.

"Wait here," she commanded, and while Thespides fumed and gnawed his velvet cap, Taurus muttered wearily under his breath, and Amalric strode back and forth, tugging at his yellow beard and grinning like a hungry lion, Yasmela disappeared again through the curtains and clapped her hands for her slaves.

At her command they brought harness to replace Conan's chain mail—gorget, sollerets, cuirass, pauldrons, jambes, cuisses, and sallet. When Yasmela again drew the curtains, a Conan in burnished steel stood before his audience. Clad in the plate armor, vizor lifted and dark face shadowed by the black plumes that nodded above his helmet, there was a grim impressiveness about him that even Thespides grudgingly noted. A jest died suddenly on Amalric's lips.

"By Mitra," said he slowly, "I never expected to see you cased in coat armor, but you do not put it to shame. By my finger bones, Conan, I have seen kings who wore their harness less regally than you!"

Conan was silent. A vague shadow crossed his mind like a prophecy. In years to come he was to remember Amalric's words, when the dream became the reality.

3

In the early haze of dawn, the streets of Khoraja were thronged by crowds of people who watched the hosts riding from the southern gate. The army was on the move at last. There were the knights, gleaming in richly wrought plate armor, colored plumes waving above their burnished sallets. Their steeds, caparisoned with silk, lacquered leather, and gold buckles, caracoled and curvetted as their riders put them through their paces. The early light struck glints from lance points that rose like a forest above the array, their pennons flowing in the breeze. Each knight wore a lady's token, a glove, scarf, or rose, bound to his helmet or fastened to his sword belt. They were the chivalry of Khoraja, five hundred strong, led by Count Thespides, who, men said, aspired to the hand of Yasmela herself.

They were followed by the light cavalry on rangy steeds. The riders were typical hillmen, lean and hawk-faced; peaked steel caps were on their heads and chain mail glinted under their flowing kaftans. Their main weapon was the terrible Shemitish bow, which could send a shaft five hundred paces. There were five thousand of these, and Shupras rode at their head, his lean face moody beneath his spired helmet.

Close on their heels marched the Khoraja spearmen, always comparatively few in any Hyborian state, where men thought cavalry the only honorable branch of service. These, like the knights, were of ancient Kothic blood —sons of ruined families, broken men, penniless youths who could not afford horses and plate armor; five hundred of them.

The mercenaries brought up the rear, a thousand horsemen, two thousand spearmen. The tall horses of the cavalry seemed hard and savage as their riders; they made no curvets or gambades. There was a grimly businesslike aspect to these professional killers, veterans of bloody campaigns. Clad from head to foot in chain mail, they wore their vizorless headpieces over linked coifs. Their shields were unadorned, their long lances without guidons. At their saddlebows hung battle axes or steel maces, and each man wore at his hip a long broadsword. The spearmen were armed in much the same manner, though they bore pikes instead of cavalry lances.

They were men of many races and many crimes. There were tall Hyperboreans, gaunt, big-boned, of slow speech and violent natures; tawny-haired Gundermen from the hills of the northwest; swaggering Corinthian renegades; swarthy Zingarans, with bristling black mustaches and fiery tempers; Aquilonians from the distant west. But all, except the Zingarans, were Hyborians.

Behind all came a camel in rich housings, led by a knight on a great war-horse and surrounded by a clump of picked fighters from the royal house-troops. Its rider, under the silken canopy of the seat, was a slim, silk-clad figure, at the sight of which the populace, always mindful of royalty, threw up its leather cap and cheered wildly.

Conan the Cimmerian, restless in his plate armor, stared at the bedecked camel with no great approval and spoke to Amalric, who rode beside him, resplendent in chain mail threaded with gold, golden breastplate, and helmet with flowing horsehair crest.

"The princess would go with us. She's supple but too soft for this work. Anyway, she'll have to get out of these robes."

Amalric twisted his yellow mustache to hide a grin. Evidently Conan supposed Yasmela intended to strap on a sword and take part in the actual fighting, as the barbarian women often fought.

"The women of the Hyborians do not fight like your Cimmerian women, Conan," he said. "Yasmela rides with us to watch the battle. Anyway," he shifted in his saddle and lowered his voice, "between you and me, I have an idea that the princess dares not remain behind. She fears something——"

"An uprising? Maybe we'd better hang a few citizens before we start——"

"No. One of her maids talked—babbled about *Something* that came into the palace by night and frightened Yasmela half out of her wits. It's some of Natohk's deviltry, I doubt not. Conan, it's more than flesh and blood we fight!"

"Well," grunted the Cimmerian, "it's better to go meet an enemy than to wait for him."

He glanced at the long line of wagons and camp-followers, gathered the reins in his mailed hand, and spoke from habit the phrase of the marching mercenaries, "Hell or plunder, comrades—march!"

Behind the long train, the ponderous gates of Khoraja closed. Eager heads lined the battlements. The citizens well knew they were watching life or death go forth. If the host was overthrown, the future of Khoraja would be written in blood. In the hordes swarming up from the savage south, mercy was a quality unknown.

All day the columns marched, through grassy rolling meadowlands, cut by small rivers, the terrain gradually beginning to slope upward. Ahead of them lay a range of low hills, sweeping in an unbroken rampart from east to west. They camped that night on the northern slopes of those hills, and hook-nosed, fiery-eyed men of the hill tribes came in scores to squat about the fires and repeat news that had come up out of the mysterious desert. Through their tales ran the name of Natohk like a crawling serpent. At his bidding the demons of the air brought thunder and wind and fog, the fiends of the underworld shook the earth with awful roaring. He brought fire out of the air and consumed the gates of walled cities, and burnt armored men to bits of charred bone. His warriors covered the desert with their numbers, and he had five thousand Stygian troops in war chariots under the rebel prince Kutamun.

Conan listened unperturbed. War was his trade. Life was a continual battle, or series of battles; since his birth Death had been a constant companion. It stalked horrifically at his side; stood at his shoulder beside the gaming-tables; its bony fingers rattled the wine cups. It loomed above him, a hooded and monstrous shadow, when he lay down to sleep. He minded its presence no more than a king minds the presence of his cupbearer. Some day its bony grasp would close; that was all. It was enough that he lived through the present.

However, others were less careless of fear than he. Striding back from the sentry lines, Conan halted as a slender, cloaked figure stayed him with an outstretched hand.

"Princess! You should be in your tent."

"I could not sleep." Her dark eyes were haunted in the shadow. "Conan, I am afraid!"

"Are there men in the host you fear?" His hand locked on his hilt.

"No man," she shuddered. "Conan, is there anything you fear?"

He considered, tugging at his chin. "Aye," he admitted at last, "the curse of the gods."

Again she shuddered. "I am cursed. A fiend from the abysses has set his mark upon me. Night after night he lurks in the shadows, whispering awful secrets to me. He will drag me down to be his queen in hell. I dare not sleep—he will come to me in my pavilion as he came in the palace. Conan, you are strong—keep me with you! I am afraid!"

She was no longer a princess, but only a terrified girl. Her pride had fallen from her, leaving her unashamed in her nakedness. In her frantic fear she had come to him who seemed strongest. The ruthless power that had repelled her, drew her now.

For answer he drew off his scarlet cloak and wrapped it about her, roughly, as if tenderness of any kind were impossible to him. His iron hand rested for an instant on her slender shoulder, and she shivered again, but not with fear. Like an electric shock a surge of animal vitality swept over her at his mere touch, as if some of his superabundant strength had been imparted to her.

"Lie here." He indicated a clean-swept space close to a small flickering fire. He saw no incongruity in a princess lying down on the naked ground beside a camp-fire, wrapped in a warrior's cloak. But she obeyed without question.

He seated himself near her on a boulder, his broadsword across his knees. With the firelight glinting from his blue steel armor, he seemed like an image of steel—dynamic power for the moment quiescent; not resting, but motionless for the instant, awaiting the signal to plunge again into terrific action. The firelight played on his features, making them seem as if carved out of substance shadowy yet hard as steel. They were immobile, but his eyes smoldered with fierce life. He was not merely a wild man; he was part of the wild, one with the untamable elements of life; in his veins ran the blood of the wolf pack; in his brain lurked the brooding depths of the northern night; his heart throbbed with the fire of blazing forests.

So, half meditating, half dreaming, Yasmela dropped off to sleep, wrapped in a sense of delicious security. Somehow she knew that no flame-eyed shadow would bend over her in the darkness, with this grim figure from the outlands standing guard above her. Yet once again she wakened, to shudder in cosmic fear, though not because of anything she saw.

It was a low mutter of voices that roused her. Opening her eyes, she saw that the fire was burning low. A feeling of dawn was in the air. She could dimly see that Conan still sat on the boulder; she glimpsed the long blue glimmer of his blade. Close beside him crouched another figure, on which the dying fire cast a faint glow. Yasmela drowsily made out a hooked beak of a nose, a glittering bead of an eye, under a white turban. The man was speaking rapidly in a Shemite dialect she found hard to understand.

"Let Bel wither my arm! I speak truth! By Derketo, Conan, I am a prince of liars, but I do not lie to an old comrade. I swear by the days when we were thieves together in the land of Zamora, before you donned hauberk!

"I saw Natohk; with the others I knelt before him when he made incantations to Set. But I did not thrust my nose in the sand as the rest did. I am a thief of Shumir, and my sight is keener than a weasel's. I squinted up and saw his veil blowing in the wind. It blew aside, and I saw —I saw—Bel aid me, Conan, I say I *saw!* My blood froze in my veins and my hair stood up. What I had seen burned my soul like a red-hot iron. I could not rest until I had made sure.

"I journeyed to the ruins of Kuthchemes. The door of the ivory dome stood open; in the doorway lay a great serpent, transfixed by a sword. Within the dome lay the body of a man, so shriveled and distorted I could scarce make it out at first—it was Shevatas, the Zamorian, the only thief in the world I acknowledged as my superior. The treasure was untouched; it lay in shimmering heaps about the corpse. That was all."

"There were no bones——" began Conan.

"There was nothing!" broke in the Shemite passionately. "Nothing! Only the *one* corpse!"

Silence reigned an instant, and Yasmela shrank with a crawling nameless horror.

"Whence came Natohk?" rose the Shemite's vibrant whisper. "Out of the desert on a night when the world was blind and wild with mad clouds driven in frenzied flight across the shuddering stars, and the howling of the wind was mingled with the shrieking of the spirits of the wastes. Vampires were abroad that night, witches rode naked on the wind, and werewolves howled across the wilderness. On a black camel he came, riding like the wind, and an unholy fire played about him, the cloven tracks of the camel glowed in the darkness. When Natohk dismounted before Set's shrine by the oasis of Aphaka, the beast swept into the night and vanished. And I have talked with tribesmen who swore that it suddenly spread gigantic wings and rushed upward into the clouds, leaving a trail of fire behind it. No man has seen that camel since that night, but a black, brutish, manlike shape shambles to Natohk's tent and gibbers to him in the blackness before dawn. I will tell you, Conan, Natohk is—look, I will show you an image of what I saw that day by Shushan when the wind blew aside his veil!"

Yasmela saw the glint of gold in the Shemite's hand,

as the men bent closely over something. She heard Conan grunt; and suddenly blackness rolled over her. For the first time in her life, princess Yasmela had fainted.

4

Dawn was still a hint of whiteness in the east when the army was again on the march. Tribesmen had raced into camp, their steeds reeling from the long ride, to report the desert horde encamped at the Well of Altaku. So through the hills the soldiers pushed hastily, leaving the wagon trains to follow. Yasmela rode with them; her eyes were haunted. The nameless horror had been taking even more awful shape, since she had recognized the coin in the Shemite's hand the night before—one of those secretly molded by the degraded Zugite cult, bearing the features of a man dead three thousand years.

The way wound between ragged cliffs and gaunt crags towering over narrow valleys. Here and there villages perched, huddles of stone huts, plastered with mud. The tribesmen swarmed out to join their kin, so that before they had traversed the hills, the host had been swelled by some three thousand wild archers.

Abruptly they came out of the hills and caught their breath at the vast expanse that swept away to the south. On the southern side the hills fell away sheerly, marking a distinct geographical division between the Kothian uplands and the southern desert. The hills were the rim of the uplands, stretching in an almost unbroken wall. Here they were bare and desolate, inhabited only by the Zaheemi clan, whose duty it was to guard the caravan road. Beyond the hills the desert stretched bare, dusty, lifeless. Yet beyond its horizon lay the Well of Altaku, and the horde of Natohk.

The army looked down on the Pass of Shamla, through which flowed the wealth of the north and the south, and through which had marched the armies of Koth,

Khoraja, Shem, Turan, and Stygia. Here the sheer wall of the rampart was broken. Promontories ran out into the desert, forming barren valleys, all but one of which were closed on the northern extremity by rugged cliffs. This one was the pass. It was much like a great hand extended from the hills; two fingers, parted, formed a fan-shaped valley. The fingers were represented by a broad ridge on either hand, the outer sides sheer, the inner, steep slopes. The vale pitched upward as it narrowed, to come out on a plateau, flanked by gully-torn slopes. A well was there, and a cluster of stone towers, occupied by the Zaheemis.

There Conan halted, swinging off his horse. He had discarded the plate armor for the more familiar chain mail. Thespides reined in and demanded, "Why do you halt?"

"We'll await them here," answered Conan.

"'Twere more knightly to ride out and meet them," snapped the count.

"They'd smother us with numbers," answered the Cimmerian. "Besides, there's no water out there. We'll camp on the plateau——"

"My knights and I camp in the valley," retorted Thespides angrily. "We are the vanguard, and *we*, at least, do not fear a ragged desert swarm."

Conan shrugged his shoulders, and the angry nobleman rode away. Amalric halted in his bellowing order, to watch the glittering company riding down the slope into the valley.

"The fools! Their canteens will soon be empty, and they'll have to ride back up to the well to water their horses."

"Let them be," replied Conan. "It goes hard for them to take orders from me. Tell the dog-brothers to ease their harness and rest. We've marched hard and fast. Water the horses and let the men munch."

No need to send out scouts. The desert lay bare to the gaze, though just now this view was limited by low-lying clouds which rested in whitish masses on the southern horizon. The monotony was broken only by a jutting tangle of stone ruins, some miles out on the desert, reputedly the remnants of an ancient Stygian temple. Conan dismounted the archers and ranged them along the ridges, with the wild tribesmen. He stationed the mercenaries and the Khoraji spearmen on the plateau about the well. Farther back, in the angle where the hill road debouched on the plateau, was pitched Yasmela's pavilion.

With no enemy in sight, the warriors relaxed. Basinets were doffed, coifs thrown back on mailed shoulders, belts let out. Rude jests flew back and forth as the fighting men gnawed beef and thrust their muzzles deep into ale jugs. Along the slopes the hillmen made themselves at ease, nibbling dates and olives. Amalric strode up to where Conan sat bareheaded on a boulder.

"Conan, have you heard what the tribesmen say about Natohk? They say—Mitra, it's too mad even to repeat. What do you think?"

"Seeds rest in the ground for centuries without rotting, sometimes," answered Conan. "But surely Natohk is a man."

"I am not sure," grunted Amalric. "At any rate, you've arranged your lines as well as a seasoned general could have done. It's certain Natohk's devils can't fall on us unawares. Mitra, what a fog!"

"I thought it was clouds at first," answered Conan. "See how it rolls!"

What had seemed clouds was a thick mist moving northward like a great unstable ocean, rapidly hiding the desert from view. Soon it engulfed the Stygian ruins, and still it rolled onward. The army watched in amazement. It was a thing unprecedented—unnatural and inexplicable.

"No use sending out scouts," said Amalric disgustedly. "They couldn't see anything. Its edges are near the outer flanges of the ridges. Soon the whole pass and these hills will be masked——"

Conan, who had been watching the rolling mist with growing nervousness, bent suddenly and laid his ear to the earth. He sprang up with frantic haste, swearing.

"Horses and chariots, thousands of them! The ground vibrates to their tread! Ho, there!" his voice thundered out across the valley to electrify the lounging men. "Burganets and pikes, you dogs! Stand to your ranks!"

At that, as the warriors scrambled into their lines, hastily donning headpieces and thrusting arms through shield straps, the mist rolled away, as something no longer useful. It did not slowly lift and fade like a natural fog; it simply vanished, like a blown-out flame. One moment the whole desert was hidden with the rolling fleecy billows, piled mountainously, stratum above stratum; the next, the sun shone from a cloudless sky on a naked desert—no longer empty, but thronged with the living pageantry of war. A great shout shook the hills.

At first glance the amazed watchers seemed to be looking down upon a glittering, sparkling sea of bronze and gold, where steel points twinkled like a myriad of stars. With the lifting of the fog, the invaders had halted as if frozen, in long serried lines, flaming in the sun.

First was a long line of chariots, drawn by the great fierce horses of Stygia, with plumes on their heads—snorting and rearing as each naked driver leaned back, bracing his powerful legs, his dusky arms knotted with muscles. The fighting men in the chariots were tall figures, their hawklike faces set off by bronze helmets crested with a crescent supporting a golden ball. Heavy bows were in their hands. No common archers, these, but nobles of the South, bred to war and the hunt, who were accustomed to bringing down lions with their arrows.

Behind these came a motley array of wild men on half-wild horses—the warriors of Kush, the first of the great black kingdoms of the grasslands south of Stygia. They were shining ebony, supple and lithe, riding stark naked and without saddle or bridle.

After these rolled a horde that seemed to encompass all the desert. Thousands on thousands of the warlike sons of Shem: ranks of horsemen in scale-mail corselets and cylindrical helmets—the *asshuri* of Nippr, Shumir, and Eruk and their sister cities; wild white-robed hordes—the nomad clans.

Now the ranks began to mill and eddy. The chariots drew off to one side while the main host came uncertainly onward. Down in the valley the knights had mounted, and now Count Thespides galloped up the slope to where Conan stood. He did not deign to dismount but spoke abruptly from the saddle.

"The lifting of the mist has confused them! Now is the time to charge! The Kushites have no bows and they mask the whole advance. A charge of my knights will crush them back into the ranks of the Shemites, disrupting their formation. Follow me! We will win this battle with one stroke!"

Conan shook his head. "Were we fighting a natural foe, I would agree. But this confusion is more feigned than real, as if to draw us into a charge. I fear a trap."

"Then you refuse to move?" cried Thespides, his face dark with passion.

"Be reasonable," expostulated Conan. "We have the advantage of position——"

With a furious oath Thespides wheeled and galloped back down the valley where his knights waited impatiently.

Amalric shook his head. "You should not have let him return, Conan. I—look there!"

Conan sprang up with a curse. Thespides had swept in beside his men. They could hear his impassioned voice faintly, but his gesture toward the approaching horde was significant enough. In another instant five hundred lances dipped and the steel-clad company was thundering down the valley.

A young page came running from Yasmela's pavilion, crying to Conan in a shrill, eager voice, "My Lord, the princess asks why you do not follow and support Count Thespides?"

"Because I am not so great a fool as he," grunted Conan, reseating himself on the boulder and beginning to gnaw a huge beef bone.

"You grow sober with authority," quoth Amalric. "Such madness as that was always your particular joy."

"Aye, when I had only my own life to consider," answered Conan. "Now—what in Hell——"

The horde had halted. From the extreme wing rushed a chariot, the naked charioteer lashing the steed like a madman; the other occupant was a tall figure whose robe floated spectrally on the wind. He held in his arms a great vessel of gold and from it poured a thin stream that sparkled in the sunlight. Across the whole front of the desert horde the chariot swept, and behind its thundering wheels was left, like the wake behind a ship, a long thin powdery line that glittered in the sands like the phosphorescent track of a serpent.

"That's Natohk!" swore Amalric. "What hellish seed is he sowing?"

The charging knights had not checked their headlong pace. Another fifty paces and they would crash into the uneven Kushite ranks, which stood motionless, spears lifted. Now the foremost knights had reached the thin line that glitered across the sands. They did not heed that crawling menace. But as the steel-shod hoofs of the horses struck it, it was as when steel strikes flint—but with more terrible result. A terrific explosion rocked the desert, which seemed to split apart along the strewn line with an awful burst of white flame.

In that instant the whole foremost line of the knights

was seen enveloped in that flame, horses and steel-clad riders withering in the glare like insects in an open blaze. The next instant, the rear ranks were piling up on their charred bodies. Unable to check their headlong velocity, rank after rank crashed into the ruins. With appalling suddenness the charge had turned into a shambles where armored figures died amid screaming mangled horses.

Now the illusion of confusion vanished as the horde settled into orderly lines. The wild Kushites rushed into the shambles, spearing the wounded, bursting the helmets of the knights with stones and iron hammers. It was all over so quickly that the watchers on the slopes stood dazed; and again the horde moved forward, splitting to avoid the charred waste of corpses. From the hills went up a cry: "We fight not men but devils!"

On either ridge the hillmen wavered. One rushed toward the plateau, froth dripping from his beard.

"Flee, flee!" he slobbered. "Who can fight Natohk's magic?"

With a snarl Conan bounded from his boulder and smote him with the beef bone; he dropped, blood starting from nose and mouth. Conan drew his sword, his eyes slits of blue balefire.

"Back to your posts!" he yelled. "Let another take a backward step and I'll shear off his head! Fight, damn you!"

The rout halted as quickly as it had begun. Conan's fierce personality was like a dash of ice water in their whirling blaze of terror.

"Take your places," he directed quickly. "And stand to it! Neither man nor devil comes up Shamla Pass this day!"

Where the plateau rim broke to the valley slope, the mercenaries braced their belts and gripped their spears. Behind them the lancers sat their steeds, and to one side were stationed the Khoraja spearmen as reserves. To Yasmela, standing white and speechless at the door of her tent, the host seemed a pitiful handful in comparison to the thronging desert horde.

Conan stood among the spearmen. He knew the invaders would not try to drive a chariot charge up the pass in the teeth of the archers, but he grunted with surprise to see the riders dismounting. These wild men had no supply trains. Canteens and pouches hung at their saddle peaks. Now they drank the last of their water and threw the canteens away.

"This is the death grip," he muttered as the lines formed on foot. "I'd rather have had a cavalry charge; wounded horses bolt and ruin formations."

The horde had formed into a huge wedge, of which the tip was the Stygians and the body, the mailed *asshuri*, flanked by the nomads. In close formation, shields lifted, they rolled onward, while behind them a tall figure in a motionless chariot lifted wide-robed arms in grisly invocation.

As the horde entered the wide valley mouth, the hillmen loosed their shafts. In spite of the protective formation, men dropped by dozens. The Stygians had discarded their bows; helmeted heads bent to the blast, dark eyes glaring over the rims of their shields, they came on in an inexorable surge, striding over their fallen comrades. But the Shemites gave back the fire, and the clouds of arrows darkened the skies. Conan gazed over the billowing waves of spears and wondered what new horror the sorcerer would invoke. Somehow he felt that Natohk, like all his kind, was more terrible in defense than in attack; to take the offensive against him invited disaster.

But surely it was magic that drove the horde on in the teeth of death. Conan caught his breath at the havoc wrought in the onsweeping ranks. The edges of the wedge seemed melting away, and already the valley was strewn with dead men. Yet the survivors came on like madmen unaware of death. By the very numbers of their bows, they began to swamp the archers on the cliffs. Clouds of shafts sped upward, driving the hillmen to cover. Panic struck at their hearts at that unwavering advance, and they plied their bows madly, eyes glaring like trapped wolves.

As the horde neared the narrower neck of the Pass, boulders thundered down, crushed men by the scores, but the charge did not waver. Conan's wolves braced themselves for the inevitable concussion. In their close formation and superior armor, they took little hurt from the arrows. It was the impact of the charge Conan feared, when the huge wedge should crash against his thin ranks. And he realized now there was no breaking of that onslaught. He gripped the shoulder of a Zaheemi who stood near.

"Is there any way by which mounted men can get down into the blind valley beyond that western ridge?"

"Aye, a steep, perilous path, secret and eternally guarded. But——"

Conan was dragging him along to where Amalric sat his great war-horse.

"Amalric!" he snapped. "Follow this man! He'll lead you into yon outer valley. Ride down it, circle the end of the ridge, and strike the horde from the rear. Speak not, but go! I know it's madness, but we're doomed anyway; we'll do all the damage we can before we die! Haste!"

Amalric's mustache bristled in a fierce grin, and a few moments later his lancers were following the guide into a tangle of gorges leading off from the plateau. Conan ran back to the pikemen, sword in hand.

He was not too soon. On either ridge Shupras' hillmen, mad with anticipation of defeat, rained down their shafts desperately. Men died like flies in the valley and along the slopes—and with a roar and an irresistible upward surge the Stygians crashed against the mercenaries.

In a hurricane of thundering steel, the lines twisted and swayed. It was war-bred noble against professional soldier.

Shields crashed against shields, and between them spears drove in and blood spurted.

Conan saw the mighty form of Prince Kutamun across the sea of swords, but the press held him hard, breast to breast with dark shapes that gasped and slashed. Behind the Stygians the *asshuri* were surging and yelling.

On either hand the nomads climbed the cliffs and came to hand-grips with their mountain kin. All along the crests of the ridges the combat raged in blind, gasping ferocity. Tooth and nail, frothing mad with fanaticism and ancient feuds, the tribesmen rent and slew and died. Wild hair flying, the naked Kushites ran howling into the fray.

It seemed to Conan that his sweat-blinded eyes looked down into a rising ocean of steel that seethed and eddied, filling the valley from ridge to ridge. The fight was at a bloody deadlock. The hillmen held the ridges, and the mercenaries, gripping their dripping pikes, bracing their feet in the bloody earth, held the pass. Superior position and armor for a space balanced the advantage of overwhelming numbers. But it could not endure. Wave after wave of glaring faces and flashing spears surged up the slope, the *asshuri* filling the gaps in the Stygian ranks.

Conan looked to see Amalric's lances rounding the western ridge, but they did not come, and the pikemen began to reel back under the shocks. And Conan abandoned all hope of victory and of life. Yelling a command to his gasping captains, he broke away and raced across the plateau to the Khoraja reserves who stood trembling with eagerness. He did not glance toward Yasmela's pavilion. He had forgotten the princess; his one thought was the wild beast instinct to slay before he died.

"This day you become knights!" he laughed fiercely, pointing with his dripping sword toward the hillmen horses, herded near by. "Mount and follow me to Hell!"

The hill steed reared wildly under the unfamiliar clash of the Kothic armor, and Conan's gusty laugh rose above the din as he led them to where the eastern ridge branched away from the plateau. Five hundred footmen —pauper patricians, younger sons, black sheep—on half-wild Shemite horses, charging an army, down a slope where no cavalry had ever dared charge before!

Past the battle-choked mouth of the pass they thundered, out onto the corpse-littered ridge. Down the steep slope they rushed, and a score lost their footing and rolled under the hoofs of their comrades. Below them men screamed and threw up their arms—and the thundering charge ripped through them as an avalanche cuts through a forest of saplings. On through the close-packed throngs the Khorajis hurtled, leaving a crushed-down carpet of dead.

And then, as the horde writhed and coiled upon itself, Amalric's lancers, having cut through a cordon of horsemen encountered in the outer valley, swept around the extremity of the western ridge and smote the host in a steel-tipped wedge, splitting it asunder. His attack carried all the dazing demoralization of a surprise on the rear. Thinking themselves flanked by a superior force and frenzied at the fear of being cut off from the desert, swarms of nomads broke and stampeded, working havoc in the ranks of their more steadfast comrades. These staggered and the horsemen rode through them. Upon the ridges the desert fighters wavered, and the hillmen fell on them with renewed fury, driving them down the slopes.

Stunned by surprise, the horde broke before they had time to see it was but a handful which assailed them. And once broken, not even a magician could weld such a horde again. Across the sea of heads and spears Conan's madmen saw Amalric's riders forging steadily through the rout, to the rise and fall of axes and maces, and a mad joy of victory exalted each man's heart and made his arm steel.

Bracing their feet in the wallowing sea of blood whose crimson waves lapped about their ankles, the pikemen in the pass mouth drove forward, crushing strongly against the milling ranks before them. The Stygians held, but behind them the pass of the *asshuri* melted; and over the bodies of the nobles of the south who died in their tracks to a man, the mercenaries rolled, to split and crumple the wavering mass behind.

Up on the cliffs old Shupras lay with an arrow through his heart; Amalric was down, swearing like a pirate, a spear through his mailed thigh. Of Conan's mounted infantry, scarce a hundred and fifty remained in the saddle. But the horde was shattered. Nomads and mailed spearmen broke away, fleeing to their camp where their horses were, and the hillmen swarmed down the slopes, stabbing the fugitives in the back, cutting the throats of the wounded.

In he swirling red chaos, a terrible apparition suddenly appeared before Conan's rearing steed. It was Prince Kutamun, naked but for a loinclout, his harness hacked away, his crested helmet dented, his limbs splashed with blood. With a terrible shout he hurled his broken hilt full into Conan's face, and leaping, seized the stallion's bridle. The Cimmerian reeled in his saddle, half stunned, and with awful strength the dark-skinned giant forced the screaming steed upward and backward, until it lost its footing and crashed into the muck of bloody sand and writhing bodies.

Conan sprang clear as the horse fell, and with a roar Kutamun was on him. In that mad nightmare of battle, the barbarian never exactly knew how he killed his man. He only knew that a stone in the Stygian's hand crashed again and again on his basinet, filling his sight with flashing sparks, as Conan drove his dagger again and again into his foe's body, without apparent effect on the prince's terrible vitality. The world was swimming to Conan's sight, when with a convulsive shudder the frame that strained against his stiffened and then went limp.

Reeling up, blood streaming down his face from under

his dented helmet, Conan glared dizzily at the profusion of destruction which spread before him. From crest to crest the dead lay strewn, a red carpet that choked the valley. It was like a red sea, with each wave a straggling line of corpses. They choked the neck of the pass, they littered the slopes. And down in the desert the slaughter continued, where the survivors of the horde had reached their horses and streamed out across the waste, pursued by the weary victors—and Conan stood appalled as he noted how few of these were left to pursue.

Then an awful scream rent the clamor. Up the valley a chariot came flying, making nothing of the heaped corpses. No horses drew it, but a great black creature that was like a camel. In the chariot stood Natohk, his robes flying; and gripping the reins and lashing like mad, crouched a black anthropomorphic being that might have been a monster ape.

With a rush of burning wind the chariot swept up the corpse-littered slope, straight toward the pavilion where Yasmela stood alone, deserted by her guards in the frenzy of pursuit. Conan, standing frozen, heard her frenzied scream as Natohk's long arm swept her up into the chariot. Then the grisly steed wheeled and came racing back down the valley, and no man dared speed arrow or spear lest he strike Yasmela, who writhed in Natohk's arms.

With an inhuman cry Conan caught up his fallen sword and leaped into the path of the hurtling horror. But even as his sword went up, the forefeet of the black beast smote him like a thunderbolt and sent him hurtling a score of feet away, dazed and bruised. Yasmela's cry came hauntingly to his stunned ears as the chariot roared by.

A yell that had nothing of the human in its timbre rang from his lips as Conan rebounded from the bloody earth and seized the rein of a riderless horse that raced past him, throwing himself into the saddle without bringing the charger to a halt. With mad abandon he raced after the rapidly receding chariot. He struck the levels flying, and passed like a whirlwind through the Shemite camp. Into the desert he fled, passing clumps of his own riders, and hard-spurring desert horsemen.

On flew the chariot, and on raced Conan, though his horse began to reel beneath him. Now the open desert lay all about them, bathed in the lurid desolate splendor of sunset. Before him rose up the ancient ruins, and with a shriek that froze the blood in Conan's veins, the unhuman charioteer cast Natohk and the girl from him. They rolled on the sand and, to Conan's dazed gaze, the chariot and its steed altered awfully. Great wings spread from a black horror that in no way resembled a camel, and it rushed upward into the sky, bearing in its wake a shape of blinding flame, in which a black man-like shape gibbered in ghastly triumph. So quickly it passed, that it was like the rush of a nightmare through a horror-haunted dream.

Natohk sprang up, cast a swift look at his grim pursuer, who had not halted but came riding hard, with sword swinging low and spattering red drops; and the sorcerer caught up the fainting girl and ran with her into the ruins.

Conan leaped from his horse and plunged after them. He came into a room that glowed with unholy radiance, though outside dusk was falling swiftly. On a black jade altar lay Yasmela, her naked body gleaming like ivory in the weird light. Her garments lay strewn on the floor, as if ripped from her in brutal haste. Natohk faced the Simmerian—inhumanly tall and lean, clad in shimmering green silk. He tossed back his veil, and Conan looked into the features he had seen depicted on the Zugite coin.

"Aye, blench, dog!" the voice was like the hiss of a giant serpent. "I am Thugra Khotan! Long I lay in my tomb, awaiting the day of awakening and release. The arts which saved me from the barbarians long ago likewise imprisoned me, but I knew one would come in time—

and he came, to fulfill his destiny, and to die as no man has died in three thousand years!

"Fool, do you think you have conquered because my people are scattered? Because I have been betrayed and deserted by the demon I enslaved? I am Thugra Khotan, who shall rule the world despite your paltry gods! The desert is filled with my people; the demons of the earth shall do my bidding, as the reptiles of the earth obey me. Lust for a woman weakened my sorcery. Now the woman is mine and, feasting on her soul, I shall be unconquerable! Back, fool! You have not conquered Thugra Khotan!"

He cast his staff and it fell at the feet of Conan, who recoiled with an involuntary cry. For as it fell it altered horribly; its outline melted and writhed, and a hooded cobra reared up hissing before the horrified Cimmerian. With a furious oath Conan struck, and his sword sheared the horrid shape in half. And there at his feet lay only the two pieces of a severed ebon staff. Thugra Khotan laughed awfully and, wheeling, caught up something that crawled loathsomely in the dust of the floor.

In his extended hand something alive writhed and slavered. No tricks of shadows this time. In his naked hand Thugra Khotan gripped a black scorpion, more than a foot in length, the deadliest creature of the desert, the stroke of whose spiked tail was instant death. Thugra Khotan's skull-like countenance split in a mummylike grin. Conan hesitated; then without warning he threw his sword.

Caught off guard, Thugra Khotan had no time to avoid the cast. The point struck beneath his heart and stood out a foot behind his shoulders. He went down, crushing the poisonous monster in his grasp as he fell.

Conan strode to the altar, lifting Yasmela in his bloodstained arms. She threw her white arms convulsively about his mailed neck, sobbing hysterically, and would not let him go.

"Crom's devils, girl!" he grunted. "Loose me! Fifty thousand men have perished today, and there is work for me to do——"

"No!" she gasped, clinging with convulsive strength, as barbaric for the instant as he in her fear and passion. "I will not let you go! I am yours, by fire and steel and blood! You are mine! Back there, I belong to others—here I am mine—and yours! You shall not go!"

He hesitated, his own brain reeling with the fierce upsurging of his violent passions. The lurid, unearthly glow still hovered in the shadowy chamber, lighting ghostily the dead face of Thugra Khotan, which seemed to grin mirthlessly and cavernously at them. Out on the desert, in the hills among the oceans of dead, men were dying, were howling with wounds and thirst and madness, and kingdoms were staggering. Then all was swept away by the crimson tide that rode madly in Conan's soul, as he crushed fiercely in his iron arms the slim white body that shimmered like a witch fire of madness before him.

Shadows in the Moonlight

Conan's pride will not let him be "Mr. Queen" to any woman, no matter how beautiful or ardent. After a time, Conan slips away to revisit his Cimmerian homeland and avenge himself on his old enemies, the Hyperboreans.

Conan is now nearly thirty. His blood brothers among the Cimmerians and the Æsir have won wives and sired sons, some of them as old and almost as big as Conan had been when he first ventured into the rat-infested slums of Zamora. His experiences as a corsair and a mercenary have stirred the spirit of battle and plunder too strongly in his blood for him to follow their example. When traders bring word of new wars in the South, Conan rides back to the Hyborian kingdoms.

A rebel prince of Koth is fighting to overthrow Strabonus, penurious king of that far-stretched nation, and Conan finds himself among old companions in the princeling's army. Unfortunately, the prince makes peace with his king, and his mercenary force becomes unemployed. Its members, Conan among them, form an outlaw band, the Free Companions, who harry the borders of Koth, Zamora, and Turan impartially. They finally gravitate to the steppes west of the Sea of Vilayet, where they join the ruffian horde known as kozaki.

Conan soon fights his way to the leadership of this lawless crew and ravages the western borders of the Turanian Empire, until his old employer, King Yildiz, adopts a policy of massive retaliation. A force under Shah Amurath lures the kozaki *deep into Turanian territory and cuts them down in a bloody battle by the river Ilbars.*

1

A swift crashing of horses through the tall reeds; a heavy fall, a despairing cry. From the dying steed there staggered up its rider, a slender girl in sandals and girdled tunic. Her dark hair fell over her white shoulders; her eyes were those of a trapped animal. She did not look at the jungle of reeds that hemmed in the little clearing, nor at the blue waters that lapped the low shore behind her. Her wide-eyed gaze was fixed in agonized intensity on the horseman who pushed through the reedy screen and dismounted before her.

He was a tall man, slender, but hard as steel. From head to heel he was clad in light, silvered mesh mail that fitted his supple form like a glove. From under the dome-shaped, gold-chased helmet his brown eyes regarded her mockingly.

"Stand back!" her voice shrilled with terror. "Touch me not, Shah Amurath, or I will throw myself into the water and drown!"

He laughed, and his laughter was like the purr of a sword sliding from a silken sheath.

"No, you will not drown, Olivia, daughter of confusion, for the marge is too shallow, and I can catch you before you can reach the deeps. You gave me a merry chase, by the gods, and all my men are far behind us. But there is no horse west of Vilayet that can distance Irem for long." He nodded at the tall, slender-legged desert stallion behind him.

"Let me go!" begged the girl, tears of despair staining her face. "Have I not suffered enough? Is there any humiliation, pain, or degradation you have not heaped on me? How long must my torment last?"

"As long as I find pleasure in your whimperings, your pleas, tears, and writhings," he answered with a smile that would have seemed gentle to a stranger. "You are strangely virile, Olivia. I wonder if I shall ever weary of you, as I have always wearied of women before. You are ever fresh and unsullied, in spite of me. Each new day with you brings a new delight.

"But come—let us return to Akif, where the people are still fêting the conqueror of the miserable *kozaki;* while he, the conqueror, is engaged in recapturing a wretched fugitive, a foolish, lovely, idiotic runaway!"

"No!" She recoiled, turning toward the waters lapping bluely among the reeds.

"Yes!" His flash of open anger was like a spark struck from flint. With a quickness her tender limbs could not approximate, he caught her wrist, twisting it in pure wanton cruelty until she screamed and sank to her knees.

"Slut! I should drag you back to Akif at my horse's tail, but I will be merciful and carry you on my saddlebow, for which favor you shall humbly thank me, while——"

He released her with a startled oath and sprang back, his saber flashing out, as a terrible apparition burst from the reedy jungle, sounding an inarticulate cry of hate.

Olivia, staring up from the ground, saw what she took to be either a savage or a madman advancing on Shah Amurath in an attitude of deadly menace. He was powerfully built, naked but for a girdled loincloth which was stained with blood and crusted with dried mire. His black mane was matted with mud and clotted blood; there were streaks of dried blood on his chest and limbs, dried blood on the long straight sword he gripped in his right hand. From under the tangle of his locks, bloodshot eyes glared like coals of blue fire.

"You Hyrkanian dog!" mouthed this apparition in a

barbarous accent. "The devils of vengeance have brought you here!"

"*Kozak!*" ejaculated Shah Amurath, recoiling. "I did not know a dog of you escaped! I thought you all lay stiff in the steepe, by Ilbars River."

"All but me, damn you!" cried the other. "Oh, I've dreamed of such a meeting as this, while I crawled on my belly through the brambles, or lay under rocks while the ants gnawed my flesh, or crouched in the mire up to my mouth—I dreamed, but never hoped it would come to pass. Oh, gods of Hell, how I have yearned for this!"

The stranger's bloodthirsty joy was terrible to behold. His jaws champed spasmodically, froth appeared on his blackened lips.

"Keep back!" ordered Shah Amurath, watching him narrowly.

"Ha!" It was like the bark of a timber wolf. "Shah Amurath, the great lord of Akif! Oh, damn you, how I love the sight of you—you, who fed my comrades to the vultures, who tore them between wild horses, blinded and maimed and mutilated them—*ai*, you dog, you filthy dog!" His voice rose to a maddened scream, and he charged.

In spite of the terror of his wild appearance, Olivia looked to see him fall at the first crossing of the blades. Madman or savage, what could he do, naked, against the mailed chief of Akif?

There was an instant when the blades flamed and licked, seeming barely to touch each other and leap apart; then the broadsword flashed past the saber and descended terrifically on Shah Amurath's shoulder. Olivia cried out at the fury of that stroke. Above the crunch of the rending mail, she distinctly heard the snap of the shoulder bone. The Hyrkanian reeled back, suddenly ashen, blood spurting over the links of his hauberk; his saber slipped from his nerveless fingers.

"Quarter!" he gasped.

"Quarter?" There was a quiver of frenzy in the stranger's voice. "Quarter such as you gave us, you swine!"

Olivia closed her eyes. This was no longer battle, but butchery, frantic, bloody, impelled by an hysteria of fury and hate, in which culminated the sufferings of battle, massacre, torture, and fear-ridden, thirst-maddened, hunger-haunted flight. Though Olivia knew that Shah Amurath deserved no mercy or pity from any living creature, yet she closed her eyes and pressed her hands over her ears, to shut out the sight of that dripping sword that rose and fell with the sound of a butcher's cleaver, and the gurgling cries that dwindled away and ceased.

She opened her eyes, to see the stranger turning away from a gory travesty that only vaguely resembled a human being. The man's breast heaved with exhaustion or passion; his brow was beaded with sweat; his right hand was splashed with blood.

He did not speak to her, or even glance toward her. She saw him stride through the reeds that grew at the water's edge, stoop, and tug at something. A boat wallowed out of its hiding place among the stalks. Then she divined his intention and was galvanized into action.

"Oh, wait!" she wailed, staggering up and running toward him. "Do not leave me! Take me with you!"

He wheeled and stared at her. There was a difference in his bearing. His bloodshot eyes were sane. It was as if the blood he had just shed had quenched the fire of his frenzy.

"Who are you?" he demanded.

"I am called Olivia. I was *his* captive. I ran away. He followed me. That's why he came here. Oh, do not leave me here! His warriors are not far behind him. They will find his corpse—they will find me near it—oh!" She moaned in her terror and wrung her white hands.

He stared at her in perplexity.

"Would you be better off with me?" he demanded. "I am a barbarian, and I know from your looks that you fear me."

"Yes, I fear you," she replied, too distracted to dissemble. "My flesh crawls at the horror of your aspect. But I fear the Hyrkanians more. Oh, let me go with you! They will put me to the torture if they find me beside their dead lord."

"Come, then." He drew aside, and she stepped quickly into the boat, shrinking from contact with him. She seated herself in the bow, and he stepped into the boat, pushed off with an oar and, using it as a paddle, worked his way tortuously among the tall stalks until they glided out into open water. Then he set to work with both oars, rowing with great, smooth, even strokes, the heavy muscles of arms and shoulders and back rippling in rhythm to his exertions.

There was silence for some time, the girl crouching in the bows, the man tugging at the oars. She watched him with timorous fascination. It was evident that he was not an Hyrkanian, and he did not resemble the Hyborian races. There was a wolfish hardness about him that marked the barbarian. His features, allowing for the strains and stains of battle and his hiding in the marshes, reflected that same untamed wildness, but they were neither evil nor degenerate.

"Who are you?" she asked. "Shah Amurath called you a *kozak*; were you of that band?"

"I am Conan, of Cimmeria," he grunted. "I was with the *kozaki*, as the Hyrkanian dogs called us."

She knew vaguely that the land he named lay far to the northwest, beyond the farthest boundaries of the different kingdoms of her race.

"I am a daughter of the king of Ophir," she said. "My father sold me to a Shemite chief, because I would not marry a prince of Koth."

The Cimmerian grunted in surprise.

Her lips twisted in a bitter smile. "Aye, civilized men sell their children as slaves to savages, sometimes. They call your race barbaric, Conan of Cimmeria."

"We do not sell our children," he growled, his chin jutting truculently.

"Well—I was sold. But the desert man did not misuse me. He wished to buy the good will of Shah Amurath, and I was among the gifts he brought to Akif of the purple gardens. Then——" She shuddered and hid her face in her hands.

"I should be lost to all shame," she said presently. "Yet each memory stings me like a slaver's whip. I abode in Shah Amurath's palace, until some weeks agone he rode out with his hosts to do battle with a band of invaders who were ravaging the borders of Turan. Yesterday he returned in triumph, and a great fête was made to honor him. In the drunkenness and rejoicing, I found an opportunity to steal out of the city on a stolen horse. I had thought to escape—but he followed and about midday came up with me. I outran his vassals, but him I could not escape. Then you came."

"I was lying hid in the reeds," grunted the barbarian. "I was one of those dissolute rogues, the Free Companions, who burned and looted along the borders. There were five thousand of us, from a score of races and tribes. We had been serving as mercenaries for a rebel prince in eastern Koth, most of us, and when he made peace with his cursed sovereign, we were out of employment; so we took to plundering the outlying dominions of Koth, Zamora and Turan impartially. A week ago, Shah Amurath trapped us near the banks of the Ilbars with fifteen thousand men. Mitra! The skies were black with vultures. When the lines broke, after a whole day of fighting, some tried to break through to the north, some to the west. I doubt if any escaped. The steppes were covered with horsemen riding down the fugitives. I broke for the east and finally reached the edge of the marshes that border this part of Vilayet.

"I've been hiding in the morasses ever since. Only the day before yesterday the riders ceased beating up the reed brakes, searching for just such fugitives as I. I've squirmed and burrowed and hidden like a snake, feasting on musk-rats I caught and ate raw, for lack of fire to cook them. This dawn I found this boat hidden among the reeds. I hadn't intended going out on the sea until night, but after I killed Shah Amurath, I knew his mailed dogs would be close at hand."

"And what now?"

"We shall doubtless be pursued. If they fail to see the marks left by the boat, which I covered as well as I could, they'll guess anyway that we took to sea, after they fail to find us among the marshes. But we have a start, and I'm going to haul at these oars until we reach a safe place."

"Where shall we find that?" she asked hopelessly. "Vilayet is an Hyrkanian pond."

"Some folk don't think so," grinned Conan grimly; "notably the slaves that have escaped from galleys and become pirates."

"But what are your plans?"

"The southwestern shore is held by the Hyrkanians for hundreds of miles. We still have a long way to go before we pass beyond their northern boundaries. I intend to go northward, until I think we have passed them. Then we'll turn westward, and try to land on the shore bordered by the uninhabited steppes."

"Suppose we meet pirates, or a storm?" she asked. "And we shall starve on the steppes."

"Well," he reminded her, "I didn't ask you to come with me."

"I am sorry." She bowed her shapely dark head. "Pirates, storms, starvation—they are all kinder than the people of Turan."

"Aye." His dark face grew somber. "I haven't done with them yet. Be at ease, girl. Storms are rare on Vilayet at this time of the year. If we make the steppes, we shall not starve. I was reared in a naked land. It was those cursed marshes, with their stench and stinging flies, that nigh unmanned me. I am at home in the high lands. As for pirates——" He grinned enigmatically and bent to the oars.

The sun sank like a dull-glowing copper ball into a lake of fire. The blue of the sea merged with the blue of the sky, and both turned to soft dark velvet, clustered with stars and the mirrors of stars. Olivia reclined in the bows of the gently rocking boat, in a state dreamy and unreal. She experienced an illusion that she was floating in mid-air, stars beneath her as well as above. Her silent companion was etched vaguely against the softer darkness. There was no break or falter in the rhythm of his oars; he might have been a fantasmal oarsman, rowing her across the dark lake of Death. But the edge of her fear was dulled, and, lulled by the monotony of motion, she passed into a quiet slumber.

Dawn was in her eyes when she awakened, aware of a ravenous hunger. It was a change in the motion of the boat that had roused her; Conan was resting on his oars, gazing beyond her. She realized that he had rowed all night without pause, and marveled at his iron endurance. She twisted about to follow his stare and saw a green wall of trees and shrubbery rising from the water's edge and sweeping away in a wide curve, enclosing a small bay whose waters lay still as blue glass.

"This is one of the many islands that dot this inland sea," said Conan. "They are supposed to be uninhabited. I've heard the Hyrkanians seldom visit them. Besides, they generally hug the shores in their galleys, and we have come a long way. Before sunset we were out of sight of the mainland."

With a few strokes, he brought the boat in to shore and

made the painter fast to the arching root of a tree, which rose from the water's edge. Stepping ashore, he reached out a hand to help Olivia. She took it, wincing slightly at the bloodstains upon it, feeling a hint of the dynamic strength that lurked in the barbarian's thews.

A dreamy quiet lay over the woods that bordered the blue bay. Then somewhere, far back among the trees, a bird lifted its morning song. A breeze whispered through the leaves and set them to murmuring. Olivia found herself listening intently for something, she knew not what. What might be lurking amid those nameless woodlands?

As she peered timidly into the shadows between the trees, something swept into the sunlight with a swift whirl of wings: a great parrot, which dropped onto a leafy branch and swayed there, a gleaming image of jade and crimson. It turned its crested head sidewise and regarded the invaders with glittering eyes of jet.

"Crom!" muttered the Cimmerian. "Here is the grandfather of all parrots. He must be a thousand years old! Look at the evil wisdom of his eyes. What mysteries do you guard, Wise Devil?"

Abruptly the bird spread its flaming wings and, soaring from its perch, cried out harshly: "*Yagkoolan yok tha, xuthalla!*" and, with a wild screech of horribly human laughter, rushed away through the trees to vanish in the opalescent shadows.

Olivia stared after it, feeling the cold hand of nameless foreboding touch her supple spine.

"What did it say?" she whispered.

"Human words, I'll swear," answered Conan; "but in what tongue I can't say."

"Nor I," returned the girl. "Yet it must have learned them from human lips. Human, or——" she gazed into the leafy fastnesses and shuddered slightly, without knowing why.

"Crom, I'm hungry!" grunted the Cimmerian. "I could eat a whole buffalo. We'll look for fruit; but first I'm going to cleanse myself of this dried mud and blood. Hiding in marshes is foul business."

So saying, he laid aside his sword and, wading out shoulder-deep into the blue water, went about his ablutions. When he emerged, his clean-cut bronze limbs shone; his streaming black mane was no longer matted. His blue eyes, though they smoldered with unquenchable fire, were no longer murky or bloodshot. But the tigerish suppleness of limb and the dangerous aspect of feature were not altered.

Strapping on his sword once more, he motioned the girl to follow him, and they left the shore, passing under the leafy arches of the great branches. Underfoot lay a short green sward, which cushioned their tread. Between the trunks of the trees they caught glimpses of faery-like vistas.

Presently Conan grunted in pleasure at the sight of golden and russet globes hanging in clusters among the leaves. Indicating that the girl should seat herself on a fallen tree, he filled her lap with the exotic delicacies, and then himself fell to with unconcealed gusto.

"Ishtar!" said he, between mouthfuls. "Since Ilbars I have lived on rats, and roots I dug out of the stinking mud. This is sweet to the palate, though not very filling. Still, it will serve if we eat enough."

Olivia was too busy to reply. The sharp edge of the Cimmerian's hunger blunted, he began to gaze at his fair companion with more interest than previously, noting the lustrous clusters of her dark hair, the peach-bloom tints of her dainty skin, and the rounded contours of her lithe figure which the scanty silk tunic displayed to full advantage.

Finishing her meal, the object of his scrutiny looked up, and meeting his burning, slit-eyed gaze, she changed color and the remnants of the fruit slipped from her fingers.

Without comment, he indicated with a gesture that

they should continue their explorations, and rising, she followed him out of the trees and into a glade, the farther end of which was bounded by a dense thicket. As they stepped into the open there was a ripping crash in the thicket, and Conan, bounding aside and carrying the girl with him, narrowly saved them from something that rushed through the air and struck a tree trunk with a thunderous impact.

Whipping out his sword, Conan bounded across the glade and plunged into the thicket. Silence ensued, while Olivia crouched on the sward, terrified and bewildered. Presently, Conan emerged, a puzzled scowl on his face.

"Nothing in that thicket," he growled. "But there was something——"

He studied the missile that had so narrowly missed them and grunted incredulously, as if unable to credit his own senses. It was a huge block of greenish stone, which lay on the sward at the foot of the tree, whose wood its impact had splintered.

"A strange stone to find on an uninhabited island," growled Conan.

Olivia's lovely eyes dilated in wonder. The stone was a symmetrical block, indisputably cut and shaped by human hands. And it was astonishingly massive. The Cimmerian grasped it with both hands, and with legs braced and the muscles standing out on his arms and back in straining knots, he heaved it above his head and cast it from him, exerting every ounce of nerve and sinew. It fell a few feet in front of him. Conan swore.

"No man living could throw that rock across this glade. It's a task for siege engines. Yet here there are no mangonels or ballistas."

"Perhaps it was thrown by some such engine from afar," she suggested.

He shook his head. "It didn't fall from above. It came from yonder thicket. See how the twigs are broken? It was thrown as a man might throw a pebble. But who? What? Come!"

She hesitantly followed him into the thicket. Inside the outer ring of leafy brush, the undergrowth was less dense. Utter silence brooded over all. The springy sward gave no sign of footprints. Yet from this mysterious thicket had hurtled that boulder, swift and deadly. Conan bent closer to the sward, where the grass was crushed down here and there. He shook his head angrily. Even to his keen eyes it gave no clue as to what had stood or trodden there. His gaze roved to the green roof above their heads, a solid ceiling of thick leaves and interwoven arches. And he froze suddenly.

Then rising, sword in hand, he began to back away, thrusting Olivia behind him.

"Out of here, quick!" he urged in a whisper that congealed the girl's blood.

"What is it? What do you see?"

"Nothing," he answered guardedly, not halting his wary retreat.

"But what is it, then? What lurks in this thicket?"

"Death!" he answered, his gaze still fixed on the brooding jade arches that shut out the sky.

Once out of the thicket, he took her hand and led her swiftly through the thinning trees, until they mounted a grassy slope, sparsely treed, and emerged upon a low plateau, where the grass grew taller and the trees were few and scattered. And in the midst of that plateau rose a long broad structure of crumbling greenish stone.

They gazed in wonder. No legends named such a building on any island of Vilayet. They approached it warily, seeing that moss and lichen crawled over the stones, and the broken roof gaped to the sky. On all sides lay bits and shards of masonry, half hidden in the waving grass, giving the impression that once many buildings rose there, perhaps a whole town. But now only the long hall-like structure rose against the sky, and its walls leaned drunkenly among the crawling vines.

Whatever doors had once guarded its portals had long rotted away. Conan and his companion stood in the broad entrance and stared inside. Sunlight streamed in through gaps in the walls and roof, making the interior a dim weave of light and shadow. Grasping his sword firmly, Conan entered, with the slouching gait of a hunting panther, sunken head and noiseless feet. Olivia tiptoed after him.

Once within, Conan grunted in surprise, and Olivia stifled a scream.

"Look! Oh, look!"

"I see," he answered. "Nothing to fear. They are statues."

"But how lifelike—and how evil!" she whispered, drawing close to him.

They stood in a great hall, whose floor was of polished stone, littered with dust and broken stones, which had fallen from the ceiling. Vines, growing between the stones, masked the apertures. The lofty roof, flat and undomed, was upheld by thick columns, marching in rows down the sides of the walls. And in each space between these columns stood a strange figure.

They were statues, apparently of iron, black and shining as if continually polished. They were life-sized, depicting tall, lithely powerful men, with cruel, hawklike faces. They were naked, and every swell, depression and contour of joint and sinew was represented with incredible realism. But the most lifelike feature was their proud, intolerant faces. These features were not cast in the same mold. Each face possessed its own individual characteristics, though there was a tribal likeness between them all. There was none of the monotonous uniformity of decorative art, in the faces at least.

"They seem to be listening—and waiting!" whispered the girl uneasily.

Conan rang his hilt against one of the images.

"Iron," he pronounced. "But Crom! in what molds were they cast?"

He shook his head and shrugged his massive shoulders in puzzlement.

Olivia glanced timidly about the great silent hall. Only the ivy-grown stones, the tendril-clasped pillars, with the dark figures brooding between them, met her gaze. She shifted uneasily and wished to be gone, but the images held a strange fascination for her companion. He examined them in detail and, barbarian-like, tried to break off their limbs. But their material resisted his best efforts. He could neither disfigure nor dislodge from its niche a single image. At last he desisted, swearing in his wonder.

"What manner of men were these copied from?" he inquired of the world at large. "These figures are black, yet they are not like Negroes. I have never seen their like."

"Let us go into the sunlight," urged Olivia, and he nodded, with a baffled glance at the brooding shapes along the walls.

So they passed out of the dusky hall into the clear blaze of the summer sun. She was surprised to note its position in the sky; they had spent more time in the ruins than she had guessed.

"Let us take to the boat again," she suggested. "I am afraid here. It is a strange, evil place. We do not know when we may be attacked by whatever cast the rock."

"I think we're safe as long as we're not under the trees," he answered. "Come."

The plateau, whose sides fell away toward the wooded shores on the east, west, and south, sloped upward toward the north to abut on a tangle of rocky cliffs, the highest point of the island. Thither Conan took his way, suiting his long stride to his companion's gait. From time to time his glance rested inscrutably upon her, and she was aware of it.

They reached the northern extremity of the plateau

and stood gazing up the steep pitch of the cliffs. Trees grew thickly along the rim of the plateau east and west of the cliffs, and clung to the precipitous incline. Conan glanced at these trees suspiciously, but he began the ascent, helping his companion on the climb. The slope was not sheer and was broken by ledges and boulders. The Cimmerian, born in a hill country, could have run up it like a cat, but Olivia found the going difficult. Again and again she felt herself lifted lightly off her feet and over some obstacle that would have taxed her strength to surmount, and her wonder grew at the sheer physical power of the man. She no longer found his touch repugnant. There was a promise of protection in his iron clasp.

At last they stood on the ultimate pinnacle, their hair stirring in the sea wind. From their feet, the cliffs fell away sheerly three or four hundred feet to a narrow tangle of woodlands bordering the beach. Looking southward, they saw the whole island lying like a great oval mirror, its bevelled edges sloping down swiftly into a rim of green, except where it broke in the pitch of the cliffs. As far as they could see, on all sides stretched the blue waters, still, placid, fading into dreamy hazes of distance.

"The sea is still," sighed Olivia. "Why should we not take up our journey again?"

Conan, poised like a bronze statue on the cliffs, pointed northward. Straining her eyes, Olivia saw a white fleck that seemed to hang suspended in the aching haze.

"What is it?"

"A sail."

"Hyrkanians?"

"Who can tell, at this distance?"

"They will anchor here—search the island for us!" she cried in quick panic.

"I doubt it. They come from the north, so they cannot be searching for us. They may stop for some other reason, in which case we'll have to hide as best we can. But I believe it's either a pirate or an Hyrkanian galley returning from some northern raid. In the latter case they are not likely to anchor here. But we can't put to sea until they've gone out of sight, for they're coming from the direction in which we must go. Doubtless they'll pass the island tonight, and at dawn we can go on our way."

"Then we must spend the night here?" She shivered.

"It's safest."

"Then let us sleep here, on the crags," she urged.

He shook his head, glancing at the stunted trees, at the marching woods below, a green mass which seemed to send out tendrils straggling up the sides of the cliffs.

"There are too many trees. We'll sleep in the ruins."

She cried out in protest.

"Nothing will harm you there," he soothed. "Whatever threw the stone at us did not follow us out of the woods. There was nothing to show that any wild thing lairs in the ruins. Besides, you are soft-skinned, and used to shelter and dainties. I could sleep naked in the snow and feel no discomfort, but the dew would give you cramps, were we to sleep in the open."

Olivia helplessly acquiesced, and they descended the cliffs, crossed the plateau, and once more approached the gloomy, age-haunted ruins. By this time the sun was sinking below the plateau rim. They had found fruit in the trees near the cliffs, and these formed their supper, both food and drink.

The southern night swept down quickly, littering the dark blue sky with great white stars, and Conan entered the shadowy ruins, drawing the reluctant Olivia after him. She shivered at the sight of those tense black shadows in their niches along the walls. In the darkness that the starlight only faintly touched, she could not make out their outlines; she could only sense their attitude of waiting—waiting as they had waited for untold centuries.

Conan had brought a great armful of tender branches,

well-leafed. These he heaped to make a couch for her, and she lay upon it, with a curious sensation as of one lying down to sleep in a serpent's lair.

Whatever her forebodings, Conan did not share them. The Cimmerian sat down near her, his back against a pillar, his sword across his knees. His eyes gleamed like a panther's in the dusk.

"Sleep, girl," said he. "My slumber is light as a wolf's. Nothing can enter this hall without awaking me."

Olivia did not reply. From her bed of leaves she watched the immobile figure, indistinct in the soft darkness. How strange, to move in fellowship with a barbarian, to be cared for and protected by one of a race, tales of which had frightened her as a child! He came of a people bloody, grim and ferocious. His kinship to the wild was apparent in his every action; it burned in his smoldering eyes. Yet he had not harmed her, and her worst oppressor had been a man the world called civilized. As a delicious languor stole over her relaxing limbs and she sank into foamy billows of slumber, her last waking thought was a drowsy recollection of the firm touch of Conan's fingers on her soft flesh.

2

Olivia dreamed, and through her dreams crawled a suggestion of lurking evil, like a black serpent writhing through flower gardens. Her dreams were fragmentary and colorful, exotic shards of a broken, unknown pattern, until they crystallized into a scene of horror and madness, etched against a background of cyclopean stones and pillars.

She saw a great hall, whose lofty ceiling was upheld by stone columns marching in even rows along the massive walls. Among these pillars fluttered great green and scarlet parrots, and the hall was thronged with black-skinned, hawk-faced warriors. They were not Negroes. Neither they nor their garments nor weapons resembled anything of the world the dreamer knew.

They were pressing about one bound to a pillar: a slender, white-skinned youth, with a cluster of golden curls about his alabaster brow. His beauty was not altogether human—like the dream of a god, chiseled out of living marble.

The black warriors laughed at him, jeered and taunted in a strange tongue. The lithe, naked form writhed beneath their cruel hands. Blood trickled down the ivory thighs to spatter on the polished floor. The screams of the victim echoed through the hall; then lifting his head toward the ceiling and the skies beyond, he cried out a name in an awful voice. A dagger in an ebon hand cut short his cry, and the golden head rolled on the ivory breast.

As if in answer to that desperate cry, there was a rolling thunder as of celestial chariot-wheels, and a figure stood before the slayers, as if materialized out of empty air. The form was of a man, but no mortal man ever wore such an aspect of inhuman beauty. There was an unmistakable resemblance between him and the youth who drooped lifeless in his chains, but the alloy of humanity that softened the godliness of the youth was lacking in the features of the stranger, awful and immobile in their beauty.

The blacks shrank back before him, their eyes slits of fire. Lifting a hand, he spoke, and his tones echoed through the silent halls in deep, rich waves of sound. Like men in a trance, the black warriors fell back until they were ranged along the walls in regular lines. Then from the stranger's chiseled lips rang a terrible invocation and command: "*Yagkoolan yok tha, xuthalla!*"

At the blast of that awful cry, the black figures stiffened and froze. Over their limbs crept a curious rigidity, an unnatural petrification. The stranger touched the limp body of the youth, and the chains fell away from it. He lifted the corpse in his arms; then ere he turned away, his tranquil gaze swept again over the silent rows of ebony figures, and he pointed to the moon, which gleamed in through the casements. And they understood, those tense, waiting statues that had been men. . . .

Olivia awoke, starting up on her couch of branches, a cold sweat beading her skin. Her heart pounded loud in the silence. She glanced wildly about. Conan slept against his pillar, his head fallen upon his massive breast. The silvery radiance of the late moon crept through the gaping roof, throwing long white lines along the dusty floor. She could see the images dimly, black, tense—waiting. Fighting down a rising hysteria, she saw the moonbeams rest lightly on the pillars and the shapes between.

What was that? A tremor among the shadows where the moonlight fell. A paralysis of horror gripped her, for where there should have been the immobility of death, there was movement: a slow twitching, a flexing and writhing of ebon limbs—an awful scream burst from her lips as she broke the bonds that held her mute and motionless. At her shriek Conan shot erect, teeth gleaming, sword lifted.

"The statues! The statues!—*Oh, my God, the statues are coming to life!*"

And with the cry she sprang through a crevice in the wall, burst madly through the hindering vines, and ran, ran, ran—blind, screaming, witless—until a grasp on her arm brought her up short and she shrieked and fought against the arms that caught her, until a familiar voice penetrated the mists of her terror, and she saw Conan's face, a mask of bewilderment in the moonlight.

"What in Crom's name, girl? Did you have a nightmare?" His voice sounded strange and far away. With a sobbing gasp she threw her arms about his thick neck and clung to him convulsively, crying in panting catches.

"Where are they? Did they follow us?"

"Nobody followed us," he answered.

She sat up, still clinging to him, and looked fearfully

about. Her blind flight had carried her to the southern edge of the plateau. Just below them was the slope, its foot masked in the thick shadows of the woods. Behind them she saw the ruins looming in the high-swinging moon.

"Did you not see them?—the statues, moving, lifting their hands, their eyes glaring in the shadows?"

"I saw nothing," answered the barbarian uneasily. "I slept more soundly than usual, because it has been so long since I have slumbered the night through; yet I don't think anything could have entered the hall without waking me."

"Nothing entered." A laugh of hysteria escaped her. "It was something there already. Ah, Mitra, we lay down to sleep among them, like sheep making their bed in the shambles!"

"What are you talking about?" he demanded. "I woke at your cry, but before I had time to look about me, I saw you rush out through the crack in the wall. I pursued you, lest you come to harm. I thought you had a nightmare."

"So I did!" She shivered. "But the reality was more grisly than the dream. Listen!" And she narrated all that she had dreamed and thought to see.

Conan listened attentively. The natural skepticism of the sophisticated man was not his. His mythology contained ghouls, goblins, and necromancers. After she had finished, he sat silent, absently toying with his sword.

"The youth they tortured was like the tall man who came?" he asked at last.

"As like as son to father," she answered, and hesitantly: "If the mind could conceive of the offspring of a union of divinity with humanity, it would picture that youth. The gods of old times mated sometimes with mortal women, our legends tell us."

"What gods?" he muttered.

"The nameless, forgotten ones. Who knows? They have gone back into the still waters of the lakes, the quiet hearts of the hills, the gulfs beyond the stars. Gods are no more stable than men."

"But if these shapes were men, blasted into iron images by some god or devil, how can they come to life?"

"There is witchcraft in the moon," she shuddered. "*He* pointed at the moon; while the moon shines on them, they live. So I believe."

"But we were not pursued," muttered Conan, glancing toward the brooding ruins. "You might have dreamed they moved. I am of a mind to return and see."

"No, no!" she cried, clutching him desperately. "Perhaps the spell upon them holds them in the hall. Do not go back! They will rend you limb from limb! Oh, Conan, let us go into our boat and flee this awful island! Surely the Hyrkanian ship has passed us now! Let us go!"

So frantic was her pleading that Conan was impressed. His curiosity in regard to the images was balanced by his superstition. Foes of flesh and blood he did not fear, however great the odds, but any hint of the supernatural roused all the dim monstrous instincts of fear that are the heritage of the barbarian.

He took the girl's hand, and they went down the slope and plunged into the dense woods, where the leaves whispered and nameless night birds murmured drowsily. Under the trees the shadows clustered thick, and Conan swerved to avoid the denser patches. His eyes roved continuously from side to side, and often flitted into the branches above them. He went quickly yet warily, his arm girdling the girl's waist so strongly that she felt as if she were being carried rather than guided. Neither spoke. The only sound was the girl's quick nervous panting, the rustle of her small feet in the grass. So they came through the trees to the edge of the water, shimmering like molten silver in the moonlight.

"We should have brought fruit for food," muttered Conan; "but doubtless we'll find other islands. As well leave now as later; it's but a few hours till dawn——"

His voice trailed away. The painter was still made fast to the looping root. But at the other end was only a smashed and shattered ruin, half submerged in the shallow water.

A stifled cry escaped Olivia. Conan wheeled and faced the dense shadows, a crouching image of menace. The noise of the night birds was suddenly silent. A brooding stillness reigned over the woods. No breeze moved the branches, yet somewhere the leaves stirred faintly.

Quick as a great cat, Conan caught up Olivia and ran. Through the shadows he raced like a phantom, while somewhere above and behind them sounded a curious rushing among the leaves, that implacably drew closer and closer. Then the moonlight burst full upon their faces, and they were speeding up the slope of the plateau.

At the crest Conan laid Olivia down, and turned to glare back at the gulf of shadows they had just quitted. The leaves shook in a sudden breeze; that was all. He shook his mane with an angry growl. Olivia crept to his feet like a frightened child. Her eyes looked up at him, dark wells of horror.

"What are we to do, Conan?" she whispered.

He looked at the ruins, stared again into the woods below.

"We'll go to the cliffs," he declared, lifting her to her feet. "Tomorrow I'll make a raft, and we'll trust our luck to the sea again."

"It was not—not *they* that destroyed our boat?" It was half question, half assertion.

He shook his head, grimly taciturn.

Every step of the way across that moon-haunted plateau was a sweating terror for Olivia, but no black shapes stole subtly from the looming ruins, and at last they reached the foot of the crags, which rose stark and gloomily majestic above them. There Conan halted in some uncertainty, at last selecting a place sheltered by a broad ledge, nowhere near any trees.

"Lie down and sleep if you can, Olivia," he said. "I'll keep watch."

But no sleep came to Olivia, and she lay watching the distant ruins and the wooded rim until the stars paled, the east whitened, and dawn in rose and gold struck fire from the dew on the grass blades.

She rose stiffly, her mind reverting to all the happenings of the night. In the morning light, some of its terrors seemed like figments of an overwrought imagination. Conan strode over to her, and his words electrified her.

"Just before dawn I heard the creak of timbers and the rasp and clack of cordage and oars. A ship has put in and anchored at the beach not far away—probably the ship whose sail we saw yesterday. We'll go up the cliffs and spy on her."

Up they went and, lying on their bellies among the boulders, saw a painted mast jutting up beyond the trees to the west.

"An Hyrkanian craft, from the cut of her rigging," muttered Conan. "I wonder if the crew——"

A distant medley of voices reached their ears; and, creeping to the southern edge of the cliffs, they saw a motley horde emerge from the fringe of trees along the western rim of the plateau and stand there a space in debate. There was much flourishing of arms, brandishing of swords, and loud rough argument. Then the whole band started across the plateau toward the ruins, at a slant that would take them close by the foot of the cliffs.

"Pirates!" whispered Conan, a grim smile on his thin lips. "It's an Hyrkanian galley they've captured. Here—crawl among these rocks.

"Don't show yourself unless I call to you," he instructed, having secreted her to his satisfaction among a tangle of boulders along the crest of the cliffs. "I'm going to meet these dogs. If I succeed in my plan, all will be well, and we'll sail away with them. If I don't succeed—

well, hide yourself in the rocks until they're gone, for no devils on this island are as cruel as these sea-wolves."

And tearing himself from her reluctant grasp, he swung quickly down the cliffs.

Looking fearfully from her eyrie, Olivia saw the band had neared the foot of the cliffs. Even as she looked, Conan stepped out from among the boulders and faced them, sword in hand. They gave back with yells of menace and surprise; then halted uncertainly to glare at this figure which had appeared so suddenly from the rocks. There were some seventy of them, a wild horde made up of men from many nations: Kothians, Zamorians, Brythunians, Corinthians, Shemites. Their features reflected the wildness of their natures. Many bore the scars of the lash or the branding iron. There were cropped ears, slit noses, gaping eye sockets, stumps of wrists—marks of the hangman as well as scars of battle. Most of them were half naked, but the garments they wore were fine: gold-braided jackets, satin girdles, silken breeches, tattered, stained with tar and blood, vied with pieces of silver-chased armor. Jewels glittered in nose rings and earrings, and in the hilts of their daggers.

Over against this bizarre mob stood the tall Cimmerian in strong contrast with his hard, bronzed limbs and clean-cut, vital features.

"Who are you?" they roared.

"Conan the Cimmerian!" His voice was like the deep challenge of a lion. "One of the Free Companions. I mean to try my luck with the Red Brotherhood. Who's your chief?"

"I, by Ishtar!" bellowed a bull-like voice, as a huge figure swaggered forward: a giant, naked to the waist, where his capacious belly was girdled by a wide sash that upheld voluminous silken pantaloons. His head was shaven except for a scalp-lock, his mustaches drooped over a rat-trap mouth. Green Shemitish slippers with upturned toes were on his feet, a long straight sword in his hand.

Conan stared and glared.

"Sergius of Khrosha, by Crom!"

"Aye, by Ishtar!" boomed the giant, his small black eyes glittering with hate. "Did you think I had forgot? Ha! Sergius never forgets an enemy. Now I'll hang you up by the heels and skin you alive. At him, lads!"

"Aye, send your dogs at me, big-belly," sneered Conan with bitter scorn. "You were always a coward, you Kothic cur."

"Coward! To me?" The broad face turned black with passion. "On guard, you northern dog! I'll cut out your heart!"

In an instant the pirates had formed a circle about the rivals, their eyes blazing, their breath sucking between their teeth in bloodthirsty enjoyment. High up among the crags Olivia watched, sinking her nails into her palms in her painful excitement.

Without formality the combatants engaged, Sergius coming in with a rush, quick on his feet as a giant cat, for all his bulk. Curses hissed between his clenched teeth as he lustily swung and parried. Conan fought in silence, his eyes slits of blue balefire.

The Kothian ceased his oaths to save his breath. The only sounds were the quick scuff of feet on the sward, the panting of the pirate, the ring and clash of steel. The swords flashed like white fire in the early sun, wheeling and circling. They seemed to recoil from each other's contact, then leap together again instantly. Sergius was giving back; only his superlative skill had saved him thus far from the blinding speed of the Cimmerian's onslaught. A louder clash of steel, a sliding rasp, a choking cry—from the pirate horde a fierce yell split the morning as Conan's sword plunged through their captain's massive body. The point quivered an instant from between Sergius' shoulders, a hand's breadth of white fire in the sunlight; then the Cimmerian wrenched back his steel and the pirate chief fell heavily, face down, and lay in a widening pool of blood, his broad hands twitching for an instant.

Conan wheeled toward the gaping corsairs.

"Well, you dogs!" he roared, "I've sent your chief to Hell—what says the law of the Red Brotherhood?"

Before any could answer, a rat-faced Brythunian, standing behind his fellows, whirled a sling swiftly and deadly. Straight as an arrow sped the stone to its mark, and Conan reeled and fell as a tall tree falls to the woodsman's ax. Up on the cliff Olivia caught at the boulders for support. The scene swam dizzily before her eyes; all she could see was the Cimmerian lying limply on the sward, blood oozing from his head.

The rat-faced one yelped in triumph and ran to stab the prostrate man, but a lean Corinthian thrust him back.

"What, Aratus, would you break the law of the Brotherhood, you dog?"

"No law is broken," snarled the Brythunian.

"No law? Why, you dog, this man you have just struck down is by just rights our captain!"

"Nay!" shouted Aratus. "He was not of our band, but an outsider. He had not been admitted to fellowship. Slaying Sergius does not make him captain, as would have been the case had one of us killed him."

"But he wished to join us," retorted the Corinthian. "He said so."

At that a great clamor arose, some siding with Aratus, some with the Corinthian, whom they called Ivanos. Oaths flew thick, challenges were passed, hands fumbled at sword hilts.

At last a Shemite spoke up above the clamor: "Why do you argue over a dead man?"

"He's not dead," answered the Corinthian, rising from beside the prostrate Cimmerian. "It was a glancing blow; he's only stunned."

At that the clamor rose anew, Aratus trying to get at the senseless man and Ivanos finally bestriding him, sword in hand, and defying all and sundry. Olivia sensed that it was not so much in defense of Conan that the Corinthian took his stand, but in opposition to Aratus. Evidently these men had been Sergius' lieutenants, and there was no love lost between them. After more arguments, it was decided to bind Conan and take him along with them, his fate to be voted on later.

The Cimmerian, who was beginning to regain consciousness, was bound with leather girdles, and then four pirates lifted him and, with many complaints and curses, carried him along with the band, which took up its journey across the plateau once more. The body of Sergius was left where it had fallen, a sprawling, unlovely shape on the sun-washed sward.

Up among the rocks, Olivia lay stunned by the disaster. She was incapable of speech or action and could only lie there and stare with horrified eyes as the brutal horde dragged her protector away.

How long she lay there, she did not know. Across the plateau she saw the pirates reach the ruins and enter, dragging their captive. She saw them swarming in and out of the doors and crevices, prodding into the heaps of debris, and clambering about the walls. After awhile a score of them came back across the plateau and vanished among the trees on the western rim, dragging the body of Sergius after them, presumably to cast into the sea. About the ruins the others were cutting down trees and securing material for a fire. Olivia heard their shouts, unintelligible in the distance, and she heard the voices of those who had gone into the woods, echoing among the trees. Presently they came back into sight, bearing casks of liquor and leathern sacks of food. They headed for the ruins, cursing lustily under their burdens.

Of all this Olivia was but mechanically cognizant. Her overwrought brain was almost ready to collapse. Left alone and unprotected, she realized how much the protection of the Cimmerian had meant to her. There intruded vaguely a wonderment at the mad pranks of Fate, that could make the daughter of a king the companion of a red-handed barbarian. With it came a revulsion toward her own kind. Her father, and Shah Amurath, they were civilized men. And from them she had had only suffering. She had never encountered any civilized man who treated her with kindness unless there was an ulterior motive behind his actions. Conan had shielded her, protected her, and—so far—demanded nothing in return. Laying her head in her rounded arms she wept, until distant shouts of ribald revelry roused her to her own danger.

She glanced from the dark ruins about which the fantastic figures, small in the distance, weaved and staggered, to the dusky depths of the green forest. Even if her terrors in the ruins the night before had been only dreams, the menace that lurked in those green, leafy depths below was no figment of nightmare. Were Conan slain or carried away captive, her only choice would lie between giving herself up to the human wolves of the sea, or remaining alone on that devil-haunted island.

As the full horror of her situation swept over her, she fell forward in a swoon.

3

The sun was hanging low when Olivia regained her senses. A faint wind wafted to her ears distant shouts and snatches of ribald song. Rising cautiously, she looked out across the plateau. She saw the pirates clustered about a great fire outside the ruins, and her heart leaped as a group emerged from the interior dragging some object she knew was Conan. They propped him against the wall, still evidently bound fast, and there ensued a long discussion, with much brandishing of weapons. At last they dragged him back into the hall, and took up anew the business of ale-guzzling. Olivia sighed; at least she knew that the Cimmerian still lived. Fresh determination steeled her. As soon as night fell, she would steal to those grim ruins and free him or be taken herself in the attempt. And she knew it was not selfish interest alone which prompted her decision.

With this in mind, she ventured to creep from her refuge to pluck and eat nuts which grew sparsely near at hand. She had not eaten since the day before. It was while so occupied that she was troubled by a sensation of being watched. She scanned the rocks nervously, then, with a shuddering suspicion, crept to the north edge of the cliff and gazed down into the waving green mass below; already dusky with the sunset. She saw nothing; it was impossible that she could be seen, when not on the cliff's edge, by anything lurking in those woods. Yet she distinctly felt the glare of hidden eyes and felt that *something* animate and sentient was aware of her presence and her hiding place.

Stealing back to her rocky eyrie, she lay watching the distant ruins until the dusk of night masked them, and she marked their position by the flickering flames about which black figures leaped and cavorted groggily.

Then she rose. It was time to make her attempt. But first she stole back to the northern edge of the cliffs, and looked down into the woods that bordered the beach. And as she strained her eyes in the dim starlight, she stiffened, and an icy hand touched her heart.

Far below her something moved. It was as if a black shadow detached itself from the gulf of shadows below her. It moved slowly up the sheer face of the cliff—a vague bulk, shapeless in the semidarkness. Panic caught Olivia by the throat, and she struggled with the scream that tugged at her lips. Turning, she fled down the southern slope.

That flight down the shadowed cliffs was a nightmare in which she slid and scrambled, catching at jagged rocks with cold fingers. As she tore her tender skin and bruised her soft limbs on the rugged boulders over which Conan had so lightly lifted her, she realized again her dependence on the iron-thewed barbarian. But this thought was but one in a fluttering maelstrom of dizzy fright.

The descent seemed endless, but at last her feet struck the grassy levels, and in a very frenzy of eagerness she sped away toward the fire that burned like the red heart of night. Behind her, as she fled, she heard a shower of stones rattle down the steep slope, and the sound lent wings to her heels. What grisly climber dislodged those stones she dared not try to think.

Strenuous physical action dissipated her blind terror somewhat, and before she had reached the ruins, her mind was clear, her reasoning faculties alert, though her limbs trembled from her efforts.

She dropped to the sward and wriggled along on her belly until, from behind a small tree that had escaped the axes of the pirates, she watched her enemies. They had completed their supper but were still drinking, dipping pewter mugs or jeweled goblets into the broken heads of the wine-casks. Some were already snoring drunkenly on the grass, while others had staggered into the ruins. Of Conan she saw nothing. She lay there, while the dew formed on the grass about her and the leaves overhead, and the men about the fire cursed, gambled, and argued. There were only a few about the fire; most of them had gone into the ruins to sleep.

She lay watching them, her nerves taut with the strain of waiting, the flesh crawling between her shoulders at the thought of what might be watching her in turn—of what might be stealing up behind her. Time dragged on leaden feet. One by one the revelers sank down in drunken slumber, until all were stretched senseless beside the dying fire.

Olivia hesitated—then was galvanized by a distant glow rising through the trees. The moon was rising!

With a gasp she rose and hurried toward the ruins. Her flesh crawled as she tiptoed among the drunken shapes that sprawled beside the gaping portal. Inside were many more; they shifted and mumbled in their besotted dreams, but none awakened as she glided among them. A sob of joy rose to her lips as she saw Conan. The Cimmerian was wide awake, bound upright to a pillar, his eyes gleaming in the faint reflection of the waning fire outside.

Picking her way among the sleepers, she approached him. Lightly as she had come, he had heard her; had seen her when first framed in the portal. A faint grin touched his hard lips.

She reached him and clung to him an instant. He felt the quick beating of her heart against his breast. Through a broad crevice in the wall stole a beam of moonlight, and the air was instantly supercharged with subtle tension. Conan felt it and stiffened. Olivia felt it and gasped. The sleepers snored on. Bending quickly, she drew a dagger from its senseless owner's belt, and set to work on Conan's bonds. They were sail cords, thick and heavy, and tied with the craft of a sailor. She toiled desperately, while the tide of moonlight crept slowly across the floor toward the feet of the crouching black figures between the pillars.

Her breath came in gasps; Conan's wrists were free, but his elbows and legs were still bound fast. She glanced fleeting at the figures along the walls—waiting, waiting. They seemed to watch her with the awful patience of the undead. The drunkards beneath her feet began to stir and groan in their sleep. The moonlight crept down the hall, touching the black feet. The cords fell from Conan's arms, and, taking the dagger from her, he ripped the bonds from his legs with a single quick slash. He stepped out from the pillar, flexing his limbs, stoically enduring the agony of returning circulation. Olivia crouched against him, shaking like a leaf. Was it some trick of the moonlight that touched the eyes of the black figures with fire, so that they glimmered redly in the shadows?

Conan moved with the abruptness of a jungle cat.

Catching up his sword from where it lay in a stack of weapons near by, he lifted Olivia lightly from her feet and glided through an opening that gaped in the ivy-grown wall.

No word passed between them. Lifting her in his arms he set off swiftly across the moon-bathed sward. Her arms about his iron neck, the Ophirean closed her eyes, cradling her dark curly head against his massive shoulder. A delicious sense of security stole over her.

In spite of his burden, the Cimmerian crossed the plateau swiftly, and Olivia, opening her eyes, saw that they were passing under the shadow of the cliffs.

"Something climbed the cliffs," she whispered. "I heard it scrambling behind me as I came down."

"We'll have to chance it," he grunted.

"I am not afraid—now," she sighed.

"You were not afraid when you came to free me, either," he answered. "Crom, what a day it has been! Such haggling and wrangling I never heard. I'm nearly deaf. Aratus wished to cut out my heart, and Ivanos refused, to spite Aratus, whom he hates. All day long they snarled and spat at one another, and the crew quickly grew too drunk to vote either way—"

He halted suddenly, an image of bronze in the moonlight. With a quick gesture he tossed the girl lightly to one side and behind him. Rising to her knees on the soft sward, she screamed at what she saw.

Out of the shadows of the cliffs moved a monstrous shambling bulk—an anthropomorphic horror, a grotesque travesty of creation.

In general outline it was not unlike a man. But its face, limned in the bright moonlight, was bestial, with close-set ears, flaring nostrils, and a great flabby-lipped mouth in which gleamed white tusklike fangs. It was covered with shaggy grayish hair shot with silver, which shone in the moonlight, and its great misshapen paws hung nearly to the earth. Its bulk was tremendous; as it stood on its short, bowed legs, its bullet-head rose above that of the man who faced it; the sweep of the hairy breast and giant shoulders was breathtaking; the huge arms were like knotted trees.

The moonlight scene swam, to Olivia's sight. This, then, was the end of the trail—for what human being could withstand the fury of that hairy mountain of thews and ferocity? Yet as she stared in wide-eyed horror at the bronzed figure facing the monster, she sensed a kinship in the antagonists that was almost appalling. This was less a struggle between man and beast than a conflict between two creatures of the wild, equally merciless and ferocious. With a flash of white tusks, the monster charged.

The mighty arms spread wide as the beast plunged, stupefyingly quick for all his vast bulk and stunted legs.

Conan's action was a blur of speed Olivia's eye could not follow. She only saw that he evaded that deadly grasp, and his sword, flashing like a jet of white lightning, sheared through one of those massive arms between shoulder and elbow. A great spout of blood deluged the sward as the severed member fell, twitching horribly, but even as the sword bit through, the other malformed hand locked in Conan's black mane.

Only the iron neck-muscles of the Cimmerian saved him from a broken neck at that instant. His left hand darted out to clamp on the beast's squat throat, his left knee was jammed hard against the brute's hairy belly. Then began a terrific struggle, which lasted only seconds, but which seemed like ages to the paralyzed girl.

The ape maintained his grasp in Conan's hair, dragging him toward the tusks that glistened in the moonlight. The Cimmerian resisted this effort, with his left arm rigid as iron, while the sword in his right hand, wielded like a butcher-knife, sank again and again into the groin, breast, and belly of his captor. The beast took its punishment in awful silence, apparently unweakened by the blood that gushed from its ghastly wounds. Swiftly the terrible strength of the anthropoid overcame the leverage of braced arm and knee. Inexorably Conan's arm bent under the strain; nearer and nearer he was drawn to the slavering jaws that gaped for his life. Now the blazing eyes of the barbarian glared into the bloodshot eyes of the ape. But as Conan tugged vainly at his sword, wedged deep in the hairy body, the frothing jaws snapped spasmodically shut, an inch from the Cimmerian's face, and he was hurled to the sward by the dying convulsions of the monster.

Olivia, half fainting, saw the ape heaving, thrashing, and writhing, gripping, manlike, the hilt that jutted from its body. A sickening instant of this, then the great bulk quivered and lay still.

Conan rose and limped over to the corpse. The Cimmerian breathed heavily, and walked like a man whose joints and muscles have been wrenched and twisted almost to their limit of endurance. He felt his bloody scalp and swore at the sight of the long, black, red-stained strands still grasped in the monster's shaggy hand.

"Crom!" he panted. "I feel as if I'd been racked! I'd rather fight a dozen men. Another instant and he'd have bitten off my head. Blast him, he's torn a handful of my hair out by the roots."

Gripping his hilt with both hands he tugged and worked it free. Olivia stole close to clasp his arm and stare down wide-eyed at the sprawling monster.

"What—what is it?" she whispered.

"A gray man-ape," he grunted. "Dumb, and man eating. They dwell in the hills that border the eastern shore of this sea. How this one got to this island, I can't say. Maybe he floated here on driftwood, blown out from the mainland in a storm."

"And it was he that threw the stone?"

"Yes; I suspected what it was when we stood in the thicket and I saw the boughs bending over our heads. These creatures always lurk in the deepest woods they can find and seldom emerge. What brought him into the open, I can't say, but it was lucky for us; I'd have had no chance with him among the trees."

"It followed me," she shivered. "I saw it climbing the cliffs."

"And following his instinct, he lurked in the shadow of the cliff, instead of following you out across the plateau. His kind are creatures of darkness and the silent places, haters of the sun and moon."

"Do you suppose there are others?"

"No, else the pirates had been attacked when they went through the woods. The gray ape is wary, for all his strength, as shown by his hesitancy in falling upon us in the thicket. His lust for you must have been great, to have driven him to attack us finally in the open. What——"

He started and wheeled back toward the way they had come. The night had been split by an awful scream. It came from the ruins.

Instantly there followed a mad medley of yells, shrieks, and cries of blasphemous agony. Though accompanied by a ringing of steel, the sounds were of massacre rather than battle.

Conan stood frozen, the girl clinging to him in a frenzy of terror. The clamor rose to a crescendo of madness, and then the Cimmerian turned and went swiftly toward the rim of the plateau, with its fringe of moon-limned trees. Olivia's legs were trembling so that she could not walk; so he carried her, and her heart calmed its frantic pounding as she nestled into his cradling arms.

They passed under the shadowy forest, but the clusters of blackness held no terrors, the rifts of silver discovered no grisly shape. Night birds murmured slumberously. The yells of slaughter dwindled behind them, masked in the distance to a confused jumble of sound. Somewhere a parrot called, like an eery echo: "*Yagkoolan yok tha, xuthalla!*" So they came to the tree-fringed water's edge and saw the galley lying at anchor, her sail shining white in the moonlight. Already the stars were paling for dawn.

4

In the ghastly whiteness of dawn a handful of tattered, bloodstained figures staggered through the trees and out on to the narrow beach. There were forty-four of them, and they were a cowed and demoralized band. With panting haste they plunged into the water and began to wade toward the galley, when a stern challenge brought them up standing.

Etched against the whitening sky they saw Conan the Cimmerian standing in the bows, sword in hand, his black mane tossing in the dawn wind.

"Stand!" he ordered. "Come no nearer. What would you have, dogs?"

"Let us come aboard!" croaked a hairy rogue, fingering a bloody stump of ear. "We'd be gone from this devil's island."

"The first man who tries to climb over the side, I'll split his skull," promised Conan.

They were forty-four to one, but he held the whip-hand. The fight had been hammered out of them.

"Let us come aboard, good Conan," whined a red-sashed Zamorian, glancing fearfully over his shoulder at the silent woods. "We have been so mauled, bitten, scratched, and rended, and are so weary from fighting and running, that not one of us can lift a sword."

"Where is that dog Aratus?" demanded Conan.

"Dead, with the others! It was devils fell upon us! They were rending us to pieces before we could awake—a dozen good rovers died in their sleep. The ruins were full of flame-eyed shadows, with tearing fangs and sharp talons."

"Aye!" put in another corsair. "They were the demons of the isle, which took the forms of molten images, to befool us. Ishtar! we lay down to sleep among them. We are no cowards. We fought them as long as mortal man may strive against the powers of darkness. Then we broke away and left them tearing at the corpses like jackals. But surely they'll pursue us."

"Aye, let us come aboard!" clamored a lean Shemite. "Let us come in peace, or we must come sword in hand, and though we be so weary you will doubtless slay many of us, yet you cannot prevail against us all."

"Then I'll knock a hole in the planks and sink her," answered Conan grimly. A frantic chorus of expostulation rose, which Conan silenced with a lionlike roar.

"Dogs! Must I aid my enemies? Shall I let you come aboard and cut out my heart?"

"Nay, nay!" they cried eagerly. "Friends—friends, Conan. We are thy comrades, lad! We be all lusty rogues together. We hate the king of Turan, not each other."

Their gaze hung on his brown, frowning face.

"Then if I am one of the Brotherhood," he grunted, "the laws of the Trade apply to me; and since I killed your chief in fair fight, then I am your captain!"

There was no dissent. The pirates were too cowed and battered to have any thought except a desire to get away from that island of fear. Conan's gaze sought out the bloodstained figure of the Corinthian.

"How, Ivanos!" he challenged. "You took my part once. Will you uphold my claims again?"

"Aye, by Mitra!" The pirate, sensing the trend of feeling, was eager to ingratiate himself with the Cimmerian. "He is right, lads; he is our lawful captain!"

A medley of acquiescence rose, lacking enthusiasm perhaps, but with sincerity accentuated by the feel of the silent woods behind them which might mask creeping ebony devils with red eyes and dripping talons.

"Swear by the hilt," Conan demanded.

Forty-four swords hilts were lifted toward him, and

forty-four voices blended in the corsair's oath of allegiance.

Conan grinned and sheathed his sword. "Come aboard, my bold swashbucklers, and take the oars."

He turned and lifted Olivia to her feet, from where she had crouched shielded by the gunwales.

"And what of me, sir?" she asked.

"What would you?" he countered, watching her narrowly.

"To go with you, wherever your path may lie!" she cried, throwing her white arms about his bronzed neck.

The pirates, clambering over the rail, gasped in amazement.

"To sail a road of blood and slaughter?" he questioned. "This keel will stain the blue waves crimson wherever it flows."

"Aye, to sail with you on blue seas or red," she answered passionately. "You are a barbarian, and I am an outcast, denied by my people. We are both pariahs, wanderers of the earth. Oh, take me with you!"

With a gusty laugh he lifted her to his fierce lips.

"I'll make you Queen of the Blue Sea! Cast off there, dogs! We'll scorch King Yildiz's pantaloons yet, by Crom!"

The Road of the Eagles

As chieftain of this mongrel Red Brotherhood, Conan is more than ever a thorn in King Yildiz's sensitive flesh. That henpecked monarch, instead of strangling his brother Teyaspa in the approved Turanian manner, has been prevailed upon to keep him cooped up in a castle deep in the Colchian Mountains, southeast of Vilayet, as a prisoner of the Zaporoskan brigand Gleg. To rid himself of another embarrassment, Yildiz sends one of Teyaspa's strongest partisans, General Artaban, to destroy the pirate stronghold at the mouth of the Zaporoska River. This he does, but he becomes the harried instead of the harrier.

The loser of the sea fight wallowed in the crimson wash. Just out of bow-shot, the winner limped away toward the rugged hills that overhung the blue water. It was a scene common enough on the Sea of Vilayet in the reign of King Yildiz of Turan.

The ship heeling drunkenly in the blue waste was a high-beaked Turanian war galley, a sister to the other. On the loser, death had reaped a plentiful harvest. Dead men sprawled on the high poop; they hung loosely over the scarred rail; they slumped along the runway that bridged the waist, where the mangled oarsmen lay among their broken benches.

Clustered on the poop stood the survivors, thirty men, many dripping blood. They were men of many nations: Kothians, Zamorians, Brythunians, Corinthians, Shemites, Zaporoskans. Their features were those of wild men, and many bore the scars of lash or branding iron. Many were half naked, but the motley clothes they wore were often of good quality, though now stained with tar and blood. Some were bareheaded, while others wore steel caps, fur caps, or strips of cloth wound turbanwise about their heads. Some wore shirts of chain mail; others were naked to their sash-girt waists, their muscular arms and shoulders burnt almost black. Jewels glittered in earrings and the hilts of daggers. Naked swords were in their hands. Their dark eyes were restless.

They stood about a man bigger than any of them, almost a giant, with thickly corded muscles. A square-cut mane of black hair surmounted his broad, low forehead, and the eyes that blazed in his dark, scarred face were a volcanic blue.

These eyes now stared at the shore. No town or harbor was visible along this stretch of lonely coast between Khawarism, the southernmost outpost of the Turanian kingdom, and its capital of Aghrapur. From the shoreline rose tree-covered hills, climbing swiftly to the snow-tipped peaks of the Colchians in the distance, on which the sinking sun shone red.

The big man glared at the slowly receding galley. Its crew had been glad to break away from the death grapple, and it crawled toward a creek that wound out of the hills between high cliffs. On the poop, the pirate captain could still make out a tall figure on whose helmet the low sun sparkled. He remembered the features under that helmet, glimpsed in the frenzy of battle: hawk-nosed, black-bearded, with slanting black eyes. That was Artaban of Shahpur, until recently the scourge of the Sea of Vilayet.

A lean Corinthian spoke: "We almost had the devil. What shall we do now, Conan?"

The gigantic Cimmerian went to one of the steering-sweeps. "Ivanos," he addressed the one who had spoken, "you and Hermio take the other sweep. Medius, pick three besides yourself and start bailing. The rest of you dog-souls tie up your cuts and then go down into the waist and bend your backs on the oars. Throw as many stiffs overboard as you need to make room."

"Are you going to follow the other galley to the creek-mouth?" asked Ivanos.

"Nay. We're too waterlogged from the holing their ram gave us to risk another grapple. But if we pull hard, we can beach her on that headland."

Laboriously they worked the galley inshore. The sun set; a haze like soft blue smoke hovered over the dusky water. Their late antagonist vanished into the creek. The starboard rail was almost awash when the bottom of the pirates' galley grounded on the sand and gravel of the headland.

The Akrim River, which wound through patches of meadow and farmland, was tinged red, and the mountains that rose on either side of the valley looked down on a scene only less old than they. Horror had come upon the peaceful valley dwellers, in the shape of wolfish riders from the outlands. They did not turn their gaze toward the castle that hung on the sheer slope of the mountains, for there too lurked oppressors.

The clan of Kurush Khan, a subchief of one of the more barbarous Hyrkanian tribes from east of the Sea of Vilayet, had been driven westward out of its native steppes by a tribal feud. Now it was taking toll of the Yuetshi villages in the valley of Akrim. Though this was mainly a simple raid for cattle, slaves, and plunder, Kurush Khan had wider ambitions. Kingdoms had been carved out of these hills before.

However, just now, like his warriors, Kurush Khan was drunk with slaughter. The huts of the Yuetshi lay in smoking ruins. The barns had been spared because they contained fodder, as well as the ricks. Up and down the valley the lean riders raced, stabbing and loosing their barbed arrows. Men howled as the steel drove home;

women screamed as they were jerked naked across the raiders' saddle bows.

Horsemen in sheepskins and high fur caps swarmed in the streets of the largest village—a squalid cluster of huts, half mud, half stone. Routed out of their pitiful hiding places, the villagers knelt, vainly imploring mercy, or as vainly fled, to be ridden down as they ran. The yataghans whistled, ending in the *zhukk* of cloven flesh and bone.

A fugitive turned with a wild cry as Kurush Khan swooped down on him with his cloak spreading out in the wind like the wings of a hawk. In that instant the eyes of the Yuetshi saw, as in a dream, the bearded face with its thin, down-curving nose, the wide sleeve falling away from the arm that rose grasping a curving glitter of steel. The Yuetshi carried one of the few effective weapons in the valley: a heavy hunting bow with a single arrow. With a screech of desperation he nocked the arrow, drew, and loosed, just as the Hyrkanian struck at him in passing. The arrow thudded home and Kurush Khan tumbled out of the saddle, instantly dead from a cloven heart.

As the riderless horse raced away, one of the two figures drew itself up on one elbow. It was the Yuetshi, whose life was welling fast from a ghastly cut across neck and shoulder. Gasping, he looked at the other form. Kurush Khan's beard jutted upwards as if in comic surprise. The Yuetshi's arm gave way and his face fell into the dirt, filling his mouth with dust. He spat red, gave a ghastly laugh from frothy lips, and fell back. When the Hyrkanians reached the spot, he, too, was dead.

The Hyrkanians squatted like vultures about a dead sheep and conversed over the body of their khan. When they rose, the doom had been sealed of every Yuetshi in the valley of Akrim.

Granaries, ricks, and stables, spared by Kurush Khan, went up in flames. All prisoners were slain, infants tossed living into the flames, young girls ripped up and flung into the bloody streets. Beside the khan's corpse grew a heap of severed heads. Riders galloped up, swinging these trophies by the hair, to toss them on the grim pyramid. Every place that might hide a shuddering wretch was ripped apart.

One tribesman, prodding into a stack of hay, discerned a movement in the straw. With a wolfish yell, he pounced upon the stack and dragged his victim to light. It was a girl, and no dumpy, apelike Yuetshi woman either. Tearing off her cloak, the Hyrkanian feasted his eyes on her scantily covered beauty.

The girl struggled silently in his grip. He dragged her toward his horse. Then, quick and deadly as a cobra, she snatched a dagger from his girdle and sank it under his heart. With a groan he crumpled, and she sprang like a she-leopard to his horse. The steed neighed and reared, and she wrenched it about and raced up the valley. Behind her the pack gave tongue and streamed out in pursuit. Arrows whistled about her head.

She guided the horse straight at the mountain wall on the south of the valley, where a narrow canyon opened out. Here the going was perilous, and the Hyrkanians reined to a less headlong pace among the stones and boulders. But the girl rode like a windblown leaf and was leading them by several hundred paces, when she came to a low wall or barrier across the mouth of the canyon, as if at some time somebody had rolled boulders together to make a crude defense. Feathery tamarisks grew out of the ridge, and a small stream cut through a narrow notch in the center. Men were there.

She saw them among the rocks, and they shouted to her to halt. At first she thought them more Hyrkanians and then saw otherwise. They were tall and strongly built, chain mail glinting under their cloaks, and spired steel caps on their heads. She made up her mind instantly. Throwing herself from her steed, she ran up to the rocks and fell on her knees, crying: "Aid, in the name of Ishtar the merciful!"

A man emerged, at the sight of whom she cried out: "General Artaban!" She clasped his knees. "Save me from those wolves that follow!"

"Why should I risk my life for you?" he asked indifferently.

"I knew you at the court of the king at Aghrapur! I danced before you. I am Roxana, the Zamorian."

"Many women have danced before me."

"Then I will give you a password," said she in desperation. "Listen!"

As she whispered a name in his ear, he started as if stung. He stared piercingly at her. Then, clambering upon a great boulder, he faced the oncoming riders with lifted hand.

"Go your way in peace, in the name of King Yildiz of Turan!"

His answer was a whistle of arrows about his ears. He sprang down and waved. Bows twanged all along the barrier and arrows sheeted out among the Hyrkanians. Men rolled from their saddles; horses screamed and bucked. The other riders fell back, yelling in dismay. They wheeled and raced back down the valley.

Artaban turned to Roxana: a tall man in a cloak of crimson silk and a chain-mail corselet threaded with gold. Water and blood had stained his apparel, yet its richness was still notable. His men gathered about him, forty stalwart Turanian mariners, bristling with weapons. A miserable-looking Yuetshi stood by with his hands bound.

"My daughter," said Artaban, "I have made enemies in this remote land on your behalf because of a name whispered in my ear. I believed you—"

"If I lied, may my skin be stripped from me."

"It will be," he promised gently. "I will see to it personally. You named Prince Teyaspa. What do you know of him?"

"For three years I have shared his exile."

"Where is he?"

She pointed down the valley to where the turrets of the castle were just visible among the crags. "In yonder stronghold of Gleg the Zaporoskan."

"It would be hard to take," mused Artaban.

"Send for the rest of your sea hawks! I know a way to bring you to the heart of that keep!"

He shook his head. "These you see are all my band." Seeing her incredulity he added: "I am not surprised that you wonder. I will tell you . . ."

With the frankness that his fellow-Turanians found so disconcerting, Artaban sketched his fall. He did not tell her of his triumphs, which were too well-known to need repetition. He was famous as a general for his swift raids into far countries—Brythunia, Zamora, Koth, and Shem—when five years before, the pirates of the Sea of Vilayet, working in league with the outlaw *kozaki* of the adjoining steppes, had become a formidable menace to that westernmost Hyrkanian kingdom, and King Yildiz had called upon Artaban to redress the situation. By vigorous action Artaban had put down the pirates, or at least driven them away from the western shores of the sea.

But Artaban, a passionate gambler, had gotten deeply in debt. To discharge his debts he had, while on a lone patrol with his flagship, seized a legitimate merchantman out of Khorusun, put all her people to the sword, and taken her cargo back to his base to sell secretly. But, though his crew was sworn to secrecy, somebody blabbed. Artaban had kept his head only at the price of a command from King Yildiz that almost amounted to suicide: to sail across the Sea of Vilayet to the mouth of the Zaporoska River and destroy the encampments of the pirates. Only two ships happened to be available for this enterprise.

Artaban had found the fortified camp of the Vilayet pirates and had taken it by storm, because only a few of the pirates were in it at the time. The rest had gone up the river to fight a band of wandering Hyrkanians, similar to Kurush Khan's band, that had attacked the native Zaporoskans along the river, with whom the pirates were on friendly terms. Artaban destroyed several pirate ships in their docks and captured a number of old or sick pirates.

To cow the absent pirates, Artaban had ordered that those taken alive should be impaled, burned by slow fires, and flayed alive all at once. This sentence was in the midst of being executed when the main body of the pirates had returned. Artaban had fled, leaving one of his ships in their hands. Knowing the penalty for failure, he had struck out for the wild stretch along the southwestern shore of Vilayet Sea where the Colchian Mountains came down to the water. He was soon pursued by the pirates in the captured ship and overtaken when the western shore was already in sight. The resulting battle had raged over the decks of both ships until dead and wounded lay everywhere. The greater numbers and superior equipment of the Turanians, together with Artaban's adroit use of his ram, had barely given them a defensive, indecisive victory.

"So we ran the galley ashore in the creek. We might have repaired it, but the king's fleet rules all of Vilayet Sea, and he will have a bowstring ready for me when he knows I've failed. We struck into the mountains, seeking we know not what—a way out of Turanian dominions or a new kingdom to rule."

Roxana listened and then without comment began her tale. As Artaban well knew, it was the custom of the kings of Turan, upon coming to the throne, to kill their brothers and their brothers' children in order to eliminate the chance of a civil war. Moreover it was the custom, when the king died, for the nobles and generals to acclaim as king the first of his sons to reach the capital after the event.

Even with this advantage, the weak Yildiz could not have conquered his aggressive brother Teyaspa had it not been for his mother, a Kothian woman named Khushia. This formidable old dame, the real ruler of Turan, preferred Yildiz because he was more docile, and Teyaspa was driven into exile. He sought refuge in Iranistan but discovered that the king of that land was corresponding with Yildiz in regard to poisoning him. In an attempt to reach Vendhya, he was captured by a nomadic Hyrkanian tribe, who recognized him and sold him to the Turanians. Teyaspa thought his fate was sealed, but his mother intervened and stopped Yildiz from having his brother strangled.

Instead, Teyaspa was confined in the castle of Gleg the Zaporoskan, a fierce semibandit chief who had come into the valley of the Akrim many years before and set himself up as a feudal lord over the primitive Yuetshi, preying on them but not protecting them. Teyaspa was furnished with all luxuries and forms of dissipation calculated to soften his fiber.

Roxana explained that she was one of the dancing girls sent to entertain him. She had fallen violently in love with the handsome prince and, instead of seeking to ruin him, had striven to lift him back to manhood.

"But," she concluded, "Prince Teyaspa has sunk into apathy. One would not know him for the young eagle who led his horsemen into the teeth of the Brythunian knights and the Shemitic *asshuri*. Imprisonment and wine and the juice of the black lotus have drugged his senses. He sits entranced on his cushions, rousing only when I sing or dance for him. But he has the blood of conquerors in him. He is a lion who but sleeps.

"When the Hyrkanians rode into the valley, I slipped out of the castle and went looking for Kurush Khan, in hope of finding a man bold enough to aid Teyaspa. But I saw Kurush Khan slain, and then the Hyrkanians became like mad dogs. I hid from them, but they dragged me out. O my lord, help us! What if you have but a handful? Kingdoms have been built on less! When it is known that the prince is free, men will flock to us! Yildiz is a fumbling mediocrity, and the people fear his son Yezdigerd, a fierce, cruel, and gloomy youth.

"The nearest Turanian garrison is three days' ride from here. Akrim is isolated, known to few but wandering nomads and the wretched Yuetshi. Here an empire can be plotted unmolested. You too are an outlaw; let us band together to free Teyaspa and place him on his throne! If he were king, all wealth and honor were yours, while Yildiz offers you naught but a bowstring!"

She was on her knees, gripping his cloak, her dark eyes ablaze with passion. Artaban stood silently, then suddenly laughed a gusty laugh.

"We shall need the Hyrkanians," he said, and the girl clapped her hands with a cry of joy.

"Hold up!" Conan the Cimmerian halted and glanced about, craning his massive neck. Behind him, his comrades shifted with a clank of weapons. They were in a narrow canyon, flanked on either hand by steep slopes grown with stunted firs. Before them, a small spring welled up among straggling trees and trickled away down a moss-green channel.

"Water here at least," grunted Conan. "Drink."

The previous evening, a quick march had brought them to Artaban's ship in its hiding place in the creek before dark. Conan had left four of his most seriously wounded men here, to work at patching up the vessel, while he pushed on with the rest. Believing that the Turanians were only a short distance ahead, Conan had pressed recklessly on in hope of coming up with them and avenging the massacre on the Zaporoska. But then, with the setting of the young moon, they had lost the trail in a maze of gullies and wandered blindly. Now at dawn they had found water but were lost and worn out. The only sign of human life they had seen since leaving the coast was a huddle of huts among the crags, housing nondescript skin-clad creatures who fled howling at their approach. Somewhere in the hills a lion roared.

Of the twenty-six, Conan was the only one whose muscles retained their spring. "Get some sleep," he growled. "Ivanos, pick two men to take the first watch with you. When the sun's over that fir, wake three others. I'm going to scout up this gorge."

He strode up the canyon and was soon lost among the straggling growth. The slopes changed to towering cliffs that rose sheer from the sloping, rock-littered floor. Then, with heart-stopping suddenness, a wild, shaggy figure sprang up from a tangle of bushes and confronted the pirate. Conan's breath hissed through his teeth as his sword flashed. Then he checked the stroke, seeing that the apparition was weaponless.

It was a Yuetshi: a wizened, gnomelike man in sheepskins, with long arms, short legs, and a flat, yellow, slant-eyed face seamed with many small wrinkles.

"Khosatral!" exclaimed the vagabond. "What does one of the Free Brotherhood in this Hyrkanian-haunted land?" The man spoke the Turanian dialect of Hyrkanian, but with a strong accent.

"Who are you?" grunted Conan.

"I was a chief of the Yuetshi," answered the other with a wild laugh. "I was called Vinashko. What do you here?"

"What lies beyond this canyon?" Conan countered.

"Over yonder ridge lies a tangle of gullies and crags. If you thread your way among them, you will come out overlooking the broad valley of the Akrim, which until yesterday was the home of my tribe, and which today holds their charred bones."

"Is there food there?"

"Aye—and death. A horde of Hyrkanian nomads holds the valley."

As Conan ruminated this, a step brought him about, to see Ivanos approaching.

"Hah!" Conan scowled. "I told you to watch while the men slept!"

"They are too hungry to sleep," retorted the Corinthian, suspiciously eyeing the Yuetshi.

"Crom!" growled the Cimmerian. "I cannot conjure food out of the air. They must gnaw their thumbs until we find a village to loot—"

"I can lead you to enough food to feed an army," interrupted Vinashko.

Conan said, his voice heavy with menace: "Don't mock me, my friend! You just said the Hyrkanians—"

"Nay! There's a place near here, unknown to them, where we stored food. I was going thither when I saw you."

Conan hefted his sword, a broad, straight, double-edged blade over four feet long, in a land where curved blades were more the rule. "Then lead on, Yuetshi, but at the first false move, off goes your head!"

Again the Yuetshi laughed that wild, scornful laugh, and motioned them to follow. He made for the nearer cliff, groped among the brittle bushes, and disclosed a crack in the wall. Beckoning, he bent and crawled inside.

"Into that wolf's den?" said Ivanos.

"What are you afraid of?" said Conan. "Mice?"

He bent and squeezed through the opening, and the other followed him. Conan found himself, not in a cave, but in a narrow cleft of the cliff. Overhead a narrow, crooked ribbon of blue morning sky appeared between the steep walls, which got higher with every step. They advanced through the gloom for a hundred paces and came out into a wide circular space surrounded by towering walls of what looked at first glance like a monstrous honeycomb. A low roaring came from the center of the space, where a small circular curbing surrounded a hole in the floor, from which issued a pallid flame as tall as a man, casting a wan illumination about the cavity.

Conan looked curiously about him. It was like being at the bottom of a gigantic well. The floor was of solid rock, worn smooth as if by the feet of ten thousand generations. The walls, too regularly circular to be altogether natural, were pierced by hundreds of black square depressions a hand's breadth deep and arranged in regular rows and tiers. The wall rose stupendously, ending in a small circle of blue sky, where a vulture hung like a dot. A spiral stairway cut in the black rock started up from ground level, made half a complete circle as it rose, and ended with a platform in front of a larger black hole in the wall, the entrance to a tunnel.

Vinashko explained: "Those holes are the tombs of an ancient people who lived here even before my ancestors came to the Sea of Vilayet. There are a few dim legends about these people; it is said they were not human, but preyed upon my ancestors until a priest of the Yuetshi by a great spell confined them to their holes in the wall and lit that fire to hold them there. No doubt their bones have all long since crumbled to dust. A few of my people have tried to chip away the slabs of stone that block these tombs, but the rock defied their efforts." He pointed to heaps of stuff at one side of the amphitheater. "My people stored food here against times of famine. Take your fill; there are no more Yuetshi to eat it."

Conan repressed a shudder of superstitious fear. "Your people should have dwelt in these caves. One man could hold that outer cleft against a horde."

The Yuetshi shrugged. "Here there is no water. Besides, when the Hyrkanians swooped down there was no time. My people were not warlike; they only wished to till the soil."

Conan shook his head, unable to understand such natures. Vinashko was pulling out leather bags of grain, rice, moldy cheese, and dried meat, and skins of sour wine.

"Go bring some of the men to help carry the stuff, Ivanos," said Conan, staring upward. "I'll stay here."

As Ivanos swaggered off, Vinashko tugged at Conan's arm. "Now do you believe I'm honest?"

"Aye, by Crom," answered Conan, gnawing a handful of dried figs. "Any man that leads me to food must be a friend. But how did you and your tribe get here from the valley of the Akrim? It must be a long steep road."

Vinashko's eyes gleamed like those of a hungry wolf. "That is our secret. I will show you, if you trust me."

"When my belly's full," said Conan with his mouth full of figs. "We're following that black devil, Artaban of Shahpur, who is somewhere in these mountains."

"He is your enemy?"

"Enemy! If I catch him, I'll make a pair of boots of his hide."

"Artaban of Shahpur is but three hours' ride from here."

"Ha!" Conan started up, feeling for his sword, his blue eyes ablaze. "Lead me to him!"

"Take care!" cried Vinashko. "He has forty armored Turanians and has been joined by Dayuki and a hundred and fifty Hyrkanians. How many warriors have you, lord?"

Conan munched silently, scowling. With such a disparity of numbers, he could not afford to give Artaban any advantages. In the months since he had become a pirate captain, he had beaten and bullied his crew into an effective force, but it was still an instrument that had to be used with care. By themselves they were reckless and improvident; well led, they could do much, but without wise leadership they would throw away their lives on a whim.

Vinashko said: "If you will come with me, *kozak*, I will show you what no man save a Yuetshi has seen for a thousand years!"

"What's that?"

"A road of death for our enemies!"

Conan took a step, then halted. "Wait; here come the red brothers. Hear the dogs swear!"

"Send them back with the food," whispered Vinashko as half a dozen pirates swaggered out of the cleft to gape at the cavern. Conan faced them with a grand gesture.

"Lug this stuff back to the spring," he said. "I told you I should find food."

"And what of you?" demanded Ivanos.

"Don't fret about me! I have words with Vinashko. Go back to camp and gorge yourselves, may the fiends bite you!"

As the pirates' footsteps faded away down the cleft, Conan gave Vinashko a clap on the back that staggered him. "Let's go," he said.

The Yuetshi led the way up the circular stairway carved in the rock wall. Above the last tier of tombs, it ended at the tunnel's mouth. Conan found that he could stand upright in the tunnel.

"If you follow this tunnel," said Vinashko, "you will come out behind the castle of the Zaporoskan, Gleg, that overlooks Akrim."

"What good will that do?" grunted Conan, feeling his way behind the Yuetshi.

"Yesterday when the slaying began, I strove for a while against the Hyrkanian dogs. When my comrades had all been cut down I fled the valley, running up to the Gorge of Diva. I had run into the gorge when I found myself among strange warriors, who knocked me down and bound me, wishing to ask me what went on in the valley. They were sailors of the king's Vilayet squadron and called their leader Artaban.

"While they questioned me, a girl came riding like mad with the Hyrkanians after her. When she sprang from her horse and begged aid of Artaban, I recognized her as the Zamorian dancing girl who dwells in Gleg's castle. A volley of arrows scattered the Hyrkanians, and then Artaban talked with the girl, forgetting about me. For three years Gleg has held a captive. I know, because I have taken grain and sheep to the castle, to be paid in the Zaporoskan fashion, with curses and blows. *Kozak*, the prisoner is Teyaspa, brother of King Yildiz!"

Conan grunted in surprise.

"The girl, Roxana, disclosed this to Artaban, and he swore to aid her in freeing the prince. As they talked, the Hyrkanians returned and halted at a distance, vengeful but cautious. Artaban hailed them and had speech with Dayuki, the new chief since Kurush Khan was slain. At last the Hyrkanian came over the wall of rocks and shared bread and salt with Artaban. And the three plotted to rescue Prince Teyaspa and put him on the throne.

"Roxana had discovered the secret way to the castle. Today, just before sunset, the Hyrkanians are to attack the castle from the front. While they thus attract the attention of the Zaporoskans, Artaban and his men are to come to the castle by a secret way. Roxana will open the door for them, and they will take the prince and flee into the hills to recruit warriors. As they talked, night fell, and I gnawed through my cords and slipped away.

"You wish vengeance. I'll show you how to trap Artaban. Slay the lot—all but Teyaspa. You can either extort a mighty price from Khushia for her son, or from Yildiz for killing him, or if you prefer you can try to be king-maker yourself."

"Show me," said Conan, eyes agleam with eagerness.

The smooth floor of the tunnel, in which three horses might have been ridden abreast, slanted downward. From time to time short flights of steps gave on to lower levels. For a while Conan could not see anything in the darkness. Then a faint glow ahead relieved it. The glow became a silvery sheen, and the sound of falling water filled the tunnel.

They stood in the mouth of the tunnel, which was

masked by a sheet of water rushing over the cliff above. From the pool that foamed at the foot of the falls, a narrow stream raced away down the gorge. Vinashko pointed out a ledge that ran from the cavern mouth, skirting the pool. Conan followed him. Plunging through the thin edge of the falls, he found himself in a gorge like a knife cut through the hills. Nowhere was it more than fifty paces wide, with sheer cliffs on both sides. No vegetation grew anywhere except for a fringe along the stream. The stream meandered down the canyon floor to plunge through a narrow crack in the opposite cliff.

Conan followed Vinashko up the twisting gorge. Within three hundred paces, they lost sight of the waterfall. The floor slanted upward. Shortly the Yuetshi drew back, clutching his companion's arm. A stunted tree grew at an angle in the rock wall, and behind this Vinashko crouched, pointing.

Beyond the angle, the gorge ran on for eighty paces and ended in an impasse. On their left the cliff seemed curiously altered, and Conan stared for an instant before he realized that he was looking at a man-made wall. They were almost behind a castle built in a notch in the cliffs. Its wall rose sheer from the edge of a deep crevice. No bridge spanned this chasm, and the only apparent entrance in the wall was a heavy, iron-braced door halfway up the wall. Opposite to it, a narrow ledge ran along the opposite side of the gorge, and this had been improved so that it could be reached on foot from where they stood.

"By this path the girl Roxana escaped," said Vinashko. "This gorge runs almost parallel to the Akrim. It narrows to the west and finally comes into the valley through a narrow notch, where the stream flows through. The Zaporoskans have blocked the entrance with stones so that the path cannot be seen from the outer valley unless one knows of it. They seldom use this road and know nothing of the tunnel behind the waterfall."

Conan rubbed his shaven chin. He yearned to loot the castle himself but saw no way to come to it. "By Crom, Vinashko, I should like to look on this noted valley."

The Yuetshi glanced at Conan's bulk and shook his head. "There is a way we call the Eagle's Road, but it is not for such as you."

"Ymir! Is a skin-clad savage a better climber than a Cimmerian hillman? Lead on!"

Vinashko shrugged and led the way back down the gorge until, within sight of the waterfall, he stopped at what looked like a shallow groove corroded in the higher cliff-wall. Looking closely, Conan saw a series of shallow handholds notched into the solid rock.

"I'd have deepened these pockmarks," grumbled Conan, but started up nevertheless after Vinashko, clinging to the shallow pits by toes and fingers. At last they reached the top of the ridge forming the southern side of the gorge and sat down with their feet hanging over the edge.

The gorge twisted like a snake's track beneath them. Conan looked out over the opposite and lower wall of the gorge into the valley of the Akrim.

On his right, the morning sun stood high over the glittering Sea of Vilayet; on his left rose the white-hooded peaks of the Colchians. Behind him he could see down into the tangle of gorges among which he knew his crew to be encamped.

Smoke still floated lazily up from the blackened patches that had been villages. Down the valley, on the left bank of the river, were pitched a number of tents of hide. Conan saw men swarming like ants around these tents. These were the Hyrkanians, Vinashko said, and pointed up the valley to the mouth of a narrow canyon where the Turanians were encamped. But the castle drew Conan's interest.

It was solidly set in a notch in the cliffs between the gorge beneath them and the valley beyond. The castle faced the valley, entirely surrounded by a massive twenty-foot wall. A ponderous gate flanked by towers pierced with slits for arrows commanded the outer slope. This slope was not too steep to be climbed or even ridden up, but afforded no cover.

"It would take a devil to storm that castle," growled Conan. "How are we to come at the king's brother in that pile of rock? Lead us to Artaban, so I can take his head back to the Zaporoska."

"Be wary if you wish to wear your own," answered Vinashko. "What do you see in the gorge?"

"A lot of bare stone with a fringe of green along the stream."

The Yuetshi grinned wolflike. "And do you notice that the fringe is denser on the right bank, where it is also higher? Listen! From behind the waterfall we can watch until the Turanians come up the gorge. Then, while they are busy at Gleg's castle, we'll hide among the bushes along the stream and waylay them as they return. We'll kill all but Teyaspa, whom we will take captive. Then we'll go back through the tunnel. Have you a ship to escape in?"

"Aye," said Conan, rising and stretching. "Vinashko, is there any way down from this knife edge you have us balanced on except that shaft we came up by?"

"There is a trail that leads east along the ridge and then down into those gullies where your men camp. Let me show you. Do you see that rock that looks like an old woman? Well, you turn right there . . ."

Conan listened attentively to the directions, but the substance of them was that this perilous path, more suitable for ibex or chamois than for men, did not provide access to the gorge beneath them.

In the midst of his explanation, Vinashko turned and stiffened. "What's this?" he said.

Men were galloping out of the distant Hyrkanian camp and lashing their horses across the shallow river.

The sun struck glints from lance points. On the castle walls helmets began to sparkle.

"The attack!" cried Vinashko. "Khosatral Khel! They've changed their plans; they were not going to attack until evening! Quickly! We must get down before the Turanians arrive!"

They levered their bodies into the shallow groove and crept down, step by step.

At last they stood in the gorge and hastened toward the waterfall. They reached the pool, crossed the ledge, and plunged through the fall. As they came into the dimness beyond, Vinashko gripped Conan's mailed arm. Above the rush of water the Cimmerian heard the clink of steel on rock. He looked out through the silver-shimmering screen that made everything ghostly and unreal, but which hid them from the eyes of anyone outside. They had not gained their refuge any too soon.

A band of men was coming along the gorge—tall men in mail hauberks and turban-bound helmets. At their head strode one taller than the rest, with black-bearded, hawklike features. Conan sighed and gripped his sword hilt, moving forward a trifle, but Vinashko caught him.

"In the gods' names, *kozak*," he whispered frantically "don't throw away our lives! We have them trapped, but if you rush out now—"

"Don't worry, little man," said Conan with a somber grin. "I am not so simple as to spoil a good vengeance by a thoughtless impulse."

The Turanians were crossing the narrow stream. On the farther bank they halted in an attitude of listening. Presently, above the rush of the waters, the men in the cave-mouth heard the distant shouting of many men.

"The attack!" whispered Vinashko.

As if it were a signal, the Turanians started swiftly up the gorge. Vinashko touched the Cimmerian's arm.

"Bide here and watch. I'll hasten back and bring your pirates."

"Hurry, then," said Conan. "It will be touch and go if you can get them here in time." And Vinashko slipped away like a shadow.

In a broad chamber luxuriant with gold-worked tapestries, silken divans, and velvet cushions, the prince Teyaspa reclined. He seemed the picture of voluptuous idleness as he lounged in silks and satins, a crystal jar of wine at his elbow. His dark eyes were those of a dreamer whose dreams are tinted with wine and drugs. His gaze rested on Roxana, who tensely gripped the bars of a casement, peering out, but his expression was placid and faraway. He seemed unaware of the yells and clamor that raged without.

Roxana moved restlessly, glancing at the prince over her slim shoulder. She had fought like a tigress to keep Teyaspa from falling into the gulf of degeneracy and resignation that his captors had prepared. Roxana, no fatalist, had stung him into life and ambition.

"It is time," she breathed, turning. "The sun hangs at the zenith. The Hyrkanians ride up the slope, lashing their steeds and loosing their arrows vainly against the walls. The Zaporoskans pour arrows and stones down upon them, until bodies litter the slope, but they come on again like madmen. I must hasten. You shall yet sit on the golden throne, my lover!"

She prostrated herself and kissed his slippers in an ecstasy of adoration, then rose and hurried out of the room, through another where ten great black mutes kept guard night and day. She traversed a corridor to the outer court that lay between the castle and the postern wall. Though Teyaspa was not allowed unguarded out of his chamber, she was free to come and go as she liked.

Crossing the court, she approached the door that led into the gorge. One warrior leaned there, disgruntled because he could not take part in the fighting. Though the rear of the castle seemed invulnerable, the cautious Gleg had posted a sentry there anyway. The man on guard was a Sogdian, his felt cap perched on the side of his head. He leaned on a pike, scowling, as Roxana approached him. "What do you here, woman?"

"I am afraid. The cries and shouts frighten me, lord. The prince is drugged with lotus juice, and there is none to soothe my fears."

She would have fired the heart of a corpse as she stood in an attitude of fear and supplication. The Sogdian plucked his thick beard.

"Nay, fear not, little gazelle," he said. "I'll soothe you." He laid a black-nailed hand on her shoulder and drew her close. "None shall touch a lock of your hair. I—ahhh!"

Snuggling in his arms, Roxana had slipped a dagger from her sash and thrust it through his thick throat. One of the Sogdian's hands clutched at his beard while the other fumbled for the hilt in his girdle. He reeled and fell heavily. Roxana snatched a bunch of keys from his girdle and ran to the door. She swung it open and gave a low cry of joy at the sight of Artaban and his Turanians on the ledge across the chasm.

A heavy plank, used as a bridge, lay inside the gate, but it was far too heavy for her to handle. Chance had enabled her to use it for her previous escape, when rare carelessness had left it in place across the chasm and unguarded for a few minutes. Artaban tossed her the end of a rope, which she made fast to the hinges of the door. The other end was gripped by half a dozen strong men, and three Turanians crossed the crevice, swinging hand over hand. They spanned the chasm with the plank for the rest to cross.

"Twenty men guard the bridge," snapped Artaban. "The rest follow me."

The sea wolves drew their steel and followed their chief. Artaban led them swiftly after the light-footed girl. As they entered the castle, a servitor sprang up and gaped at them. Before he could cry out, Dayuki's razor-edged yataghan sliced through his throat, and the band rushed into the chamber where the ten mutes sprang up, gripping scimitars. There was a flurry of fierce, silent fighting, noiseless except for the hiss and rasp of steel and the gasps of the wounded. Three Turanians died, and the rest strode into the inner chamber over the mangled bodies of the blacks.

Teyaspa rose, his quiet eyes gleaming with old fire, as Artaban dramatically knelt before him and lifted the hilt of his bloody scimitar.

"These are the warriors who shall set you on your throne!" cried Roxana.

"Let us go quickly, before the Zaporoskan dogs are aware of us," said Artaban.

He drew up his men in a clump around Teyaspa. Swiftly they traversed the chambers, crossed the court, and approached the gate. But the clang of steel had been heard. Even as the raiders were crossing the bridge, savage yells rose behind them. Across the courtyard rushed a stocky, powerful figure in silk and steel, followed by fifty helmeted archers and swordsmen.

"Gleg!" screamed Roxana.

"Cast down the plank!" roared Artaban, springing to the bridgehead.

On each side of the chasm bows twanged until the air over the plank was clouded with shafts whistling in both directions. Several Zaporoskans fell, but so did the two Turanians who stooped to lift the plank, and across the bridge rushed Gleg, his cold gray eyes blazing under his spired helmet. Artaban met him breast to breast. In a glittering whirl of steel the Turanian's scimitar grated around Gleg's blade, and the keen edge cut through the camail and the thick muscles of the Zaporoskan's neck. Gleg staggered and, with a wild cry, pitched off into the chasm.

In an instant the Turanians had cast the bridge after him. On the far side, the Zaporoskans halted with furious yells and began shooting their thick horn bows as fast as they could draw and nock. Before the Turanians, running down the ledge, could get out of range, three more had been brought down and a couple of others had received minor wounds from the vicious arrow storm. Artaban cursed at his losses.

"All but six of you go forward to see that the way is clear," he ordered. "I follow with the prince. My lord, I could not bring a horse up this defile, but I will have the dogs make you a litter of spears—"

"The gods forbid that I ride on my deliverers' shoulders!" cried Teyaspa. "Again I am a man! I shall never forget this day!"

"The gods be praised!" whispered Roxana.

They came within sight of the waterfall. All but the small group in the rear had crossed the stream and were straggling down the left bank, when there came a multiple snap of bowstrings, as though a hand had swept across the strings of a muted harp. A sheet of arrows hissed across the stream into their ranks, and then another and another. The foremost Turanians went down like wheat under the scythe and the rest gave back, shouting alarm.

"Dog!" shouted Artaban, turning on Dayuki. "This is your work."

"Do I order my men to shoot at me?" squalled the Hyrkanian, his dark face pale. "This is some new enemy!"

Artaban ran down the gorge toward his demoralized men, cursing. He knew that the Zaporoskans would rig up some sort of bridge across the chasm and pursue him, catching him between two forces. Who his assailants were he had no idea. From the castle he heard the shouts of battle, and then a great rumble of hooves and shouting and clang of steel seemed to come from the outer valley. But, pent in that narrow gorge, which muffled sound, he could not be sure.

The Turanians continued to fall before the storm of arrows from their invisible opponents. Some loosed blindly into the bushes. Artaban knocked their bows aside, shouting:

"Fools!" Why waste arrows on shadows? Draw steel and follow me!"

With a fury of desperation, the remaining Turanians charged the ambush, cloaks flowing and eyes blazing. Arrows brought down some, but the rest leaped into the water and splashed across. From the bushes on the farther bank rose wild figures, mail-clad or half-naked, swords in hands. "Up and at them!" bellowed a great voice. "Cut and thrust!"

A yell of amazement rose from the Turanians at the sight of the Vilayet pirates. Then they closed with a roar. The rasp and clangor of steel echoed from the cliffs. The first Turanians to spring up the higher bank fell back into the stream with heads split. Then the pirates leaped down the bank to meet their foes hand-to-hand, thigh-deep in water that soon swirled crimson. Pirate and Turanian slashed and slew in a blind frenzy, sweat and blood running into their eyes.

Dayuki ran into the mêlée, glaring. His double-curved blade split a pirate's head. Then Vinashko leaped upon him barehanded and screaming.

The Hyrkanian recoiled from the mad ferocity in the Yuetshi's features, but Vinashko caught Dayuki around the neck and sank his teeth in the man's throat. He hung on, chewing deeper and deeper, heedless of the dagger that Dayuki drove again and again into his side. Blood spurted around his jaws until both lost their footing and fell into the stream. Still tearing and rending, they were washed down with the current, now one face showing above water, now another, until both vanished forever.

The Turanians were driven back up the left bank, where they made a brief, bloody stand. Then they broke and fled toward the place where Prince Teyaspa stared entranced in the shadow of the cliff, with the small knot of warriors whom Artaban had detailed to guard him.

Thrice he moved as though to draw his sword and cast himself into the fray, but Roxana, clinging to his knees, stopped him.

Artaban, breaking away from the battle, hastened to Teyaspa. The admiral's sword was red to the hilt, his mail was hacked, and blood dripped from beneath his helmet. After him through the mêlée came Conan, brandishing his great sword in his sledgelike fist. He beat down his foes with strokes that shattered bucklers, caved in helmets, and clove through mail, flesh, and bone.

"Ho, you rascals!" he roared in his barbarous Hyrkanian. "I want your head, Artaban, and the fellow beside you there—Teyaspa. Fear not, my pretty prince; I'll not hurt you."

Artaban, looking about for an avenue of escape, saw the groove leading up the cliff and divined its purpose.

"Quick, my lord!" he whispered. "Up the cliff! I'll hold off the barbarian while you climb!"

"Aye, hasten!" urged Roxana. "I'll follow!"

But the fatalistic mask had descended again on Prince Teyaspa. He shrugged. "Nay, the gods do not will that I should press the throne. Who can escape his destiny?"

Roxana clutched her hair with a look of horror. Artaban sheathed his sword, sprang for the groove, and started up with the agility of a sailor. But Conan, coming up behind him at a run, reached up, caught his ankle, and plucked him out of his cranny like a fowler catching a bird by the leg. Artaban struck the ground with a clang. As he tried to roll over to wrench loose, the Cimmerian drove his sword into the Turanian's body, crunching through mail links, and into the ground beneath.

Pirates approached with dripping blades. Teyaspa spread his hands, saying: "Take me if you will. I am Teyaspa."

Roxana swayed, her hands over her eyes. Then like a flash she thrust her dagger through Teyaspa's heart, and he died on his feet. As he fell, she drove the point into her own breast and sank down beside her lover. Moaning, she cradled his head in her arms, while the pirates stood about, awed and incomprehending.

A sound up the gorge made them lift their heads. They were but a handful, weary and dazed with battle, their garments soaked with blood and water.

Conan said: "Men are coming down the gorge. Get back into the tunnel."

They obeyed, but slowly, as if they only half understood him. Before the last of them had ducked under the waterfall, a stream of men poured down the path from the castle. Conan, cursing and beating his rearmost men to make them hurry, looked around to see the gorge thronged with armed figures. He recognized the fur caps of the Zaporoskans and with them the white turbans of the Imperial Guards from Aghrapur. One of these wore a spray of bird-of-paradise feathers in his turban, and Conan stared to recognize, from these and other indications, the general of the Imperial Guards, the third man of the Turanian Empire.

The general saw Conan and the tail of his procession too and shouted an order. As Conan, the last in line, plunged through the waterfall, a body of Turanians detached themselves from the rest and ran to the pool.

Conan yelled to his men to run, then turned and faced the sheet of water from the inner side, holding up a buckler from a dead Turanian and his great sword.

Presently a guardsman came through the sheet of water. He started to yell, but the sound was cut off by a meaty *chunk* as Conan's sword sheared through his neck. His head and body tumbled separately off the ledge into the pool. The second guard had time to strike at the dim figure that towered over him, but his sword rebounded from the Cimmerian's buckler. The next instant he in turn fell back into the pool with a cloven skull.

There were shouts, partly muffled by the sound of the water. Conan flattened himself against the side of the tunnel, and a storm of arrows whipped through the sheet of water, bringing little splashes of droplets with them and rebounding with a clatter from the walls and floor of the tunnel.

A glance back showed Conan that his men had vanished into the gloom of the tunnel. He ran after them, so that when, a few moments later, the guardsmen again burst through the waterfall, they found nobody in front of them.

Meanwhile in the gorge, voices filled with horror rose as the newcomers halted among the corpses. The general knelt beside the dead prince and the dying girl.

"It is Prince Teyaspa!" he cried.

"He is beyond your power," murmured Roxana. "I would have made him king, but you robbed him of his manhood . . . so I killed him . . ."

"But I bring him the crown of Turan!" cried the general. "Yildiz is dead, and the people will rise against his son Yezdigerd if they have anyone else to follow—"

"Too late!" whispered Roxana, and her dark head sank on her arm.

Conan ran up the tunnel with the feet of the pursuing Turanians echoing after him. Where the tunnel opened into the great natural chimney lined with the tombs of the forgotten race, he saw his men grouped uncertainly on the floor of the pit below him, some looking at the hissing flame and some up at the stair down which they had come.

"Go on to the ship!" he bellowed through cupped hands. The words rattled back from the black cylindrical walls.

The men ran out into the cleft that led to the outer world. Conan turned again and leaned against the side of the chimney just alongside the tunnel entrance. He waited as the footsteps grew louder.

An Imperial Guard popped out of the tunnel. Again Conan's sword swished and struck, biting into the man's back through mail and skin and spine. With a shriek the guard pitched head-first off the platform. His momentum carried him out from the spiral stair toward the middle of the floor below. His body plunged into the hole in the rocky floor from which issued the flame and wedged there like a cork in a bottle. The flame went out with a pop, plunging the chamber into gloom only faintly relieved by the opening to the sky far above.

Conan did not see the body strike the floor, for he was watching the tunnel opening for his next foe. The next guard looked out but leaped back as Conan struck at him with a ferocious backhand. There came a jabber of voices; an arrow whizzed out of the tunnel past Conan's face, to strike the far side of the chamber and shatter against the black rock.

Conan turned and started down the stone steps, taking three at a time. As he reached the bottom, he saw Ivanos herding the last of the pirates into the cleft across the floor, perhaps ten strides away. To the left of the cleft, five times Conan's height from the floor, the Turanian guards boiled out of the tunnel and clattered down the stairs. A couple loosed arrows at the Cimmerian as they ran, but between the speed of his motion and the dimness of the light their shots missed.

But, as Conan reached the bottom steps, another group of beings appeared. With a grinding sound, the slabs of stone blocking the ends of the tomb cavities swung inward, first a few, then by scores. Like a swarm of larvae issuing from their cells, the inhabitants of the tombs came forth. Conan had not taken three strides toward the cleft when he found the way blocked by a dozen of the things.

They were of vaguely human form, but white and hairless, lean and stringy as if from a long fast. Their toes and fingers ended in great, hooked claws. They had large, staring eyes set in faces that looked more like those of bats than of human beings, with great, flaring ears, little snub noses, and wide mouths that opened to show needle-pointed fangs.

The first to reach the floor were those who crawled out of the bottom tiers of cells. But the upper tiers were opening too and the creatures were spelling out of them by hundreds, climbing swiftly down the pitted walls of the chamber by their hooked claws. Those that reached the floor first glimpsed the last pirates as they entered the cleft. With a pointing of clawed fingers and a shrill twittering, those nearest the cleft rushed toward and into it.

Conan, the hairs of his neck prickling with a barbarian's horror of supernatural menaces, recognized the newcomers as the dreaded *brylukas* of Zaporoskan legend—creatures neither man nor beast nor demon, but a little of all three. Their near-human intelligence served their bestial lust for human blood, while their supernatural powers enabled them to survive even though entombed for centuries. Creatures of darkness, they had been held at bay by the light of the flame. When this was put out they emerged, as ferocious as ever and even more avid for blood.

Those that struck the floor near Conan rushed upon him, claws outstretched. With an inarticulate roar he whirled, making wide sweeps with his great sword to keep them from piling on his back. The blade sheared off a head here, an arm there, and cut one *bryluka* in half. Still they clustered, twittering, while from the spiral staircase rose the shrieks of the leading Turanians as *brylukas* leaped upon them from above and climbed up from below to fasten their claws and fangs in their bodies.

The stair was clustered with writhing, battling figures as the Turanians hacked madly at the things crowding upon them. A cluster consisting of one guard with several *brylukas* clinging to him rolled off the stair to strike the floor. The entrance to the cleft was solidly jammed with twittering *brylukas* trying to force their way in to chase Conan's pirates. In the seconds before they overwhelmed him too, Conan saw that neither way out would serve him. With a bellow of fury he ran across the floor, but not in the direction the *brylukas* expected. Weaving and zigzagging, his sword a whirling glimmer in the gloom, he reached the wall directly below the platform that formed the top of the stair and the entrance to the tunnel, leaving a trail of still or writhing figures behind him. Hooked claws snatched at him as he ran, glancing off his mail, tearing his clothes to ribbons, and drawing blood from deep scratches on his arms and legs.

As he reached the wall, Conan dropped his buckler, took his sword in his teeth, sprang high in the air, and caught the lower sill of one of the cells in the third tier above the floor, a cell that had already discharged its occupant. With simian agility the Cimmerian mountaineer went up the wall, using the cell openings as hand and foot-holds. Once, as his face came opposite a cell opening, a hideous batlike visage looked into his as the *bryluka* started to emerge. Conan's fist lashed out and struck the grinning face with a crunch of bone; then, without waiting to see what execution he had done, he swarmed on up.

Below him, other *brylukas* climbed the wall in pursuit. Then with a heave and a grunt he was on the platform. Those guards who had been behind the ones who first started down the stair, seeing what was happening in the chamber, had turned and raced back through the tunnel. A few *brylukas* crowded into the tunnel in pursuit just as Conan reached the platform.

Even as they turned toward him he was among them like a whirlwind. Bodies, whole or dismembered, spilled off the platform as his sword sheared through white, unnatural flesh. For an instant the platform was cleared of the gibbering horrors. Conan plunged into the tunnel and ran with all his might.

Ahead of him ran a few of the vampires, and ahead of them the guards who had been coming along the tunnel. Conan, coming to the *brylukas* from behind, struck down one, then another, then another, until they were all writhing in their blood behind him. He kept on until he came to the end of the tunnel, where the last of the guards had just ducked through the waterfall.

A glance back showed Conan another swarm of *brylukas* rushing upon him with outstretched claws. Conan bolted through the sheet of water in his turn and found himself looking down upon the scene of the recent battle with the Turanians. The general and the rest of his escort were standing about, shouting and gesticulating as their fellows emerged from the water and ran down the ledge to the ground. When Conan appeared right after the last of these, the yammer continued without a break until a louder shout from the general cut through it:

"It is one of the pirates! Shoot!"

Conan, running down the ledge, was already halfway to the ladder shaft. Those in front of him, who had just reached the floor of the gorge, turned to stare as he raced past them with such tremendous strides that the archers, misjudging his speed, sent a flight of arrows clattering against the rocks behind him. Before they had nocked their second arrows, he had reached the vertical groove in the cliff face.

The Cimmerian slipped into the shaft, whose concavity protected him momentarily from the arrows of the Turanians standing near the general. He caught at the indentations with hands and toes and went up like a monkey. By the time the Turanians had recovered their wits enough to run up the gorge to a position in front of the groove, where they could see him to shoot at, Conan was fifteen paces up and rising fast.

Another storm of arrows whistled about him, clattering as they glanced from the rock. A couple struck his body but were prevented from piercing his flesh by his mail shirt. A couple of others struck his clothing and caught in the cloth. One hit his right arm, the point passing shallowly under the skin and then out again.

With a fearful oath Conan tore the arrow out of the wound point-first, threw it from him, and continued his climb. Blood from the flesh wound soaked up his arm and down his body. By the next volley, he was so high that the arrows had little force left when they reached him. One struck his boot but failed to penetrate.

Up and up he went, the Turanians becoming small beneath him. When their arrows no longer reached him, they ceased shooting. Snatches of argument floated up. The general wanted his men to climb the shaft after Conan, and the men protested that this would be futile, as he would simply wait at the top of the cliff and cut their heads off one by one as they emerged. Conan smiled grimly.

Then he reached the top. He sat gasping on the edge with his feet hanging down into the shaft while he bandaged his wounds with strips torn from his clothing, meantime looking about him. Glancing ahead over the rock wall into the valley of the Akrim, he saw sheepskin-clad Hyrkanians riding hard for the hills, pursued by horsemen in glittering mail—Turanian soldiers. Below him, the Turanians and Zaporoskans milled around like ants and finally set off up the gorge to the castle, leaving a few of their number on watch in case Conan should come back down the groove.

Some time later Conan rose, stretched his great muscles, and turned to look eastward toward the Sea of Vilayet. He started as his keen vision picked up a ship, and shading his eyes with his hand he made out a galley of the Turanian navy crawling away from the mouth of the creek where Artaban had left his ship.

"Crom!" he muttered. "So the cowards piled aboard and pulled out without waiting!"

He struck his palm with his fist, growling deep in his

throat like an angry bear. Then he relaxed and laughed shortly. It was no more than he should have expected. Anyway, he was getting tired of the Hyrkanian lands, and there were still many countries in the West that he had never visited.

He started to hunt for the precarious route down from the ridge that Vinashko had shown him.

A Witch Shall Be Born

Conan appropriates a stallion abandoned by one of the Hyrkanian soldiers and heads back by land to the steppes of his kozak *friends. But he finds the* kozaki *still scattered. Yezdigerd, now on the throne of Turan, is already proving himself a far more astute and energetic ruler than his late sire. He is submerging the fortunes and energies of would-be rivals in a program of imperialism, which will eventually make him master of the greatest empire of the Hyborian Age.*

After some narrow escapes from the far-ranging Turanians, Conan reaches the small border kingdom of Khauran, between the eastern tip of Koth and the steppes and deserts over which the Turanians are methodically extending their control. Soon, Conan wins himself the command of the royal guard of Queen Taramis of Khauran.

1. The Blood-Red Crescent

Taramis, Queen of Khauran, awakened from a dream-haunted slumber to a silence that seemed more like the stillness of nighted catacombs than the normal quiet of a sleeping palace. She lay staring into the darkness, wondering why the candles in their golden candelabra had gone out. A flecking of stars marked a gold-barred casement that lent no illumination to the interior of the chamber. But, as Taramis lay there, she became aware of a spot of radiance glowing in the darkness before her.

She watched, puzzled. It grew, and its intensity deepened as it expanded, a widening disk of lurid light hovering against the dark velvet hangings of the opposite wall. Taramis caught her breath, starting up to a sitting position. A dark object was visible in that circle of light—*a human head.*

In a sudden panic the queen opened her lips to cry out for her maids; then she checked herself. The glow was more lurid, the head more vividly limned. It was a woman's head, small, delicately molded, superbly poised, with a high-piled mass of lustrous black hair. The face grew distinct as she stared—and it was the sight of this face which froze the cry in Taramis' throat. The features were her own! She might have been looking into a mirror which subtly altered her reflection, lending it a tigerish gleam of eye, a vindictive curl of lip.

"Ishtar!" gasped Taramis. "I am bewitched!"

Appallingly, the apparition spoke, and its voice was like honeyed venom.

"Bewitched? No, sweet sister! Here is no sorcery."

"Sister?" stammered the bewildered girl. "I have no sister."

"You never had a sister?" came the sweet, poisonously mocking voice. "Never a twin sister whose flesh was as soft as yours to caress or hurt?"

"Why, once I had a sister," answered Taramis, still convinced that she was in the grip of some sort of nightmare. "But she died."

The beautiful face in the disk was convulsed with the aspect of a fury; so hellish became its expression that Taramis, cowering back, half expected to see snaky locks writhe hissing about the ivory brow.

"You lie!" The accusation was spat from between the snarling red lips. "She did not die! Fool! Oh, enough of this mummery! Look—and let your sight be blasted!"

Light ran suddenly along the hangings like flaming serpents, and incredibly the candles in the golden sticks flared up again. Taramis crouched on her velvet couch, her lithe legs flexed beneath her, staring wide-eyed at the pantherish figure which posed mockingly before her. It was as if she gazed upon another Taramis, identical with herself in every contour of feature and limb, yet animated by an alien and evil personality. The face of this stranger waif reflected the opposite of every characteristic the countenance of the queen denoted. Lust and mystery sparkled in her scintillant eyes, cruelty lurked in the curl of her full red lips. Each movement of her supple body was subtly suggestive. Her coiffure imitated that of the queen's, on her feet were gilded sandals such as Taramis wore in her boudoir. The sleeveless, low-necked silk tunic, girdled at the waist with a cloth-of-gold cincture, was a duplicate of the queen's night-garment.

"Who are you?" gasped Taramis, an icy chill she could not explain creeping along her spine. "Explain your presence before I call my ladies-in-waiting to summon the guard!"

"Scream until the roof beams crack," callously answered the stranger. "Your sluts will not wake till dawn, though the palace spring into flames about them. Your guardsmen will not hear your squeals; they have been sent out of this wing of the palace."

"What!" exclaimed Taramis, stiffening with outraged majesty. "Who dared give my guardsmen such a command?"

"I did, sweet sister," sneered the other girl. "A little while ago, before I entered. They thought it was their darling adored queen. Ha! How beautifully I acted the part! With what imperious dignity, softened by womanly sweetness, did I address the great louts who knelt in their armor and plumed helmets!"

Taramis felt as if a stifling net of bewilderment was being drawn about her.

"Who are you?" she cried desperately. "What madness is this? Why do you come here?"

"Who am I?" There was the spite of a she-cobra's hiss in the soft response. The girl stepped to the edge of the couch, grasped the queen's white shoulders with fierce fingers, and bent to glare full into the startled eyes of Taramis. And under the spell of that hypnotic glare, the queen forgot to resent the unprecedented outrage of violent hands laid on regal flesh.

"Fool!" gritted the girl between her teeth. "Can you ask? Can you wonder? I am Salome!"

"Salome!" Taramis breathed the word, and the hairs prickled on her scalp as she realized the incredible, numbing truth of the statement. "I thought you died within the hour of your birth," she said feebly.

"So thought many," answered the woman who called herself Salome. "They carried me into the desert to die, damn them! I, a mewing, puling babe whose life was so young it was scarcely the flicker of a candle. And do you know why they bore me forth to die?"

"I—I have heard the story——" faltered Taramis.

Salome laughed fiercely, and slapped her bosom. The low-necked tunic left the upper parts of her firm breasts bare, and between them there shone a curious mark—a crescent, red as blood.

"The mark of the witch!" cried Taramis, recoiling.

"Aye!" Salome's laughter was dagger-edged with hate. "The curse of the kings of Khauran! Aye, they tell the tale in the marketplaces, with wagging beards and rolling eyes, the pious fools! They tell how the first queen of our line had traffic with a fiend of darkness and bore him a daughter who lives in foul legendry to this day. And thereafter, in each century, a girl baby was born into the Askhaurian dynasty, with a scarlet half-moon between her breasts, that signified her destiny.

"'Every century a witch shall be born.' So ran the ancient curse. And so it has come to pass. Some were slain at birth, as they sought to slay me. Some walked the earth as witches, proud daughters of Khauran, with the moon of hell burning upon their ivory bosoms. Each was named Salome. I, too, am Salome. It was always Salome, the witch. It will always be Salome, the witch, even when the mountains of ice have roared down from the pole and ground the civilizations to ruin, and a new world has risen from the ashes and dust—even then there shall be Salomes to walk the earth, to trap men's hearts by their sorcery, to dance before the kings of the world, and see the heads of the wise men fall at their pleasure."

"But—but you——" stammered Taramis.

"I?" The scintillant eyes burned like dark fires of mystery. "They carried me into the desert far from the city, and laid me naked on the hot sand, under the flaming sun. And then they rode away and left me for the jackals and the vultures and the desert wolves.

"But the life in me was stronger than the life in common folk, for it partakes of the essence of the forces that seethe in the black gulfs beyond mortal ken. The hours passed, and the sun slashed down like the molten flames of Hell, but I did not die—aye, something of that torment I remember, faintly and far away, as one remembers a dim, formless dream. Then there were camels, and yellow-skinned men who wore silk robes and spoke in a weird tongue. Strayed from the caravan road, they passed close by, and their leader saw me, and recognized the scarlet crescent on my bosom. He took me up and gave me life.

"He was a magician from far Khitai, returning to his native kingdom after a journey to Stygia. He took me with him to purple-towered Paikang, its minarets rising amid the vine-festooned jungles of bamboo, and there I grew to womanhood under his teaching. Age had steeped him deep in black wisdom, not weakened his powers of evil. Many things he taught me——"

She paused, smiling enigmatically, with wicked mystery gleaming in her dark eyes. Then she tossed her head.

"He drove me from him at last, saying that I was but

a common witch in spite of his teachings, and not fit to command the mighty sorcery he would have taught me. He would have made me queen of the world and ruled the nations through me, he said, but I was only a harlot of darkness. But what of it? I could never endure to seclude myself in a golden tower, and spend the long hours staring into a crystal globe, mumbling over incantations written on serpent's skin in the blood of virgins, poring over musty volumes in forgotten languages.

"He said I was but an earthly sprite, knowing naught of the deeper gulfs of cosmic sorcery. Well, this world contains all I desire—power, and pomp, and glittering pageantry, handsome men and soft women for my paramours and my slaves. He had told me who I was, of the curse and my heritage. I have returned to take that to which I have as much right as you. Now it is mine by right of possession."

"What do you mean?" Taramis sprang up and faced her sister, stung out of her bewilderment and fright. "Do you imagine that by drugging a few of my maids and tricking a few of my guardsmen you have established a claim to the throne of Khauran? Do not forget that I am queen of Khauran! I shall give you a place of honor, as my sister, but——"

Salome laughed hatefully.

"How generous of you, dear, sweet sister! But before you begin putting me in my place—perhaps you will tell me whose soldiers camp in the plain outside the city walls?"

"They are the Shemitish mercenaries of Constantius, the Kothic *voivode* of the Free Companies."

"And what do they in Khauran?" cooed Salome.

Taramis felt that she was being subtly mocked, but she answered with an assumption of dignity which she scarcely felt.

"Constantius asked permission to pass along the borders of Khauran on his way to Turan. He himself is hostage for their good behavior as long as they are within my domains."

"And Constantius," pursued Salome. "Did he not ask your hand today?"

Taramis shot her a clouded glance of suspicion.

"How did you know that?"

An insolent shrug of the slim, naked shoulders was the only reply.

"You refused, dear sister?"

"Certainly I refused!" exclaimed Taramis angrily. "Do you, an Askhaurian princess yourself, suppose that the queen of Khauran could treat such a proposal with anything but disdain? Wed a bloody-handed adventurer, a man exiled from his own kingdom because of his crimes, and the leader of organized plunderers and hired murderers?

"I should never have allowed him to bring his black-bearded slayers into Khauran. But he is virtually a prisoner in the south tower, guarded by my solders. Tomorrow I shall bid him order his troops to leave the kingdom. He himself shall be kept captive until they are over the border. Meantime, my soldiers man the walls of the city, and I have warned him that he will answer for any outrages perpetrated on the villagers or shepherds by his mercenaries."

"He is confined in the south tower?" asked Salome.

"That is what I said. Why do you ask?"

For answer Salome clapped her hands, and lifting her voice, with a gurgle of cruel mirth in it, called: "The queen grants you an audience, Falcon!"

A gold-arabesqued door opened and a tall figure entered the chamber, at the sight of which Taramis cried out in amazement and anger.

"Constantius! You dare enter my chamber!"

"As you see, Your Majesty!" He bent his dark, hawk-like head in mock humility.

Constantius, whom men called Falcon, was tall, broad-shouldered, slim-waisted, lithe and strong as pliant steel. He was handsome in an aquiline, ruthless way. His face was burnt dark by the sun, and his hair, which grew far back from his high, narrow forehead, was black as a raven. His dark eyes were penetrating and alert, the hardness of his thin lips not softened by his thin black mustache. His boots were of Kordavan leather, his hose and doublet of plain, dark silk, tarnished with the wear of the camps and the stains of armor rust.

Twisting his mustache, he let his gaze travel up and down the shrinking queen with an effrontery that made her wince.

"By Ishtar, Taramis," he said silkily, "I find you more alluring in your night-tunic than in your queenly robes. Truly, this is an auspicious night!"

Fear grew in the queen's dark eyes. She was no fool; she knew that Constantius would never dare this outrage unless he was sure of himself.

"You are mad!" she said. "If I am in your power in this chamber, you are no less in the power of my subjects, who will rend you to pieces if you touch me. Go at once, if you would live."

Both laughed mockingly, and Salome made an impatient gesture.

"Enough of this farce; let us on to the next act in the comedy. Listen, dear sister: it was I who sent Constantius here. When I decided to take the throne of Khauran, I cast about for a man to aid me, and chose the Falcon, because of his utter lack of all characteristics men call good."

"I am overwhelmed, princess," murmured Constantius sardonically, with a profound bow.

"I sent him to Khauran and, once his men were camped in the plain outside and he was in the palace, I entered the city by that small gate in the west wall—the fools guarding it thought it was you returning from some nocturnal adventure——"

"You hell-cat!" Taramis' cheeks flamed and her resentment got the better of her regal reserve.

Salome smiled hardly.

"They were properly surprised and shocked, but admitted me without question. I entered the palace the same way and gave the order to the surprised guards that sent them marching away, as well as the men who guarded Constantius in the south tower. Then I came here, attending to the ladies-in-waiting on the way."

Taramis' fingers clenched and she paled.

"Well, what next?" she asked in a shaky voice.

"Listen!" Salome inclined her head. Faintly through the casement there came the clank of marching men in armor; gruff voices shouted in an alien tongue, and cries of alarm mingled with the shouts.

"The people awaken and grow fearful," said Constantius sardonically. "You had better go and reassure them, Salome!"

"Call me Taramis," answered Salome. "We must become accustomed to it."

"What have you done?" cried Taramis. "What have you done?"

"I have gone to the gates and ordered the soldiers to open them," answered Salome. "They were astounded, but they obeyed. That is the Falcon's army you hear, marching into the city."

"You devil!" cried Taramis. "You have betrayed my people, in my guise! You have made me seem a traitor! Oh, I shall go to them——"

With a cruel laugh Salome caught her wrist and jerked her back. The magnificent suppleness of the queen was helpless against the vindictive strength that steeled Salome's slender limbs.

"You know how to reach the dungeons from the palace, Constantius?" said the witch-girl. "Good. Take this spitfire and lock her into the strongest cell. The jailers are all sound in drugged sleep. I saw to that. Send a man to cut their throats before they can awaken. None must ever know what has occurred tonight. Henceforward I am Taramis, and Taramis is a nameless prisoner in an unknown dungeon."

Constantius smiled with a glint of strong white teeth under his thin mustache.

"Very good; but you would not deny me a little—ah—amusement first?"

"Not I! Tame the scornful hussy as you will." With a wicked laugh Salome flung her sister into the Kothian's arms, and turned away through the door that opened into the outer corridor.

Fright widened Taramis' lovely eyes, her supple figure rigid and straining against Constantius' embrace. She forgot the men marching in the streets, forgot the outrage to her queenship, in the face of the menace to her womanhood. She forgot all sensations but terror and shame as she faced the complete cynicism of Constantius' burning, mocking eyes, felt his hard arms crushing her writhing body.

Salome, hurrying along the corridor outside, smiled spitefully as a scream of despair and agony rang shuddering through the palace.

2. *The Tree of Death*

The young soldier's hose and shirt were smeared with dried blood, wet with sweat and gray with dust. Blood oozed from the deep gash in his thigh, from the cuts on his breast and shoulder. Perspiration glistened on his livid face and his fingers were knotted in the cover of the divan on which he lay. Yet his words reflected mental suffering that outweighed physical pain.

"She must be mad!" he repeated again and again, like one still stunned by some monstrous and incredible happening. "It's like a nightmare! Taramis, whom all Khauran loves, betraying her people to that devil from Koth!

Oh, Ishtar, why was I not slain? Better die than live to see our queen turn traitor and harlot!"

"Lie still, Valerius," begged the girl who was washing and bandaging his wounds with trembling hands. "Oh, please lie still, darling! You will make your wounds worse, I dared not summon a leech——"

"No," muttered the wounded youth. "Constantius' blue-bearded devils will be searching the quarters for wounded Khauranis; they'll hang every man who has wounds to show he fought against them. Oh, Taramis, how could you betray the people who worshipped you?" In his fierce agony he writhed, weeping in rage and shame, and the terrified girl caught him in her arms, straining his tossing head against her bosom, imploring him to be quiet.

"Better death than the black shame that has come upon Khauran this day," he groaned. "Did you see it, Ivga?"

"No, Valerius." Her soft, nimble fingers were again at work, gently cleansing and closing the gaping edges of his raw wounds. "I was awakened by the noise of fighting in the streets—I looked out a casement and saw the Shemites cutting down people; then presently I heard you calling me faintly from the alley door."

"I had reached the limits of my strength," he muttered. "I fell in the alley and could not rise. I knew they'd find me soon if I lay there—I killed three of the blue-bearded beasts, by Ishtar! They'll never swagger through Khauran's streets, by the gods! The fiends are tearing their hearts in Hell!"

The trembling girl crooned soothingly to him, as to a wounded child, and closed his panting lips with her own cool sweet mouth. But the fire that raged in his soul would not allow him to lie silent.

"I was not on the wall when the Shemites entered," he burst out. "I was asleep in the barracks, with the others not on duty. It was just before dawn when our captain entered, and his face was pale under his helmet. 'The Shemites are in the city,' he said. 'The queen came to the southern gate and gave orders that they should be admitted. She made the men come down from the walls, where they've been on guard since Constantius entered the kingdom. I don't understand it, and neither does anyone else, but I heard her give the order, and we obeyed as we always do. We are ordered to assemble in the square before the palace. Form ranks outside the barracks and march—leave your arms and armor here. Ishtar knows what this means, but it is the queen's order.'

"Well, when we came to the square the Shemites were drawn up on foot opposite the palace, ten thousand of the blue-bearded devils, fully armed, and people's heads were thrust out of every window and door on the square. The streets leading into the square were thronged by bewildered folk. Taramis was standing on the steps of the palace, alone except for Constantius, who stood stroking his mustache like a great lean cat who has just devoured a sparrow. But fifty Shemites with bows in their hands were ranged below them.

"That's where the queen's guard should have been, but they were drawn up at the foot of the palace stair, as puzzled as we, though they had come fully armed, in spite of the queen's order.

"Taramis spoke to us then, and told us that she had reconsidered the proposal made her by Constantius—why, only yesterday she threw it in his teeth in open court!—and that she had decided to make him her royal consort. She did not explain why she had brought the Shemites into the city so treacherously. But she said that, as Constantius had control of a body of professional fighting-men, the army of Khauran would no longer be needed, and therefore she disbanded it, and ordered us to go quietly to our homes.

"Why, obedience to our queen is second nature to us,

but we were struck dumb and found no word to answer. We broke ranks almost before we knew what we were doing, like men in a daze.

"But, when the palace guard was ordered to disarm likewise and disband, the captain of the guard, Conan, interrupted. Men said he was off duty the night before, and drunk. But he was wide awake now. He shouted to the guardsmen to stand as they were until they received an order from him—and such is his dominance of his men, that they obeyed in spite of the queen. He strode up to the palace steps and glared at Taramis—and then he roared: 'This is not the queen! This isn't Taramis! It's some devil in masquerade!'

"Then Hell was to pay! I don't know just what happened. I think a Shemite struck Conan, and Conan killed him. The next instant the square was a battleground. The Shemites fell on the guardsmen, and their spears and arrows struck down many soldiers who had already disbanded.

"Some of us grabbed up such weapons as we could and fought back. We hardly knew what we were fighting for, but it was against Constantius and his devils—not against Taramis, I swear it! Constantius shouted to cut the traitors down. We were not traitors!" Despair and bewilderment shook his voice. The girl murmured pityingly, not understanding it all, but aching in sympathy with her lover's suffering.

"The people did not know which side to take. It was a madhouse of confusion and bewilderment. We who fought didn't have a chance, in no formation, without armor and only half armed. The guards were fully armed and drawn up in a square, but there were only five hundred of them. They took a heavy toll before they were cut down, but there could be only one conclusion to such a battle. And while her people were being slaughtered before her, Taramis stood on the palace steps, with Constantius' arm about her waist, and laughed like a heartless, beautiful fiend! Gods, it's all mad—mad!

"I never saw a man fight as Conan fought. He put his back to the courtyard wall, and before they overpowered him the dead men were strewn in heaps thigh-deep about him. But at last they dragged him down, a hundred against one. When I saw him fall I dragged myself away, feeling as if the world had burst under my very fingers. I heard Constantius call to his dogs to take the captain alive—stroking his mustache, with that hateful smile on his lips!"

That smile was on the lips of Constantius at that very moment. He sat his horse among a cluster of his men—thick-bodied Shemites with curled blue-black beards and hooked noses; the low-swinging sun struck glints from their peaked helmets and the silvered scales of their corselets. Nearly a mile behind, the walls and towers of Khauran rose sheer out of the meadowlands.

By the side of the caravan road a heavy cross had been planted, and on this grim tree a man hung, nailed there by iron spikes through his hands and feet. Naked but for a loincloth, the man was almost a giant in stature, and his muscles stood out in thick corded ridges on limbs and body, which the sun had long ago burned brown. The perspiration of agony beaded his face and his mighty breast, but from under the tangled black mane that fell over his low, broad forehead, his blue eyes blazed with an unquenched fire. Blood oozed sluggishly from the lacerations in his hands and feet.

Constantius saluted him mockingly.

"I am sorry, captain," he said, "that I can not remain to ease your last hours, but I have duties to perform in yonder city—I must not keep our delicious queen waiting!" He laughed softly. "So I leave you to your own devices—and those beauties!" He pointed meaningly at the black shadows which swept incessantly back and forth, high above.

"Were it not for them, I imagine that a powerful brute like yourself should live on the cross for days. Do not cherish any illusions of rescue because I am leaving you unguarded. I have had it proclaimed that anyone seeking to take your body, living or dead, from the cross, will be flayed alive, together with all the members of his family, in the public square. I am so firmly established in Khauran that my order is as good as a regiment of guardsmen. I am leaving no guard, because the vultures will not approach as long as anyone is near, and I do not wish them to feel any constraint. That is also why I brought you so far from the city. These desert vultures approach the walls no closer than this spot.

"And so, brave captain, farewell! I will remember you when, in an hour, Taramis lies in my arms."

Blood started afresh from the pierced palms as the victim's mallet-like fists clenched convulsively on the spikeheads. Knots and bunches of muscle started out on the massive arms, and Conan bent his head forward and spat savagely at Constantius' face. The *voivode* laughed coolly, wiped the saliva from his gorget and reined his horse about.

"Remember me when the vultures are tearing at your living flesh," he called mockingly. "The desert scavengers are a particularly voracious breed. I have seen men hang for hours on a cross, eyeless, earless, and scalpless, before the sharp beaks had eaten their way into his vitals."

Without a backward glance he rode toward the city, a supple, erect figure, gleaming in his burnished armor, his stolid, bearded henchmen jogging beside him. A faint rising of dust from the worn trail marked their passing.

The man hanging on the cross was the one touch of sentient life in a landscape that seemed desolate and deserted in the late evening. Khauran, less than a mile away, might have been on the other side of the world, and existing in another age.

Shaking the sweat out of his eyes, Conan stared blankly at the familiar terrain. On either side of the city, and beyond it, stretched the fertile meadowlands, with cattle browsing in the distance where fields and vineyards checkered the plain. The western and northern horizons were dotted with villages, miniature in the distance. A lesser distance to the southeast, a silvery gleam marked the course of a river, and beyond that river sandy desert began abruptly, to stretch away and away beyond the horizon. Conan stared at that expanse of empty waste, shimmering tawnily in the late sunlight, as a trapped hawk stares at the open sky. A revulsion shook him when he glanced at the gleaming towers of Khauran. The city had betrayed him—trapped him into circumstances that left him hanging to a wooden cross like a hare nailed to a tree.

A red lust for vengeance swept away the thought. Curses ebbed fitfully from the man's lips. All his universe contracted, focused, became incorporated in the four iron spikes that held him from life and freedom. His great muscles quivered, knotting like iron cables. With the sweat starting out on his graying skin, he sought to gain leverage, to tear the nails from the wood. It was useless. They had been driven deep. Then he tried to tear his hands off the spikes, and it was not the knifing abysmal agony that finally caused him to cease his efforts, but the futility of it. The spike heads were broad and heavy; he could not drag them through the wounds. A surge of helplessness shook the giant for the first time in his life. He hung motionless, his head resting on his breast, shutting his eyes against the aching glare of the sun.

A beat of wings caused him to look up, just as a feathered shadow shot down out of the sky. A keen beak, stabbing at his eyes, cut his cheek, and he jerked his head aside, shutting his eyes involuntarily. He shouted, a croaking, desperate shout of menace, and the vultures swerved away and retreated, frightened by the sound. They resumed their wary circling above his head. Blood trickled over Conan's mouth, and he licked his lips involuntarily, spat at the salty taste.

Thirst assailed him savagely. He had drunk deeply of wine the night before, and no water had touched his lips since before the battle in the square, that dawn. And killing was thirsty, salt-sweaty work. He glared at the distant river as a man in Hell glares through the opened grille. He thought of gushing freshets of white water he had breasted, laved to the shoulders in liquid jade. He remembered great horns of foaming ale, jacks of sparkling wine gulped carelessly or spilled on the tavern floor. He bit his lip to keep from bellowing in intolerable anguish as a tortured animal bellows.

The sun sank, a lurid ball in a fiery sea of blood. Against a crimson rampart that banded the horizon, the towers of the city floated unreal as a dream. The very sky was tinged with blood to his misted glare. He licked his blackened lips and stared with bloodshot eyes at the distant river. It, too, seemed crimson like blood, and the shadows crawling up from the east seemed black as ebony.

In his dulled ears sounded the louder beat of wings. Lifting his head he watched with the burning glare of a wolf the shadows wheeling above him. He knew that his shouts would frighten them away no longer. One dipped—dipped—lower and lower. Conan drew his head back as far as he could, waiting with terrible patience. The vulture swept in with a swift roar of wings. Its beak flashed down, ripping the skin on Conan's chin as he jerked his head aside; then, before the bird could flash away, Conan's head lunged forward on his mighty neck muscles, and his teeth, snapping like those of a wolf, locked on the bare, wattled neck.

Instantly, the vulture exploded into squawking, flapping hysteria. Its thrashing wings blinded the man, and its talons ripped his chest. But grimly he hung on, the muscles starting out in lumps on his jaws. And the scavenger's neck-bones crunched between those powerful teeth. With a spasmodic flutter the bird hung limp. Conan let go, spat blood from his mouth. The other vultures, terrified by the fate of their companion, were in full flight to a distant tree, where they perched like black demons in conclave.

Ferocious triumph surged through Conan's numbed brain. Life beat strongly and savagely through his veins. He could still deal death; he still lived. Every twinge of sensation, even of agony, was a negation of death.

"By Mitra!" Either a voice spoke, or he suffered from hallucination. "In all my life I have never seen such a thing!"

Shaking the sweat and blood from his eyes, Conan saw four horsemen sitting their steeds in the twilight and staring up at him. Three were lean, white-robed hawks, Zuagir tribesmen without a doubt, nomads from beyond the river. The other was dressed like them in a white, girdled *khalat* and a flowing headdress which, banded about the temples with a triple circlet of braided camel-hair, fell to his shoulders. But he was not a Shemite. The dusk was not so thick, nor Conan's hawklike sight so clouded, that he could not perceive the man's facial characteristics.

He was as tall as Conan, though not so heavy-limbed. His shoulders were broad, and his supple figure was hard as steel and whalebone. A short black beard did not altogether mask the aggressive jut of his lean jaw, and gray eyes cold and piercing as a sword gleamed from the shadow of the kaffia. Quieting his restless steed with a quick, sure hand, this man spoke: "By Mitra, I should know this man!"

"Aye!" It was the guttural accents of a Zuagir. "It is the Cimmerian who was captain of the queen's guard!"

"She must be casting off all her old favorites," muttered the rider. "Who'd have ever thought it of Queen Taramis? I'd rather have had a long, bloody war. It would have given us desert folk a chance to plunder. As it is, we've come this close to the walls and found only this nag"—he glanced at a fine gelding led by one of the nomads—"and this dying dog."

Conan lifted his bloody head.

"If I could come down from this beam I'd make a dying dog out of you, you Zaporoskan thief!" he rasped through blackened lips.

"Mitra, the knave knows me!" exclaimed the other. "How, knave, do you know me?"

"There's only one of your breed in these parts," muttered Conan. "You are Olgerd Vladislav, the outlaw chief."

"Aye! and once a hetman of the *kozaki* of the Zaporoskan River, as you have guessed. Would you like to live?"

"Only a fool would ask that question," panted Conan.

"I am a hard man," said Olgerd, "and toughness is the only quality I respect in a man. I shall judge if you are a man, or only a dog after all, fit only to lie here and die."

"If we cut him down we may be seen from the walls," objected one of the nomads.

Olgerd shook his head.

"The dusk is too deep. Here, take this ax, Djebal, and cut down the cross at the base."

"If it falls forward it will crush him," objected Djebal. "I can cut it so it will fall backward, but then the shock of the fall may crack his skull and tear loose all his entrails."

"If he's worthy to ride with me he'll survive it," answered Olgerd imperturbably. "If not, then he doesn't deserve to live. Cut!"

The first impact of the battle-ax against the wood and its accompanying vibrations sent lances of agony through Conan's swollen feet and hands. Again and again the blade fell, and each stroke reverberated on his bruised brain, setting his tortured nerves aquiver. But he set his teeth and made no sound. The ax cut through, the cross reeled on its splintered base and toppled backward. Conan made his whole body a solid knot of iron-hard muscle, jammed his head back hard against the wood and held it rigid there. The beam struck the ground heavily and rebounded slightly. The impact tore his wounds and dazed him for an instant. He fought the rushing tide of blackness, sick and dizzy, but realized that the iron muscles that sheathed his vitals had saved him from permanent injury.

And he had made no sound, though blood oozed from his nostrils and his belly muscles quivered with nausea. With a grunt of approval, Djebal bent over him with a pair of pincers used to draw horsehoe nails and gripped the head of the spike in Conan's right hand, tearing the skin to get a grip on the deeply embedded head. The pincers were small for that work. Djebal sweated and tugged, swearing and wrestling with the stubborn iron, working it back and forth—in swollen flesh as well as in wood. Blood started, oozing over the Cimmerian's fingers. He lay so still he might have been dead, except for the spasmodic rise and fall of his great chest. The spike gave way, and Djebal held up the bloodstained thing with a grunt of satisfaction, then flung it away and bent over the other.

The process was repeated, and then Djebal turned his attention to Conan's skewered feet. But the Cimmerian, struggling up to a sitting posture, wrenched the pincers from his fingers and sent him staggering backward with a violent shove. Conan's hands were swollen to almost twice their normal size. His fingers felt like misshapen thumbs, and closing his hands was an agony that brought blood streaming from under his grinding teeth. But somehow, clutching the pincers clumsily with both hands, he managed to wrench out first one spike and then the other.

They were not driven so deeply into the wood as the others had been.

He rose stiffly and stood upright on his swollen, lacerated feet, swaying drunkenly, the icy sweat dripping from his face and body. Cramps assailed him, and he clamped his jaws against the desire to retch.

Olgerd, watching him impersonally, motioned him toward the stolen horse. Conan stumbled toward it, and every step was a stabbing, throbbing hell that flecked his lips with bloody foam. One misshapen, groping hand fell clumsily on the saddle bow, a bloody foot somehow found the stirrup. Setting his teeth, he swung up, and he almost fainted in midair; but he came down in the saddle—and as he did so, Olgerd struck the horse sharply with his whip. The startled beast reared, and the man in the saddle swayed and slumped like a sack of sand, almost unseated. Conan had wrapped a rein about each hand, holding it in place with a clamping thumb. Drunkenly he exerted the strength of his knotted biceps, wrenching the horse down; it screamed, its jaw almost dislocated.

One of the Shemites lifted a water flask questioningly.

Olgerd shook his head.

"Let him wait until we get to camp. It's only ten miles. If he's fit to live in the desert, he'll live that long without a drink."

The group rode like swift ghosts toward the river; among them Conan swayed like a drunken man in the saddle, bloodshot eyes glazed, foam drying on his blackened lips.

3. *A Letter to Nemedia*

The savant Astreas, traveling in the East in his never-tiring search for knowledge, wrote a letter to his friend and fellow philosopher Alcemides, in his native Nemedia, which constitutes the entire knowledge of the Western nations concerning the events of that period in the East, always a hazy, half-mythical region in the minds of the Western folk.

Astreas wrote, in part: "You can scarcely conceive, my dear old friend, of the conditions now existing in this tiny kingdom since Queen Taramis admitted Constantius and his mercenaries, an event which I briefly described in my last, hurried letter. Seven months have passed since then, during which time it seems as though the Devil himself had been loosed in this unfortunate realm. Taramis seems to have gone quite mad; whereas formerly she was famed for her virtue, justice, and tranquility, she is now notorious for qualities precisely opposite to those just enumerated. Her private life is a scandal—or perhaps 'private' is not the correct term, since the queen makes no attempt to conceal the debauchery of her court. She constantly indulges in the most infamous revelries, in which the unfortunate ladies of the court are forced to join, young married women as well as virgins.

"She herself has not bothered to marry her paramour, Constantius, who sits on the throne beside her and reigns as her royal consort, and his officers follow his example and do not hesitate to debauch any woman they desire, regardless of her rank or station. The wretched kingdom groans under exorbitant taxation, the farms are stripped to the bone, and the merchants go in rags, which are all that is left them by the tax gatherers. Nay, they are lucky if they escape with a whole skin.

"I sense your incredulity, good Alcemides; you will fear that I exaggerate conditions in Khauran. Such conditions would be unthinkable in any of the Western countries, admittedly. But you must realize the vast difference that exists between West and East, especially this part of the East. In the first place, Khauran is a kingdom of no great size, one of the many principalities which at one time formed the eastern part of the empire of Koth, and which later regained the independence which was theirs at a still earlier age. This part of the world is made up of these tiny realms, diminutive in comparison with the great kingdoms of the West, or the great sultanates of the farther East, but important in their control of the caravan routes and in the wealth concentrated in them.

"Khauran is the most southeasterly of these principalities, bordering on the very deserts of eastern Shem. The city of Khauran is the only city of any magnitude in the realm and stands within sight of the river which separates the grasslands from the sandy desert, like a watch-tower to guard the fertile meadows behind it. The land is so rich that it yields three and four crops a year, and the plains north and west of the city are dotted with villages. To one accustomed to the great plantations and stock farms of the West, it is strange to see these tiny fields and vineyards; yet wealth in grain and fruit pours from them as from a horn of plenty. The villagers are agriculturists, nothing else. Of a mixed, aboriginal race, they are unwarlike, unable to protect themselves, and forbidden the possession of arms. Dependent wholly upon the soldiers of the city for protection, they are helpless under the present conditions. So the savage revolt of the rural sections, which would be a certainty in any Western nation, is here impossible.

"They toil supinely under the iron hand of Constantius, and his black-bearded Shemites ride incessantly through the fields with whips in their hands like the slave drivers of the black serfs who toil in the plantations of southern Zingara.

"Nor do the people of the city fare any better. Their wealth is stripped from them, their fairest daughters taken to glut the insatiable lust of Constantius and his mercenaries. These men are utterly without mercy or compassion, possessed of all the characteristics our armies learned to abhor in our wars against the Shemitish allies of Argos—inhuman cruelty, lust, and wild-beast ferocity.

The people of the city are Khauran's ruling caste, predominantly Hyborian, and valorous and warlike. But the treachery of their queen delivered them into the hands of their oppressors. The Shemites are the only armed force in Khauran, and the most hellish punishment is inflicted on any Khauran found possessing weapons. A systematic persecution to destroy the young Khaurani men able to bear arms has been savagely pursued. Many have ruthlessly been slaughtered, others sold as slaves to the Turanians. Thousands have fled the kingdom and either entered the service of other rulers, or become outlaws, lurking in numerous bands along the borders.

"At present there is some possibility of invasion from the desert, which is inhabited by tribes of Shemitish nomads. The mercenaries of Constantius are men from the Shemitish cities of the west, Pelishtim, Anakim, Akkharim, and are ardently hated by the Zuagirs and other wandering tribes. As you know, good Alcemides, the countries of these barbarians are divided into the western meadowlands which stretch to the distant ocean, and in which rise the cities of the town-dwellers, and the eastern deserts, where the lean nomads hold sway; there is incessant warfare between the dwellers of the cities and the dwellers of the desert.

"The Zuagirs have fought with and raided Khauran for centuries without success, but they resent its conquest by their western kin. It is rumored that their natural antagonism is being fomented by the man who was formerly the captain of the queen's guard, and who, somehow escaping the hate of Constantius, who actually had him upon the cross, fled to the nomads. He is called Conan, and is himself a barbarian, one of those gloomy Cimmerians whose ferocity our soldiers have more than once learned to their bitter cost. It is rumored that he has become the right-hand man of Olgerd Vladislav, the *kozak* adventurer who wandered down from the northern steppes and made himself chief of a band of Zuagirs.

There are also rumors that this band has increased vastly in the last few months, and that Olgerd, incited no doubt by this Cimmerian, is even considering a raid on Khauran.

"It cannot be anything more than a raid, as the Zuagirs are without siege machines or the knowledge of investing a city, and it has been proven repeatedly in the past that the nomads in their loose formation, or rather lack of formation, are no match in hand-to-hand fighting for the well-disciplined, fully-armed warriors of the Shemitish cities. The natives of Khauran would perhaps welcome this conquest, since the nomads could deal with them no more harshly than their present masters, and even total extermination would be preferable to the suffering they have to endure. But they are so cowed and helpless that they could give no aid to the invaders.

"Their plight is most wretched. Taramis, apparently possessed of a demon, stops at nothing. She has abolished the worship of Ishtar and turned the temple into a shrine of idolatry. She has destroyed the ivory image of the goddess which these eastern Hyborians worship (and which, inferior as it is to the true religion of Mitra which we Western nations recognize, is still superior to the devil worship of the Shemites) and filled the temple of Ishtar with obscene images of every imaginable sort—gods and goddesses of the night, portrayed in all the salacious and perverse poses and with all the revolting characteristics that a degenerate brain could conceive. Many of these images are to be identified as foul deities of the Shemites, the Turanians, the Vendhyans, and the Khitans, but others are reminiscent of a hideous and half-remembered antiquity, vile shapes forgotten except in the most obscure legends. Where the queen gained the knowledge of them I dare not even hazard a guess.

"She has instituted human sacrifice, and since her mating with Constantius, no less than five hundred men, women, and children have been immolated. Some of these have died on the altar she has set up in the temple, herself wielding the sacrificial dagger, but most have met a more horrible doom.

"Taramis has placed some sort of monster in a crypt in the temple. What it is, and whence it came, none knows. But shortly after she had crushed the desperate revolt of her soldiers against Constantius, she spent a night alone in the desecrated temple, alone except for a dozen bound captives, and the shuddering people saw thick, foul-smelling smoke curling up from the dome, heard all night the frenetic chanting of the queen, and the agonized cries of her tortured captives; and toward dawn another voice mingled with these sounds—a strident, inhuman croaking that froze the blood of all who heard.

"In the full dawn, Taramis reeled drunkenly from the temple, her eyes blazing with demoniac triumph. The captives were never seen again, nor the croaking voice heard. But there is a room in the temple into which none ever goes but the queen, driving a human sacrifice before her. And this victim is never seen again. All know that in that grim chamber lurks some monster from the black night of ages, which devours the shrieking humans Taramis delivers up to it.

"I can no longer think of her as a mortal woman, but as a rabid she-fiend, crouching in her blood-fouled lair amongst the bones and fragments of her victims, with taloned, crimsoned fingers. That the gods allow her to pursue her awful course unchecked almost shakes my faith in divine justice.

"When I compare her present conduct with her deportment when first I came to Khauran, seven months ago, I am confused with bewilderment, and almost inclined to the belief held by many of the people—that a demon has possessed the body of Taramis. A young soldier, Valerius, had another belief. He believed that a witch had assumed a form identical with that of Khauran's adored ruler. He believed that Taramis had been spirited away in the night and confined in some dungeon, and that this being ruling in her place was but a female sorcerer. He swore that he would find the real queen, if she still lived, but I greatly fear that he himself has fallen victim to the cruelty of Constantius. He was implicated in the revolt of the palace guards, escaped, and remained in hiding for some time, stubbornly refusing to seek safety abroad, and it was during this time that I encountered him and he told me his beliefs.

"But he has disappeared, as so many have, whose fate one dares not conjecture, and I fear he has been apprehended by the spies of Constantius.

"But I must conclude this letter and slip it out of the city by means of a swift carrier pigeon, which will carry it to the post whence I purchased it, on the borders of Koth. By rider and camel train it will eventually come to you. I must haste, before dawn. It is late, and the stars gleam whitely on the gardened roofs of Khauran. A shuddering silence envelops the city, in which I hear the throb of a sullen drum from the distant temple. I doubt not that Taramis is there, concocting more deviltry."

But the savant was incorrect in his conjecture concerning the whereabouts of the woman he called Taramis. The girl whom the world knew as queen of Khauran stood in a dungeon, lighted only by a flickering torch which played on her features, etching the diabolical cruelty of her beautiful countenance.

On the bare stone floor before her crouched a figure whose nakedness was scarcely covered with tattered rags.

This figure Salome touched contemptuously with the upturned toe of her gilded sandal, and smiled vindictively as her victim shrank away.

"You do not love my caresses, sweet sister?"

Taramis was still beautiful, in spite of her rags and the imprisonment and abuse of seven weary months. She did not reply to her sister's taunts, but bent her head as one grown accustomed to mockery.

This resignation did not please Salome. She bit her red lip, and stood tapping the toe of her shoe against the flags as she frowned down at the passive figure. Salome was clad in the barbaric splendor of a woman of Shushan. Jewels glittered in the torchlight on her gilded sandals, on her gold breast-plates and the slender chains that held them in place. Gold anklets clashed as she moved, jeweled bracelets weighted her bare arms. Her tall coiffure was that of a Shemitish woman, and jade pendants hung from gold hoops in her ears, flashing and sparkling with each impatient movement of her haughty head. A gem-crusted girdle supported a silk skirt so transparent that it was in the nature of a cynical mockery of convention.

Suspended from her shoulders and trailing down her back hung a darkly scarlet cloak, and this was thrown carelessly over the crook of one arm and the bundle that arm supported.

Salome stooped suddenly and with her free hand grasped her sister's disheveled hair and forced back the girl's head to stare into her eyes. Taramis met that tigerish glare without flinching.

"You are not so ready with your tears as formerly, sweet sister," muttered the witch-girl.

"You shall wring no more tears from me," answered Taramis. "Too often you have reveled in the spectacle of the queen of Khauran sobbing for mercy on her knees. I know that you have spared me only to torment me; that is why you have limited your tortures to such torments as neither slay nor permanently disfigure. But I fear you no longer; you have strained out the last vestige of hope, fright, and shame from me. Slay me and be done with it, for I have shed my last tear for your enjoyment, you she-devil from Hell!"

"You flatter yourself, my dear sister," purred Salome. "So far it is only your handsome body that I have caused to suffer, only your pride and self-esteem that I have crushed. You forget that, unlike myself, you are capable of mental torment. I have observed this when I have regaled you with narratives concerning the comedies I have enacted with some of your stupid subjects. But this time I have brought more vivid proof of these farces. Did you know that Krallides, your faithful councillor, had come sulking back from Turan and been captured?"

Taramis turned pale.

"What—what have you done to him?"

For answer Salome drew the mysterious bundle from under her cloak. She shook off the silken swathings and held it up—the head of a young man, the features frozen in a convulsion as if death had come in the midst of inhuman agony.

Taramis cried out as if a blade had pierced her heart.

"Oh, Ishtar! Krallides!"

"Aye! He was seeking to stir up the people against me, poor fool, telling them that Conan spoke the truth when he said I was not Taramis. How would the people rise against the Falcon's Shemites? With sticks and pebbles? Bah! Dogs are eating his headless body in the marketplace, and this foul carrion shall be cast into the sewer to rot.

"How, sister!" She paused, smiling down at her victim. "Have you discovered that you still have unshed tears? Good! I reserved the mental torment for the last. Hereafter I shall show you many such sights as—this!"

Standing there in the torchlight with the severed head in her hand she did not look like anything ever born of a human woman, in spite of her awful beauty. Taramis did not look up. She lay face down on the slimy floor, her slim body shaken in sobs of agony, beating her clenched hands against the stones. Salome sauntered toward the door, her anklets clashing at each step, her ear pendants winking in the torch-glare.

A few moments later, she emerged from a door under a sullen arch that let into a court, which in turn opened upon a winding alley. A man standing there turned toward her—a giant Shemite, with somber eyes and shoulders like a bull, his great black beard falling over his mighty; silver-mailed breast.

"She wept?" His rumble was like that of a bull, deep, low-pitched, and stormy. He was the general of the mercenaries, one of the few even of Constantius' associates who knew the secret of the queen of Khauran.

"Aye, Khumbanigash. There are whole sections of her sensibilities that I have not touched. When one sense is dulled by continual laceration, I will discover a newer, more poignant pang.—Here, dog!" A trembling, shambling figure in rags, filth, and matted hair approached, one of the beggars that slept in the alleys and open courts. Salome tossed the head to him. "Here, deaf one; cast that in the nearest sewer.—Make the sign with your hands, Khumbanigash. He cannot hear."

The general complied, and the tousled head bobbed, as the man turned painfully away.

"Why do you keep up this farce?" rumbled Khumbanigash. "You are so firmly established on the throne that nothing can unseat you. What if the Khaurani fools learn the truth? They can do nothing. Proclaim yourself in your true identity! Show them their beloved ex-queen—and cut off her head in the public square!"

"Not yet, good Khumbanigash——"

The arched door slammed on the hard accents of Salome, the stormy reverberations of Khumbanigash. The mute beggar crouched in the courtyard, and there was none to see that the hands which held the severed head were quivering strongly—brown, sinewy hands, strangely incongruous with the bent body and filthy tatters.

"I knew it!" It was a fierce, vibrant whisper, scarcely audible. "She lives! Oh, Krallides, your martyrdom was not in vain! They have her locked in that dungeon! Oh, Ishtar, if you love true men, aid me now!"

4. *Wolves of the Desert*

Olgerd Vladislav filled his jeweled goblet with crimson wine from a golden jug and thrust the vessel across the ebony table to Conan the Cimmerian. Olgerd's apparel would have satisfied the vanity of any Zaporoskan hetman.

His *khalat* was of white silk, with pearls sewn on the bosom. Girdled at the waist with a Bakhauriot belt, its skirts were drawn back to reveal his wide silken breeches, tucked into short boots of soft green leather, adorned with gold thread. On his head was a green silk turban, wound about a spired helmet chased with gold. His only weapon was a broad curved Cherkees knife in an ivory sheath girdled high on his left hip, *kozak* fashion. Throwing himself back in his gilded chair with its carven eagles, Olgerd spread his booted legs before him and gulped down the sparkling wine noisily.

To his splendor the huge Cimmerian opposite him offered a strong contrast, with his square-cut black mane, brown, scarred countenance and burning blue eyes. He was clad in black mesh mail, and the only glitter about him was the broad gold buckle of the belt which supported his sword in its worn leather scabbard.

They were alone in the silk-walled tent, which was hung with gild-worked tapestries and littered with rich carpets and velvet cushions, the loot of the caravans. From outside came a low, incessant murmur, the sound that always accompanies a great throng of men, in camp or otherwise. An occasional gust of desert wind rattled the palm leaves.

"Today in the shadow, tomorrow in the sun," quoth Olgerd, loosening his crimson girdle a trifle and reaching again for the wine jug. "That's the way of life. Once I was a hetman on the Zaporoska; now I'm a desert chief. Seven months ago you were hanging on a cross outside Khauran. Now you're lieutenant to the most powerful raider between Turan and the western meadows. You should be thankful to me!"

"For recognizing my usefulness?" Conan laughed and lifted the jug. "When you allow the elevation of a man, one can be sure that you'll profit by his advancement. I've earned everything I've won, with my blood and sweat." He glanced at the scars on the insides of his palms. There were scars, too, on his body, scars that had not been there seven months ago.

"You fight like a regiment of devils," conceded Olgerd. "But don't get to thinking that you've had anything to do with the recruits who've swarmed in to join us. It was our success at raiding, guided by my wit, that brought them in. These nomads are always looking for a successful leader to follow, and they have more faith in a foreigner than in one of their own race.

"There's no limit to what we may accomplish! We have eleven thousand men now. In another year we may have three times that number. We've contented ourselves, so far, with raids on the Turanian outposts and the city-states to the west. With thirty or forty thousand men we'll raid no longer. We'll invade and conquer and establish ourselves as rulers. I'll be emporor of all Shem yet, and you'll be my vizier, so long as you carry out my orders unquestioningly. In the meantime, I think we'll ride eastward and storm that Turanian outpost at Vezek, where the caravans pay toll."

Conan shook his head. "I think not."

Olgerd glared, his quick temper irritated.

"What do you mean, *you* think not? *I* do the thinking for this army!"

"There are enough men in this band now for my purpose," answered the Cimmerian. "I'm sick of waiting. I have a score to settle."

"Oh!" Olgerd scowled, and gulped wine, then grinned. "Still thinking of that cross, eh? Well, I like a good hater. But that can wait."

"You told me once you'd aid me in taking Khauran," said Conan.

"Yes, but that was before I began to see the full possibilities of our power," answered Olgerd. "I was only thinking of the loot in the city. I don't want to waste our strength unprofitably. Khauran is too strong a nut for us to crack now. Maybe in a year——"

"Within the week," answered Conan, and the *kozak* stared at the certainty in his voice.

"Listen," said Olgerd, "even if I were willing to throw away men on such a harebrained attempt—what could you expect, Do you think these wolves could besiege and take a city like Khauran?"

"There'll be no siege," answered the Cimmerian. "I know how to draw Constantius out into the plain."

"And what then?" cried Olgerd with an oath. "In the arrow play our horsemen would have the worst of it, for the armor of the *asshuri* is the better, and when it came to sword strokes their close-marshaled ranks of trained swordsmen would cleave through our loose lines and scatter our men like chaff before the wind."

"Not if there were three thousand desperate Hyborian horsemen fighting in a solid wedge such as I could teach them," answered Conan.

"And where would you secure three thousand Hyborians?" asked Olgerd with vast sarcasm. "Will you conjure them out of the air?"

"I *have* them," answered the Cimmerian imperturbably. "Three thousand men of Khauran camp at the oasis of Akrel, awaiting my orders."

"*What?*" Olgerd glared like a startled wolf.

"Aye. Men who had fled from the tyranny of Constantius. Most of them have been living the lives of outlaws in the deserts east of Khauran and are gaunt and hard and desperate as man-eating tigers. One of them will be a match for any three squat mercenaries. It takes oppression and hardship to stiffen men's guts and put the fire of Hell into their thews. They were broken up into small bands; all they needed was a leader. They believed the word I sent them by my riders, and assembled at the oasis and put themselves at my disposal."

"All this without my knowledge?" A feral light began to gleam in Olgerd's eyes. He hitched at his weapon-girdle.

"It was *I* they wished to follow, not *you*."

"And what did you tell these outcasts to gain their allegiance?" There was a dangerous ring in Olgerd's voice.

"I told them that I'd use this horde of desert wolves to help them destroy Constantius and give Khauran back into the hands of its citizens."

"You fool!" whispered Olgerd. "Do you deem yourself chief already?"

The men were on their feet, facing each other across the ebony board, devil-lights dancing in Olgerd's cold gray eyes, a grim smile on the Cimmerian's hard lips.

"I'll have you torn between four palm trees," said the *kozak* calmly.

"Call the men and bid them do it!" challenged Conan. "See if they obey you!"

Baring his teeth in a snarl, Olgerd lifted his hand—then paused. There was something about the confidence in the Cimmerian's dark face that shook him. His eyes began to burn like those of a wolf.

"You scum of the western hills," he muttered, "have you dared to seek to undermine my power?"

"I didn't have to," answered Conan. "You lied when you said I had nothing to do with bringing in the new recruits. I had everything to do with it. They took your orders, but they fought for me. There is not room for two chiefs of the Zuagirs. They know I am the stronger man. I understand them better than you, and they, me; because I am a barbarian too."

"And what will they say when you ask them to fight for the Khauranis?" asked Olgerd sardonically.

"They'll follow me. I'll promise them a camel train of

gold from the palace. Khauran will be willing to pay that as a guerdon for getting rid of Constantius. After that, I'll lead them against the Turanians as you have planned. They want loot, and they'd as soon fight Constantius for it as anybody."

In Olgerd's eyes grew a recognition of defeat. In his red dreams of empire he had missed what was going on about him. Happenings and events that had seemed meaningless before now flashed into his mind, with their true significance, bringing a realization that Conan spoke no idle boast. The giant black-mailed figure before him was the real chief of the Zuagirs.

"Not if you die!" muttered Olgerd, and his hand flickered toward his hilt. But quick as the stroke of a great cat Conan's arm shot across the table and his fingers locked on Olgerd's forearm. There was a snap of breaking bones, and for a tense instant the scene held: the men facing each other as motionless as images, perspiration starting out on Olgerd's forehead. Conan laughed, never easing his grip on the broken arm.

"Are you fit to live, Olgerd?"

His smile did not alter as the corded muscles rippled in knotting ridges along his forearm and his fingers ground into the *kozak's* quivering flesh. There was the sound of broken bones grating together and Olgerd's face turned the color of ashes; blood oozed from his lip where his teeth sank, but he uttered no sound.

With a laugh Conan released him and drew back, and the *kozak* swayed, caught the table edge with his good hand to steady himself.

"I give you life, Olgerd, as you gave it to me," said Conan tranquilly, "though it was for your own ends that you took me down from the cross. It was a bitter test you gave me then; you couldn't have endured it; neither could anyone but a western barbarian.

"Take your horse and go. It's tied behind the tent, and food and water are in the saddlebags. None will see your going, but go quickly. There's no room for a fallen chief on the desert. If the warriors see you, maimed and deposed, they'll never let you leave the camp alive."

Olgerd did not reply. Slowly, without a word, he turned and stalked across the tent, through the flapped opening. Unspeaking he climbed into the saddle of the great white stallion that stood tethered there in the shade of a spreading palm tree; and unspeaking, with his broken arm thrust in the bosom of his *khalat*, he reined the steed about and rode eastward into the open desert, out of the life of the people of the Zuagir.

Inside the tent Conan emptied the wine jug and smacked his lips with relish. Tossing the empty vessel into a corner, he braced his belt and strode out through the front opening, halting for a moment to let his gaze sweep over the lines of camel-hair tents that stretched before him, and the white-robed figures that moved among them, arguing, singing, mending bridles, or whetting tulwars.

He lifted his voice in a thunder that carried to the farthest confines of the encampment: "*Aie*, you dogs, sharpen your ears and listen! Gather around here. I have a tale to tell you."

5. *The Voice from the Crystal*

In a chamber in a tower near the city wall, a group of men listened attentively to the words of one of their number. They were young men, but hard and sinewy, with the bearing that comes only to men rendered desperate by adversity. They were clad in mail shirts and worn leather; swords hung at their girdles.

"I knew that Conan spoke the truth when he said it was not Taramis!" the speaker exclaimed. "For months I have haunted the outskirts of the palace, playing the part of a deaf beggar. At last I learned what I had believed—that our queen was a prisoner in the dungeons that adjoin the palace. I watched my opportunity and captured a Shemitish jailer—knocked him senseless as he left the courtyard late one night—dragged him into a cellar nearby and questioned him. Before he died, he told me what I have just told you, and what we have suspected all along—that the woman ruling Khauran is a witch: Salome. Taramis, he said, is imprisoned in the lowest dungeon.

"This invasion of the Zuagirs gives us the opportunity we sought. What Conan means to do, I cannot say. Perhaps he merely wishes vengeance on Constantius. Perhaps he intends sacking the city and destroying it. He is a barbarian, and no one can understand their minds.

"But this is what we must do: rescue Taramis while the battle rages! Constantius will march out into the plain to give battle. Even now his men are mounting. He will do this because there is not sufficient food in the city to stand a siege. Conan burst out of the desert so suddenly that there was no time to bring in supplies. And the Cimmerian is equipped for a siege. Scouts have reported that the Zuagirs have siege engines, built, undoubtedly, according to the instructions of Conan, who learned all the arts of war among the Western nations.

"Constantius does not desire a long siege; so he will march with his warriors into the plain, where he expects to scatter Conan's forces at one stroke. He will leave only a few hundred men in the city, and they will be on the walls and in the towers commanding the gates.

"The prison will be left all but unguarded. When we have freed Taramis, our next actions will depend upon circumstances. If Conan wins, we must show Taramis to the people and bid them rise—they will! Oh, they will! With their bare hands they are enough to overpower the Shemites left in the city and close the gates against both the mercenaries and the nomads. Neither must get within the walls! Then we will parley with Conan. He was always loyal to Taramis. If he knows the truth, and she appeals to him, I believe he will spare the city. If, which is more probable, Constantius prevails, and Conan is routed, we must steal out of the city with the queen and seek safety in flight.

"Is all clear?"

They replied with one voice.

"Then let us loosen our blades in our scabbards, commend our souls to Ishtar, and start for the prison, for the mercenaries are already marching through the southern gate."

This was true. The dawnlight glinted on peaked helmets pouring in a steady stream through the broad arch, on the bright housings of the chargers. This would be a battle of horsemen, such as is possible only in the lands of the East. The riders flowed through the gates like a river of steel—somber figures in black and silver mail, with their curled beards and hooked noses, and their inexorable eyes in which glimmered the fatality of their race—the utter lack of doubt or of mercy.

The streets and the walls were lined with throngs of people who watched silently these warriors of an alien race riding forth to defend their native city. There was no sound; dully, expressionlessly they watched, those gaunt people in shabby garments, their caps in their hands.

In a tower that overlooked the broad street that led to the southern gate, Salome lolled on a velvet couch, cynically watching Constantius as he settled his broad sword belt about his lean hips and drew on his gauntlets. They were alone in the chamber. Outside, the rhythmical clank of harness and shuffle of horses' hooves welled up through the gold-barred casements.

"Before nightfall," quoth Constantius, giving a twirl to his thin mustache, "you'll have some captives to feed to your temple devil. Does it not grow weary of soft, city-bred flesh? Perhaps it would relish the harder thews of a desert man."

"Take care you do not fall prey to a fiercer beast than Thaug," warned the girl. "Do not forget who it is that leads these desert animals."

"I am not likely to forget," he answered. "That is one reason why I am advancing to meet him. The dog has fought in the West and knows the art of siege. My scouts had some trouble in approaching his columns, for his outriders have eyes like hawks; but they did get close enough to see the engines he is dragging on oxcart wheels drawn by camels—catapults, rams, ballistas, mangonels—by Ishtar! he must have had ten thousand men working day and night for a month. Where he got the material for their construction is more than I can understand. Perhaps he has a treaty with the Turanians and gets supplies from them.

"Anyway, they won't do him any good. I've fought these desert wolves before—an exchange of arrows for a while, in which the armor of my warriors protects them—then a charge and my squadrons sweep through the loose swarms of the nomads, wheel and sweep back through, scattering them to the four winds. I'll ride back through the south gate before sunset, with hundreds of naked captives staggering at my horse's tail. We'll hold a fête tonight, in the great square. My soldiers delight in flaying their enemies alive—we will have a wholesale skinning, and make these weak-kneed townsfolk watch. As for Conan, it will afford me intense pleasure, if we can take him alive, to impale him on the palace steps."

"Skin as many as you like," answered Salome indifferently. "I would like a dress made of human hide. But at least a hundred captives you must give to me—for the altar, and for Thaug."

"It shall be done," answered Constantius, with his gauntleted hand brushing back the thin hair from his high, bald forehead, burned dark by the sun. "For victory and the fair honor of Taramis!" he said sardonically, and, taking his vizored helmet under his arm, he lifted a hand in salute and strode clanking from the chamber. His voice drifted back, harshly lifted in orders to his officers.

Salome leaned back on the couch, yawned, stretched herself like a great, supple cat, and called: "Zang!"

A cat-footed priest, with features like yellowed parchment stretched over a skull, entered noiselessly.

Salome turned to an ivory pedestal on which stood two crystal globes and, taking from it the smaller, she handed the glistening sphere to the priest.

"Ride with Constantius," she said. "Give me the news of the battle. Go!"

The skull-faced man bowed low and, hiding the globe under his dark mantle, hurried from the chamber.

Outside in the city there was no sound, except the clank of hoofs and after a while the clang of a closing gate. Salome mounted a wide marble stair that led to the flat, canopied, marble-battlemented roof. She was above all other buildings of the city. The streets were deserted, the great square in front of the palace was empty. In normal times folk shunned the grim temple which rose on the opposite side of that square, but now the town looked like a dead city. Only on the southern wall and the roofs that overlooked it was there any sign of life. There the people massed thickly. They made no demonstration, did not know whether to hope for the victory or defeat of Constantius. Victory meant further misery under his intolerable rule; defeat probably meant the sack of the city and red massacre. No word had come from Conan. They did not know what to expect at his hands. They remembered that he was a barbarian.

The squadrons of the mercenaries were moving out into the plain. In the distance, just this side of the river, other dark masses were moving, barely recognizable as men on horses. Objects dotted the farther bank; Conan had not brought his siege engines across the river, apparently fearing an attack in the midst of the crossing. But he had crossed with his full force of horsemen. The sun rose and struck glints of fire from the dark multitudes. The squadrons from the city broke into a gallop; a deep roar reached the ears of the people on the wall.

The rolling masses merged, intermingled; at that distance it was a tangled confusion in which no details stood out. Charge and countercharge were not to be identified. Clouds of dust rose from the plains, under the stamping hoofs, veiling the action. Through these swirling clouds masses of riders loomed, appearing and disappearing, and spears flashed.

Salome shrugged her shoulders and descended the stair. The palace lay silent. All the slaves were on the wall, gazing vainly southward with the citizens.

She entered the chamber where she had talked with Constantius and approached the pedestal, noting that the crystal globe was clouded, shot with bloody streaks of crimson. She bent over the ball, swearing under her breath.

"Zang!" she called. "Zang!"

Mists swirled in the sphere, resolving themselves into billowing dust clouds through which black figures rushed unrecognizably; steel glinted like lightning in the murk. Then the face of Zang leaped into startling distinctness; it was as if the wide eyes gazed up at Salome. Blood trickled from a gash in the skull-like head, the skin was gray with sweat-runneled dust. The lips parted, writhing; to other ears than Salome's it would have seemed that the face in the crystal contorted silently. But sound to her came as plainly from those ashen lips as if the priest had been in the same room with her, instead of miles away, shouting into the smaller crystal. Only the gods of darkness knew what unseen, magic filaments linked together those shimmering spheres.

"Salome!" shrieked the bloody head. "*Salome!*"

"I hear!" she cried. "Speak! How goes the battle?"

"Doom is upon us!" screamed the skull-like apparition. "Khauran is lost! *Aie*, my horse is down and I cannot win clear! Men are falling around me! They are dying like flies, in their silvered mail!"

"Stop yammering and tell me what happened!" she cried harshly.

"We rode at the desert dogs, and they came on to meet us!" yowled the priest. "Arrows flew in clouds between the hosts, and the nomads wavered. Constantius ordered the charge. In even ranks we thundered upon them.

"Then the masses of their horde opened to right and left, and through the cleft rushed three thousand Hyborian horsemen whose presence we had not even suspected. Men of Khauran, mad with hate! Big men in full armor on massive horses! In a solid wedge of steel they smote us like a thunderbolt. They split our ranks asunder before we knew what was upon us, and then the desert men swarmed on us from either flank.

"They have ripped our ranks apart, broken and scattered us! It is a trick of that devil Conan! The siege engines are false—mere frames of palm trunks and painted silk, that fooled our scouts who saw them from afar. A trick to draw us out to our doom! Our warriors flee! Khumbanigash is down—Conan slew him. I do not see Constantius. The Khauranis rage through our milling masses like blood-mad lions, and the desert men feather us with arrows. I—ahhh!"

There was a flicker as of lightning, or trenchant steel, a burst of bright blood—then abruptly the image vanished, like a bursting bubble, and Salomé was staring into an empty crystal ball that mirrored only her own furious features.

She stood perfectly still for a few moments, erect and staring into space. Then she clapped her hands and another skull-like priest entered, as silent and immobile as the first.

"Constantius is beaten," she said swiftly. "We are doomed. Conan will be crashing at our gates within the hour. If he catches me, I have no illusions as to what I can expect. But first I am going to make sure that my cursed sister never ascends the throne again. Follow me! Come what may, we shall give Thaug a feast."

As she descended the stairs and galleries of the palace, she heard a faint, rising echo from the distant walls. The people there had begun to realize that the battle was going against Constantius. Through the dust clouds masses of horsemen were visible, racing toward the city.

Palace and prison were connected by a long closed gallery, whose vaulted roof rose on gloomy arches. Hurrying along this, the false queen and her slave passed through a heavy door at the other end that let them into the dim-lit recesses of the prison. They had emerged into a wide, arched corridor at a point near where a stone stair descended into the darkness. Salome recoiled suddenly, swearing. In the gloom of the hall lay a motionless form —a Shemitish jailer, his short beard tilted toward the roof as his head hung on a half-severed neck. As panting voices from below reached the girl's ears, she shrank back into the black shadow of an arch, pushing the priest behind her, her hand groping in her girdle.

6. *The Vulture's Wings*

It was the smoky light of a torch which roused Taramis, queen of Khauran, from the slumber in which she sought forgetfulness. Lifting herself on her hand, she raked back her tangled hair and blinked up, expecting to meet the mocking countenance of Salome, malign with new torments. Instead a cry of pity and horror reached her ears.

"Taramis! Oh, my queen!"

The sound was so strange to her ears that she thought she was still dreaming. Behind the torch she could make out figures now, the glint of steel, then five countenances bent toward her, not swarthy and hook-nosed, but lean, aquiline faces, browned by the sun. She crouched in her tatters, staring wildly.

One of the figures sprang forward and fell on one knee before her, arms stretched appealingly toward her.

"Oh, Taramis! Thank Ishtar we have found you! Do you not remember me, Valerius? Once with your own lips you praised me, after the battle of Korveka!"

"Valerius!" she stammered. Suddenly tears welled into her eyes. "Oh, I dream! It is some magic of Salome's, to torment me!"

"No!" The cry rang with exultation. "It is your own true vassals come to rescue you! Yet we must hasten. Constantius fights in the plain against Conan, who has brought the Zuagirs across the river, but three hundred Shemites yet hold the city. We slew the jailer and took his keys, and have seen no other guards. But we must be gone. Come!"

The queen's legs gave way, not from weakness but from the reaction. Valerius lifted her like a child, and with the torchbearer hurrying before them, they left the dungeon and went up a slimy stone stair. It seemed to mount endlessly, but presently they emerged into a corridor.

They were passing a dark arch when the torch was suddenly struck out, and the bearer cried out in fierce, brief agony. A burst of blue fire glared in the dark corridor, in which the furious face of Salome was limned momentarily, with a beastlike figure crouching beside her—then the eyes of the watchers were blinded by that blaze.

Valerius tried to stagger along the corridor with the queen; dazedly he heard the sound of murderous blows driven deep in flesh, accompanied by gasps of death and a bestial grunting. Then the queen was torn brutally from his arms, and a savage blow on his helmet dashed him to the floor.

Grimly he crawled to his feet, shaking his head in an effort to rid himself of the blue flame, which seemed still to dance devilishly before him. When his blinded sight cleared, he found himself alone in the corridor—alone except for the dead. His four companions lay in their blood, heads and bosoms cleft and gashed. Blinded and dazed in that hell-born glare, they had died without an opportunity of defending themselves. The queen was gone.

With a bitter curse Valerius caught up his sword, tearing his cleft helmet from his head to clatter on the flags; blood ran down his cheek from a cut in his scalp.

Reeling, frantic with indecision, he heard a voice calling his name in desperate urgency: "Valerius! *Valerius!*"

He staggered in the direction of the voice, and rounded a corner just in time to have his arms filled with a soft, supple figure which flung itself frantically at him.

"Ivga! Are you mad!"

"I had to come!" she sobbed. "I followed you—hid in an arch of the outer court. A moment ago I saw *her* emerge with a brute who carried a woman in his arms. I knew it was Taramis, and that you had failed! Oh, you are hurt!"

"A scratch!" He put aside her clinging hands. "Quick, Ivga, tell me which way they went!"

"They fled across the square toward the temple."

He paled. "Ishtar! Oh, the fiend! She means to give Taramis to the devil she worships! Quick, Ivga! Run to the south wall where the people watch the battle! Tell them that their real queen has been found—that the imposter has dragged her to the temple! Go!"

Sobbing, the girl sped away, her light sandals pattering across the court, plunged into the street, dashed into the square upon which it debouched, and raced for the great structure that rose on the opposite side.

His own flying feet spurned the marble as he darted up the broad stair and through the pillared portico. Evidently their prisoner had given them some trouble. Taramis, sensing the doom intended for her, was fighting against it with all the strength of her splendid young body. Once she had broken away from the brutish priest, only to be dragged down again.

The group was half way down the broad nave, at the other end of which stood the grim altar and beyond that the great metal door, obscenely carven, through which many had gone but from which only Salome had ever emerged. Taramis' breath came in panting gasps; her tattered garment had been torn from her in the struggle. She writhed in the grasp of her apish captor like a white, naked nymph in the arms of a satyr. Salome watched cynically, though impatiently, moving toward the carven door; and from the dusk that lurked along the lofty walls the obscene gods and gargoyles leered down, as if imbued with salacious life.

Choking with fury, Valerius rushed down the great hall, sword in hand. At a sharp cry from Salome, the skull-faced priest looked up, then released Taramis, drew a heavy knife, already smeared with blood, and ran at the oncoming Khaurani.

But cutting down men blinded by the devil's flame loosed by Salome was different from fighting a wiry young Hyborian afire with hate and rage.

Up went the dripping knife, but before it could fall Valerius' keen narrow blade slashed through the air, and the fist that held the knife jumped from its wrist in a shower of blood. Valerius, berserk, slashed again and yet again before the crumpling figure could fall. The blade licked through flesh and bone. The skull-like head fell one way, the half-sundered torso the other.

Valerius whirled on his toes, quick and fierce as a jungle cat, glaring about for Salome. She must have exhausted her fire dust in the prison. She was bending over Taramis, grasping her sister's black locks in one hand, in the other lifting a dagger. Then with a fierce cry, Valerius' sword was sheathed in her breast with such fury that the point sprang out between her shoulders. With an awful shriek the witch sank down, writhing in convulsions, grasping at the naked blade as it was withdrawn, smoking and dripping. Her eyes were unhuman; with a more than human vitality she clung to the life that ebbed through the wound that split the crimson crescent on her ivory bosom. She groveled on the floor, clawing and biting at the naked stones in her agony.

Sickened at the sight, Valerius stooped and lifted the half-fainting queen. Turning his back on the twisting figure upon the floor, he ran toward the door, stumbling in his haste. He staggered out upon the portico, halted at the head of the steps. The square thronged with people. Some had come at Ivga's incoherent cries; others had deserted the walls in fear of the onsweeping hordes out of the desert, fleeing unreasoningly toward the center of the city. Dumb resignation had vanished. The throng seethed and milled, yelling and screaming. About the road there sounded somewhere the splintering of stone and timbers.

A band of grim Shemites cleft the crowd—the guards of the northern gates, hurrying toward the south gate to reinforce their comrades there. They reined up short at sight of the youth on the steps, holding the limp, naked figure in his arms. The heads of the throng turned toward the temple; the crowd gaped, a new bewilderment added to their swirling confusion.

"Here is your queen!" yelled Valerius, straining to make himself understood above the clamor. The people gave back a bewildered roar. They did not understand, and Valerius sought in vain to lift his voice above their bedlam. The Shemites rode toward the temple steps, beating a way through the crowd with their spears.

Then a new, grisly element introduced itself into the frenzy. Out of the gloom of the temple behind Valerius wavered a slim white figure, laced with crimson. The people screamed; there in the arms of Valerius hung the woman they thought their queen; yet there in the temple door staggered another figure, like a reflection of the other. Their brains reeled. Valerius felt his blood congeal as he stared at the swaying witch-girl. His sword had transfixed her, sundered her heart. She should be dead; by all laws of nature she should be dead. Yet there she swayed, on her feet, clinging horribly to life.

"Thaug!" she screamed, reeling in the doorway. "*Thaug!*" As in answer to that frightful invocation there boomed a thunderous croaking from within the temple, the snapping of wood and metal.

"That is the queen!" roared the captain of the Shemites, lifting his bow. "Shoot down the man and the other woman!"

But the roar of a roused hunting pack rose from the people; they had guessed the truth at last, understood Valerius' frenzied appeals, knew that the girl who hung limply in his arms was their true queen. With a soul-shaking yell they surged on the Shemites, tearing and smiting with tooth and nail and naked hands, with the desperation of hard-pent fury loosed at last. Above them Salome swayed and tumbled down the marble stair, dead at last.

Arrows flickered about him as Valerius ran back between the pillars of the portico, shielding the body of the queen with his own. Shooting and slashing ruthlessly, the mounted Shemites were holding their own with the maddened crowd. Valerius darted to the temple door—with one foot on the threshold he recoiled, crying out in horror and despair.

Out of the gloom at the other end of the great hall, a vast dark form heaved up—came rushing toward him in gigantic froglike hops. He saw the gleam of great unearthly eyes, the shimmer of fangs or talons. He fell back from the door, and then the whir of a shaft past his ear warned him that death was also behind him. He wheeled desperately. Four or five Shemites had cut their way through the throng and were spurring their horses up the steps, their bows lifted to shoot him down. He sprang behind a pillar, on which the arrows splintered. Taramis had fainted. She hung like a dead woman in his arms.

Before the Shemites could loose again, the doorway

was blocked by a gigantic shape. With affrighted yells the mercenaries wheeled and began beating a frantic way through the throng, which crushed back in sudden, galvanized horror, trampling one another in their stampede.

But the monster seemed to be watching Valerius and the girl. Squeezing its vast, unstable bulk through the door, it bounded toward him, as he ran down the steps. He felt it looming behind him, a giant shadowy thing, like a travesty of nature cut out of the heart of night, a black shapelessness in which only the staring eyes and gleaming fangs were distinct.

There came a sudden thunder of hoofs; a rout of Shemites, bloody and battered, streamed across the square from the south, plowing blindly through the packed throng. Behind them swept a horde of horsemen yelling in a familiar tongue, waving red swords—the exiles, returned! With them rode fifty black-bearded desert riders, and at their head a giant figure in black mail.

"Conan!" shrieked Valerius. "*Conan!*"

The giant yelled a command. Without checking their headlong pace, the desert men lifted their bows, drew and loosed. A cloud of arrows sang across the square, over the seething heads of the multitudes, and sank feather-deep in the black monster. It halted, wavered, reared, a black blot against the marble pillars. Again the sharp cloud sang, and yet again, and the horror collapsed and rolled down the steps, as dead as the witch who had summoned it out of the night of ages.

Conan drew rein beside the portico, leaped off. Valerius had laid the queen on the marble, sinking beside her in utter exhaustion. The people surged about, crowding in. The Cimmerian cursed them back, lifted her dark head, pillowed it against his mailed shoulder.

"By Crom, what is this? The real Taramis! But who is that yonder?"

"The demon who wore her shape," panted Valerius.

Conan swore heartily. Ripping a cloak from the shoulders of a soldier, he wrapped it about the naked queen. Her long dark lashes quivered on her cheeks; her eyes opened, stared up unbelievingly into the Cimmerian's scarred face.

"Conan!" Her soft fingers caught at him. "Do I dream? *She* told me you were dead——"

"Scarcely!" He grinned hardly. "You do not dream. You are queen of Khauran again. I broke Constantius, out there by the river. Most of his dogs never lived to reach the walls, for I gave orders that no prisoners be taken—except Constantius. The city guard closed the gate in our faces, but we burst it in with rams swung from our saddles. I left all my wolves outside, except this fifty. I didn't trust them in here, and these Khaurani lads were enough for the gate guards."

"It has been a nightmare!" she whimpered. "Oh, my poor people! You must help me try to repay them for all they have suffered, Conan, henceforth councilor as well as captain!"

Conan laughed, but shook his head. Rising, he set the queen upon her feet, and beckoned to a number of his Khaurani horsemen who had not continued the pursuit of the fleeing Shemites. They sprang from their horses, eager to do the bidding of their new-found queen.

"No, lass, that's over with. I'm chief of the Zuagirs now and must lead them to plunder the Turanians, as I promised. This lad, Valerius, will make you a better captain than I. I wasn't made to dwell among marble walls, anyway. But I must leave you now and complete what I've begun. Shemites still live in Khauran."

As Valerius started to follow Taramis across the square toward the palace, through a lane opened by the wildly cheering multitude, he felt a soft hand slipped timidly into his sinewy fingers and turned to receive the slender body of Ivga in his arms. He crushed her to him and drank her kisses with the gratitude of a weary fighter who has attained rest at last through tribulation and storm.

But not all men seek rest and peace; some are born with the spirit of the storm in their blood, restless harbingers of violence and bloodshed, knowing no other path. . . .

The sun was rising. The ancient caravan road was thronged with white-robed horsemen, in a wavering line that stretched from the walls of Khauran to a spot far out in the plain. Conan the Cimmerian sat at the head of that column, near the jagged end of a wooden beam that stuck up out of the ground. Near that stump rose a heavy cross, and on that cross a man hung by spikes through his hands and feet.

"Seven months ago, Constantius," said Conan, "it was I who hung there, and you who sat here."

Constantius did not reply; he licked his gray lips and his eyes were glassy with pain and fear. Muscles writhed like cords along his lean body.

"You are more fit to inflict torture than to endure it," said Conan tranquilly. "I hung there on a cross as you are hanging, and I lived, thanks to circumstances and a stamina peculiar to barbarians. But you civilized men are soft; your lives are not nailed to your spines as are ours. Your fortitude consists mainly in inflicting torment, not in enduring it. You will be dead before sundown. And so, Falcon of the desert, I leave you to the companionship of another bird of the desert."

He gestured toward the vultures whose shadows swept across the sands as they wheeled overhead. From the lips of Constantius came an inhuman cry of despair and horror.

Conan lifted his reins and rode toward the river that shone like silver in the morning sun. Behind him the white-clad riders struck into a trot; the gaze of each, as he passed a certain spot, turned impersonally and with the desert man's lack of compassion, toward the cross and the gaunt figure that hung there, black against the sunrise. Their horses' hooves beat out a knell in the dust. Lower and lower swept the wings of the hungry vultures.